THE
LAMBDA
FACTOR

DIMPLE PATEL DESAI

ISBN: 978-1-954614-29-1

Desai. Dimple Patel.
The Lambda Factor

Edited by: Karli Jackson

Published by Warren Publishing
Charlotte, NC
www.warrenpublishing.net
Printed in the United States

*I would like to sincerely thank my
family and friends for putting up with my writing.*

*Thanks to my brother who always listens to me
and lets me bounce ideas off of him.*

Thank you to my parents who support me unconditionally.

*I would especially like to thank my husband
and two boys who inspire me everyday.*

*This is for everyone who wants to do something out of
their comfort zone. This is for anyone who struggles with
a mental health disorder and needs a creative outlet.*

The possibilities are endless when you believe in yourself.

Prologue

The National Biocontainment Lab, Galveston University Hospital

The awful thing about a Chemturion HAZMAT suit is not only its weight, but the fact that you can't rub your eyes.

Cory Finch felt as though he'd been counting the same cells for hours. Behind the built-in visor, one of his eyes started to water. He sighed and blinked rapidly. In the suit, his hands were useless to stop the itch. Cory felt as though his eyes felt ready to fall out of his head. Out of the corner of his eye, he spotted his fellow post-doc, Billy Andersen, fidgeting anxiously over the closed-circuit television. Although Billy looked much too comfortable in the lab manager's office in denim shorts and BIRKENSTOCK sandals, Cory was still reassured that another senior lab member was close by. Just in case there was an emergency.

Billy paused, scowling at a muted TV screen in his office. "You see that, Finch?" He called over the headset. "Category three already. And still seventy-two hours from landfall. This one's going to be a monster."

Cory glanced up, annoyed. "Calm down, will you? Waiting for this thing is like waiting for a turtle. Besides, all the reports are like that now. Every single storm is 'the *worst* that ever happened.' Why do they have to make everybody crazy? It's not as though this is the first time the island has seen a hurricane, is it? Galveston has had its fair share."

Billy started pacing. "Yeah, I know. But the further south they come, the bigger they get. And I don't want to get stuck in all the evac traffic. It's going to be nuts by the time our shift is over. I promised my mom I'd make it to Houston by midnight. She's all alone up there. She worries."

Cory hid a smile. "Geez, dude. You'd think she'd be more worried about you working here. Researching deadly viruses in a bio-containment lab isn't exactly hazard-proof."

Cory's phone vibrated in his pocket beneath the suit, along with a deafening tone signaling a new message. Billy jumped and reached for the phone in his pocket as a loud buzzing sounded like an AMBER Alert. A notification boomed overhead, "Nonessential personnel advised to evacuate ASAP."

"Yeah, we know that already." He glanced back up at Billy. "What's everybody so spooked about, anyhow?"

Billy shrugged. "Liability. They don't want to get sued for not advising people to evacuate early enough."

Scowling over the oculars of his microscope, Cory went back to splitting the cell culture. "Two hundred and fifty-two by my count in this flask."

Billy shook his head. "Crimean Congo Hemorrhagic Fever. I can't believe that of all the pathogens studied in this facility, this was the proposal that got funded. And by the Department of Defense, no less."

"I'm not in the mood to talk about office politics. I joined this lab to do good science and maybe get a publication in *Nature* or *Science*," Cory said.

Billy only shrugged. "So, tell me what do you know about this obscure CCHF virus ... thing?"

Cory spouted off from memory, "Level-4 security risk. Forty to fifty percent mortality rate. First emerged in the 1940s. Found in Eastern Europe, Russia, the Mediterranean, Africa, the Middle East, and India. Believed to be tickborne. Found in livestock mammals, birds, and vertebrates all over the world, but only kills human hosts. Infection is believed to spread through contact with the victim's blood and/or bodily fluids; symptoms present within one to five days after exposure ... and here's the weird part: when exposed for prolonged periods, some people, even outside a controlled environment, never get it at all."

Billy glanced at the clock. "Yeah, okay. Skip ahead."

Feeling a headache taking shape at the base of his neck, Cory sighed heavily. "The virus attacks the cell membrane of endothelial cells in blood vessels at multiple points." He broke off again. "You know what I think? This is all BS. We are working with modified lab-produced samples that are probably eighty percent inert, from some place called Dugway Proving Ground. We can't really say for certain what it does. I mean, when you have wild-type samples, how are you supposed to be able to track anything if you can't see it in action?"

Billy shuffled a few steps back. "Whoa there. Live virus? That's above my pay grade. The stuff we handle is creepy enough. And the CDC knows it. Why else would we do the suits and the freezers and the decontamination? Don't go asking for trouble you don't need."

Cory rolled his head to ease the tension in his shoulders. "I know, I know. I'm just frustrated. I have all these questions and no answers."

"Like what?"

"Like, other similar viruses in the Norovirus group don't cause disease in humans. How did CCHF make the jump to humans? And why is it still so deadly? This virus has been around for nearly seventy years. You'd think it would adapt to its host and become less virulent overtime like other viruses have." Cory proposed.

"You sure *this* virus has been around that long?"

Cory went on. "Not entirely. But CCHF in humans has been documented as early as 1944 when it was first described by Soviets in Crimea."

Billy walked a circle around the room. "HIV, Ebola, SARS, MERS, COVID-19—if you ask me, it's all about biowarfare."

"Huh? Have you been playing video games again? You know the United States and practically every country in the world signed the Biologic Weapons Convention in the '70s. We aren't soldiers. We are scientists."

"Sure, man. Don't you get it?" Billy swung around a nearby chair and perched on it backwards as he went on talking seemingly to the ceiling. "Biological warfare has been practiced since colonial times when natives were gifted blankets smothered with smallpox. Post-World War II, everybody was under the impression that we were curing the world. The golden age of immunization. Research money everywhere. So, the Centers of Disease Control and Prevention along with the World Health Organization developed a truckload of vaccines and antibiotics for stuff that had already been around forever. Tuberculosis, malaria, diphtheria, measles, smallpox, etc. But you've got to remember that during the war, they also blasted a whole bunch of new crap into the environment as biological weapons. Think about all those medical experiments the Japanese did with Unit 731. Part of it—maybe most of it—was all about developing new kinds of bio-weapons. Only, nature adapts, right?"

As he peered at Billy, trying to gauge whether his friend had lost his mind, Cory managed to meekly respond, "Nature evolves."

"So existent viruses interact with new environmental toxins, mutate, mutate again, and before you know it, you got something like CCHF, still tickborne, but not transmitted through any vertebrates, except humans. And infectious enough to make Lyme disease look like a day on the Riviera. Super bugs. Why do you think the DoD is interested in a virus that also happens to be endemic to the Middle East? Biological warfare is the perfect vehicle to give a government the ability to retaliate with plausible deniability. You can't fly around Blackhawks emblazoned with the US flag anymore without someone tweeting about it or livestreaming it to YouTube. Just look at how the *New York Times* investigated the Russians' secret bombing campaign of *Médecins Sans Frontières* hospitals in Syria. There is no smoking gun with biological weapons. People assume disease is something that happens during conflict. No one questions what's happened, and those who do are ostracized like a schizophrenic wearing a tinfoil hat."

Cory could only stare at him, gaping like a guppy. Billy could be a real pain sometimes, but he had a point. Maybe he was all about the broad strokes, but he never lost sight of the big picture. Cory himself was more a "God is in the details" type of research nerd. Maybe that was why they made a good team. Cory shook his head. "Hard to believe you went into science, you know? You're more like a combo of House and Dexter from television. Crazy, maybe. But smart."

Billy grinned and pointed to his temple. "Job security, dude. It's what pays our salary, man. National Institute of Health funding has been drying up for decades. The golden age of research money everywhere ended. The CDC and WHO aren't what they used to be. COVID-19 proved that. If the DoD is willing to fund this, I'm ready to work on it."

"Don't be so cynical. You make it sound as if our science is just part of some worldwide conspiracy or something. Make people sick, then cure them with drugs. We're supposed to be the good guys, remember?"

Billy laughed. "Oh, I remember, dude. You go into science wanting to be on the cutting-edge, maybe even save the world. But look at the reality. We are spending the best years of our youth in dead-end science fair projects in graduate school. I'd rather be working directly for the DoD rather than living this post-doc life."

Cory stacked his files, not saying anything. Billy had him there.

Billy swung a long leg over the chair, stood, and stretched, sighing elaborately. "Say, can we get out of here yet? If you want to talk philosophy, I'm going to need a beer."

"Go. Go see your mama in Houston. I won't rat you out to Dr. Wong. And if we all don't get blown away, I'll see you back here next week."

Billy was already heading for the door. "You sure you don't want me to double-check security and decon procedures?"

"I got this," Cory said, more sharply than he'd intended. "Just sign off and don't skip anything. Now go. You're making me nervous and I have to lock down the vials and samples in the freezer. We can't have this stuff getting loose."

"I owe you," said Billy as he left the office.

Cory waited until Billy had gone before he headed toward the showers.

"I got this, I got this ..." he murmured the words like an incantation as he twisted the pipette back into its slim glass vial and replaced the lab slides into their sleeves. Then, he tucked everything safely into the Pandora's box with the automatic temperature control and put everything to sleep until the box opened again. He locked the unit with a digital combination he knew by heart, certain that it would not be him who let loose some plague upon the unsuspecting world. He gave a last glance around before he turned out the lights. A place for everything and everything safely in its place. The blue light from the digital freezer blinked at him as he closed the door. He entered the decontamination shower and closed the door behind him. Everything was as it should be. He made his way back to the antechamber and struggled out of the suffocating suit. Grateful to be able to wiggle his shoulders and ease his aching neck, he allowed the heat of the shower to sink deep in his muscles.

And when he was finished, he spent a long moment studying his freckled face in the mirror, all dark eyes, red hair, and full lips and a serious expression that never seemed to leave him. "I'm one of the good guys," he said to no one as he gathered his things, turned out the light, and headed out.

But even as he hit the button for the elevator in the hallway outside, hearing the wind whistling softly over the great glass wall that faced the sea, *something* in that mournful sound bothered him. A thought flickered on the edge of his mind, taunting him.

Someone else might have called it intuition, but Cory Finch was a scientist and placed little stock in such things.

And yet it persisted. A nameless, nagging sensation.

Something, somewhere, was terribly wrong.

CHAPTER ONE
Galveston University Hospital
Forty-eight hours until Hurricane Beatrix makes landfall

"Can you please show up on time? We've been waiting for you to start."

Dr. Amy Dunn, the ICU fellow, frowned as Dr. Danica Diza skittered to a stop in the Intensive Care Unit's outer corridor.

"It's only 6:03," Danica protested. "Besides, I got held up helping out with the bagging and tagging at the nurses' station for the mandatory evac to Houston."

The administrators wanted three hundred and fifty patients gone today and another two hundred by tomorrow. And every single one of them had to travel with their charts, their meds, and their essential personal belongings. It was a logistics nightmare. The long, slow procession of wheelchairs, shuffling patients dragging their IV drips, and walking casts had snaked their way toward the elevator banks all afternoon. The least serious were to be loaded onto waiting buses and the more serious cases were to be airlifted by a small army of medivac helicopters that buzzed like some eerie invasion of dragonflies, over the hospital helipads in a never-ending succession.

"The circumstances are irrelevant," Dr. Dunn insisted. "Rounds begin promptly at 6:00 p.m."

From somewhere behind her, Danica heard a low murmur: "And the horse you rode in on." She stifled a snicker. As much she hated to be called out, Danica had to admit that Dr. Amy Dunn was one of those doctors who wasn't out to win any popularity contests—with the residents, the patients, or anybody else.

But regardless of incoming hurricanes, every hospital with a residency program in the country goes through a similar ritual of evening checkout. The day team passes on information about each patient and the events that unfolded during the day to the incoming night team. Details about individual patient plans are passed on along with pitfalls to watch out for. The medical intensive care unit rotation at University Hospital was a time-consuming process, and rounds took a minimum of three to four hours.

The day-and-night team entered room 212. Dr. Dunn cleared her throat loudly. "First patient, Mr. Garcia. He's a sixty-year-old who presented with an ST-elevation myocardial infarction today and is status post percutaneous coronary intervention on a heparin drip. He was stable throughout the day with no cardiac events. We had been drawing his cardiac enzymes every eight hours and will need to continue to trend the troponins tonight."

Danica scribbled "Trend trops" in her notes, next to Garcia's name and record number. Then she followed Dr. Dunn to room 214.

"Next, Mrs. Myers. She's a seventy-two-year-old female nursing home resident who presented with septic shock, likely from a decubitus ulcer. She's on antibiotics and IV fluids. We need to follow up the lactic acid."

She duly noted the follow-up, suddenly aware of weatherman Wolf Blitzer's voice echoing from the TV monitor. She listened for a few seconds. He was doing a special on climate change. "This is the busiest hurricane season on record," he said. "Just today, we learned of another tropical depression developing in the Atlantic off the coast of Africa."

As Dr. Dunn's voice droned on, Danica's mind wandered for a moment. *Funny thing about disasters*, Danica thought, *when you get right down to it, they are all relative.* As big as climate change is, as scary as an impending hurricane might be, what did they mean, really? In the end, it was easy to get caught up in the downward spiral of impending doom and global catastrophe.

Breaking Danica's trance, Alondra, the charge nurse, rushed into the room. "Mr. Garcia in 212 just went into cardiac arrest!"

The MICU nurses were seasoned veterans. They could run a code better than anyone else in the hospital. By the time Danica got to Mr. Garcia's room, they had already connected defibrillator pads to Mr. Garcia's bare chest and were performing chest compressions.

"Do we have vascular access?" shouted the anesthesiology resident, who set up at the head of the bed, preparing to intubate.

"Twenty-seven, twenty-eight, twenty-nine, thirty," said Julio, another MICU nurse, counting the compressions aloud. Both day and night staff piled into Mr. Garcia's room.

"Analyzing rhythm. Shock advised." A loud metallic voice emanated from the external defibrillator.

"Everybody cleared?"

It was a moment before Danica realized it was she who'd asked the question. Her own heart pounded. She knew full well that codes were never as organized or successful as they seemed. Only about twenty percent of patients who arrested actually made it out of the hospital.

"Delivering shock," continued the metallic voice.

The team performed a rhythm check and someone announced he felt a pulse.

Danica's eyes flickered to the monitor and she verified a bounding, regular radial pulse. It was a small victory. Mr. Garcia wasn't out of the woods yet.

She looked up at the clock. 7:10 p.m. It was going to be another long night.

***

"*Beep! Beep!*"

Still asleep, Danica fumbled for her phone to silence the alarm she'd set. Five more minutes, just five more precious minutes … .

"*Beep! Beep!*"

This time, the sound was overlaid with another sound: a human voice mimicking the electronic signal.

Annoyed, she opened one eye to see Dr. Shaka Sen standing over her, a steaming, foam cup of coffee in his hand. The intoxicating smell of caffeine alone was enough to get her to open the other eye. She struggled to sit upright from her place on the couch in the residents' lounge. Once up, she swept her hair from her eyes. "Damn! What time is it?"

Shaka handed her the cup. "Half past hurry-up-for-rounds. You got five before we're due in ICU."

She took it and gulped gratefully. "Thanks," she said. "How come 'we'? I thought you would've evacuated by now."

Shaka shrugged and smiled wickedly, reminding Danica of her narcissistic ex-boyfriend. "What can I say? They needed the best surgeon they had to stay on as essential personnel. And we all know who that is, don't we?"

Danica shook her head. Arrogant didn't begin to describe him. All the surgeons were egotistical, of course. It was a quality she figured a person had to have to some degree before aspiring to cut people open on a regular basis, but Shaka took it to new heights and not without reason.

His skills were already legendary—both as a surgeon and, according to any number of the female staff, in the bedroom as well. She couldn't say she blamed them. Shaka was one of the most handsome men she'd ever laid eyes on. If he hadn't gone into medicine, he could have been a model or one of those Bollywood legends like Ranveer Singh. Deep down Shaka just reminded her of her first love in medical school who she thought she would marry and grow old with. He was the cockiest person she had ever met. He would make his mediocre surgeon skills seem like they were God's gift to humanity, constantly overshadowing Danica's own accomplishments. Danica spent three excruciating years waiting for him to put a ring on it. She was so blinded by the idea of love that she didn't see he was cheating on her during their whole relationship and he ended up knocking up her friend. It devastated her.

In retrospect, she should have seen he was the absolute worst person for her, but hindsight is always twenty-twenty.

Since then, she'd had a string of failed encounters amounting to nothing more than casual dates, not allowing herself to experience that heartbreak again. All marriages and relationships were shams, a power dynamic used to control each other through the façade of affection. Relationships were prisons of unhappiness, and she didn't want to be stuck in one.

Swallowing the last of her coffee, she jumped to her feet, suddenly acutely aware of her own appearance. She swept past him into the restroom, getting just close enough to catch a whiff of his cologne and feel the warmth that emanated from every cell of his body.

Danica scowled at her own reflection in the bathroom mirror. She looked worse than she thought. She'd been at the hospital for more than twenty-four hours, and the evidence—the dark bags under her hazel eyes and the lines of tension etched into her forehead—was prominent. By working abnormal, sometimes grueling, hours, she felt she'd aged five years just being in residency. She straightened her dark blue scrubs, fixed her brunette hair into a high, messy ponytail, and took out some tinted lip balm from her back pocket, slapping it on at the last moment in order to look somewhat presentable.

Danica followed hard on Shaka's long, easy strides as they navigated to the ICU, where Dr. Hardy, the attending, and the rest of the team awaited them, ready to round. Starting at one end of the department, they discussed the first patient, who happened to be hers. Hastily, she filled them in and offered her overnight updates.

Dr. Hardy appeared uninterested as they moved on to the next patient, who belonged to the intern. Dr. Hardy's face, suddenly amused, brightened with a grin as he gazed at the intern. Relentlessly, he spat out a whole barrage of questions about the pathophysiology of sepsis.

Unaccustomed to the attention, the intern looked down at her notes and stammered, "It's from an infection that goes into the bloodstream that leads to septic shock and multi-organ failure."

"What tests have you done to monitor severity?"

"Complete blood count and cultures." By this time, the intern was red-faced with embarrassment.

He faced her and pushed for more answers. "What else?"

She looked down, searching for the correct answer.

Danica finally jumped in to save her. "Glucose levels, creatinine, urine output, serum lactate level."

Dr. Hardy's eyes were cold as he glared at her.

Danica faced him, her expression composed. "We still have forty other patients to talk about."

Not to be outdone, Dr. Hardy whirled around and proceeded down the hallway. "And as you are doubtlessly aware, none of the patients in the ICU are cleared for evacuation as yet. So be prepared for your new patient assignments at the end of shift. As designated essential personnel, you will remain here at the hospital for the duration, or until further notice."

Just then, the group was slowed by yet another line of evacuees, shuffling slowly toward the elevator bank that led down to the parking level. Some appeared frightened, some annoyed, and others merely resigned to the turn things had taken.

Almost reluctantly, the team moved on.

After rounds, Danica made her way to the nearest computer station. As she pondered placing orders in for her new patient roster, the young intern skittered up behind Danica, rubber soles squeaking loudly against the flooring tile. "Thanks for saving me back there," the intern said, holding out her hand and blushing furiously. "Dr. Hardy … I mean, I know he's probably very good and everything, but some days it's like … ."

Danica smiled warmly. "Don't worry about him. He's tough on new interns until he's sure they know their stuff, that's all. Believe me, his bark is worse than his bite."

"No kidding!" She stuck out her hand. "I'm Beth, by the way. Beth Windsor."

"Nice to meet you, Beth. Don't worry, you're doing fine. Hey! I guess it's kind of an honor, an intern getting pegged as essential personnel this early in the game. Even if it means we have to go through a hurricane."

Beth's face darkened and she blinked rapidly, as though she was on the verge of tears. "Aren't you scared? I am. Ugh, I'd give anything to be in Houston right now."

Danica took a left, heading toward the cafeteria. "Look, I have to get something to eat before I fall down, okay? And don't worry. Just take care of your patients. You won't have time to be scared."

As she walked into the cafeteria, the news was blasting from the TV screens mounted on the walls. The reporter was interviewing a Galvestonian couple who were saying that they had survived Hurricane Ike and Hurricane Harvey, and they weren't going to evacuate for this hurricane. They were going to stay put and ride out the storm.

"Nice to have a choice, I guess," she muttered glumly as she waited for her order. She pulled out her phone and began scrolling through her texts, mostly from her family wanting to know if she was safe.

"Tsk, tsk." A familiar voice interrupted her thoughts. "Talking to ourselves, are we, Dr. Diza?"

She glanced up to see Shaka's sparkling black eyes studying her with an amused expression. She couldn't help but be drawn in by his warm, caramel-colored skin, full lips, white teeth, and movie star smile. In a hospital full of tired, overworked, and terribly ill people, he stood out like a beacon of radiant health—robust and strong and sexy as hell. She felt a slow blush creeping up her neck.

Danica slid her tray down the tubular tray slide as a cafeteria employee set out her sandwich. "No," she insisted more sharply than she'd intended. "That is—it was more to the TV."

If he was put off, he didn't show it. "Good. Mind if I join you?"

Actually, she *did* mind. All she wanted in the world was to eat her sandwich in peace. He grabbed her tray and his without waiting for an answer and slid them onto a booth table in the corner. For a moment, neither of them spoke, each too preoccupied and hungry to do anything more than rip into their sandwiches. Hers was a grilled cheese and his was a bacon cheeseburger. She closed her eyes and chewed gratefully. People could say what they wanted about hospital food, but after the past couple of days, it might as well have come from a fancy restaurant. She paused and sucked greedily at her sweet tea.

Shaka observed her thoughtfully. "You've had better days."

She rolled her eyes. "Gee, thanks. Is that your official diagnosis?"

The corner of his mouth curved into a grin as he tore into a bag of chips. "Just an observation." His eyes drifted to the TV in the corner. "So, what do you think about this storm coming in? I heard it was upgraded to a category three and expect to do it again before it's all over. What do you think? How rough is it going to be?"

Feeling somewhat fortified by the food, Danica picked at a tired-looking orange slice from her fruit cup and then eyed Shaka skeptically. "Dr. Sen, did you really want to sit down here and talk to me about the weather?"

His smile faltered momentarily and he shrugged. "Pretty hot topic of conversation these days, doctor. In case you haven't noticed."

Poor thing, she thought. Probably so used to women falling at his feet, he didn't know what to do. "Sorry," she relented.

Like magic, his smile returned. "Just making conversation. I figure since we're stuck here for the duration it couldn't hurt to get better acquainted."

"I don't mean to be rude. It's been a real long day. Guess I'm a little punchy."

"Besides," he went on smoothly, "you wouldn't be half bad-looking with a little sleep."

She bristled again before she realized he was only teasing. In spite of herself, she smiled.

"That's more like it," he said. "Relax a little when you get the chance."

As if in answer, Danica's pager signaled and she fumbled for her phone. "Damn … Dr. Sen, I'm sorry—"

"Call me Shaka. And you're Danica, is it?"

"Yup." Danica punched the number that was paged to her into her cell phone and waited for an answer. Someone on the other end responded with an update and a beckon. After murmuring into the receiver, "I am on my way," Danica hung up.

"What's up?"

"I have to go. Mr. Ruiz's family is here. We have to have *the* talk."

His handsome face fell. "Oh, *that* talk. Why doesn't the attending doctor do it? Why pick on you?"

She tilted her head and stared at him oddly. "Ruiz is my patient. I don't think any of the Ruiz family has even met Dr. Hardy. It wouldn't be fair."

Resigned, Shaka rose to his feet and gathered the trays. "I got these. But Danica?"

Already halfway across the room, she turned around.

"Don't work too hard, okay? Or be too hard on yourself. I mean it."

She heard the sincerity in his tone. Maybe he wasn't as arrogant as she presumed. "Thanks," she said. "I'll try."

***

After Danica left the room, the scent of vanilla and lavender still lingered in the air, intoxicating him. Shaka had been trying to get Danica's attention since the first time he crossed paths with her eight months ago. She was the primary doctor on one of his patients and had consulted him for surgery. The patient needed emergency surgery and subsequently needed chemotherapy. The patient was not insured, so getting post-op chemotherapy would have been difficult. But not for Danica. She brilliantly advocated for the patient and set that patient up for an assistance program, then convinced the attending physicians to do the treatments urgently. The memory brought a smile to his face.

He'd tried to pursue her multiple times, mustering the courage to talk to her once or twice, but the hierarchy of medicine frowns down on fraternization among colleagues. As far as he could tell, Danica was driven enough that she barely looked at other men and was seldom friendly with other staff.

One-night stands and casual hooks ups had been a ton of fun, but as of late, they were getting mundane and redundant. Wine and dine a girl, take her home to bed, and wave her out the next day under false pretenses of calling her later, yet they never piqued his interest enough to do. Shaka had never had any problems with forgetting about a girl and moving onto the next one. But when it came to Danica, he couldn't stop thinking about her. At work, when he was operating, when he went to bed, and the first thing when he woke up, she was always in his thoughts.

Danica wasn't the casual dating or hookup type of girl. With her it would be something different. Shuffling through his thoughts, he was determined to find out what this was and where it might lead. He wasn't the type to walk away from a challenge, and she had piqued his interest even more now that they were stuck together.

CHAPTER TWO
Galveston University Hospital

Needing time to prepare herself for the conversation ahead with Mr. Ruiz's family, Danica decided to take the long way back from the cafeteria. The alternate route gave her an opportunity to cross the long walkway that served to link the two major wings of the hospital. One wall was made entirely of glass windows that faced the seawall. She paused for a moment, marveling at the sunlight dancing over the water in a sparkling display, seagulls circling the beach. A breeze fluttered through the towering palms that decorated the landscape with a view that was nearly devoid of pedestrians. It might have been just another day at the beach, with no indication of the impending storm. She inhaled deeply, longing to smell the scent of the ocean and feel the sea spray on her skin. How long had it been since she'd gotten some fresh air? It felt like days.

Her reverie was interrupted as Dr. Kirsten Stone, the chief medical officer, hustled off the elevator in her direction, staring angrily at the phone in her hand. "Damn it!" she shouted, then glanced up, clearly embarrassed that someone had heard her outburst.

Danica smiled a little, trying to put her at her ease.

Dr. Stone squinted at Danica's ID. "Oh, hello. Dr. Diza, is it? Am I pronouncing that right?"

Danica quickly corrected the pronunciation to "DEE-za."

Dr. Stone slid her phone into the pocket of her blazer. "My apologies, but this morning has been … ."

"I completely understand," said Danica. "It can't be an easy time for the administration office."

"You're telling me. I was called down to the east entrance. There had to be two hundred people down there. Most from that homeless camp down on the beach. Apparently, those who couldn't or didn't want to follow the mandatory evacuation order decided to head over here and demand shelter in the hospital till the storm passes."

Danica looked concerned. "Isn't there something we can do? We're a state institution after all."

Dr. Stone pressed her lips together in an angry line. "No, there isn't. We have, at best, a skeleton crew—no way to monitor their activities, no place to put them except in the wards we've already shut down, and no way to feed them, either. This is a hospital, not a hotel."

Danica could see the older woman's point. She nodded in apparent agreement.

"Do you have any idea what a move like that would cost us?" Dr. Stone asked. "So, suddenly they're out there chanting and holding up signs and the TV news crew shows up. I'm trying to explain. I directed them to St. Mary's, even. I figured maybe the church had a basement or something they could stay in."

Danica agreed. "It's something, anyway."

Dr. Stone's phone buzzed frantically. She plucked it out and displayed a screenshot of a very frustrated acting chief of staff waving a microphone out of her face as the hostile crowd rose in the background.

Danica shook her head. "I'm so sorry," she offered lamely.

"Me, too. The piece is going viral on Twitter. 'Heartless Hospital Admin turns away homeless.' Great. Now I'm the Wicked Witch of the Week. I just hope the board doesn't decide to fire me before it has a chance to blow over."

With that, she turned and continued down the hall without so much as a wave of her hand. Danica couldn't blame her. Dr. Stone had a great reputation as a problem solver, but this one didn't seem to have a ready solution.

***

Steeling herself for an extremely difficult conversation with the Ruiz family, Danica inhaled deeply before turning the doorknob to his room. Inside, she tried to muster an understanding smile.

"Hi, I am Dr. Diza. I'm a third-year family medicine resident on ICU and have been taking care of Mr. Ruiz since he has been here at the hospital. I know I've met some of you, but if I haven't, then let's get acquainted."

Slowly, she made her way around the room, shook everyone's hand, and asked how they were related. They were cousins, in-laws, even a sister from New York that no one had expected. Mr. Ruiz was well-loved. Somehow, knowing this about Mr. Ruiz made what she had to do next easier.

As many times as she'd had this same conversation, she couldn't help but wonder what she would do if it were one of her own family members. Despite all her training, would she be able to withdraw life support from a loved one when they were most vulnerable? It was one of those decisions she hoped she never had to make.

Her stomach churned, and she cleared her throat uncomfortably. "I know you must have some questions for me. I'm happy to answer any of your concerns."

Mrs. Ruiz rose unsteadily to her feet. In her late forties, she had long, black hair and was dressed in jeans and a gray T-shirt. Recent events had clearly taken their toll, and deep exhaustion showed in her face. Her black eyes glistened with moisture. "So, what happened? He was fine a week ago and now you are telling me he's basically dead."

Danica couldn't help but notice how beautiful the woman was. Danica shook her head, acknowledging Mrs. Ruiz's statement.

"Mr. Ruiz had a stroke from a ruptured brain aneurysm, an abnormal outpouching in a blood vessel in his brain," Danica said. "Most likely, he'd had it for a while. His smoking and high blood pressure probably contributed to its formation. It wasn't causing him problems until it burst. That's why he came to us with the worst headache of his life. Our neuroradiologist did his best to secure the aneurysm with coils so it wouldn't rebleed. After that, as you know, he was transferred to the ICU, where we monitored him very closely. Today he developed signs of severe vasospasm—or narrowing of the arteries—in the brain after subarachnoid hemorrhage."

Danica took a deep breath, her eyes glistening as she continued. "We tried everything to augment blood flow back to the brain, but it wasn't enough. The vasospasm affected a blood vessel that supplies most of the left hemisphere of the brain, causing another type of stroke called an ischemic stroke, which resulted in brain swelling. Our neurosurgeon performed a hemicraniectomy to help relieve this pressure, but it was too late. His intracranial pressure had increased so much so that his brain stem herniated through the hole at the bottom of the skull. This caused Mr. Ruiz to progress to brain-death, an irreversible loss of brain function. He can't feel pain and he can't breathe on his own. Unfortunately, we believe that he will not wake up."

Mrs. Ruiz stood in the center of the room, shaking her hands in a gesture of utter helplessness, then she screamed at the top of her lungs and sobbed uncontrollably.

An older man rose to his feet and gently placed his arm around Mrs. Ruiz's shoulders. "*Pobrecita,*" he said, and tried to lead her to a chair.

Danica discreetly turned her gaze out the window as the rest of the group erupted into sobs, trying to process the awful news. Another woman took up the rosary in her lap, made the sign of the cross, and kissed it in a final prayer. Outside, the earlier dance of sunlight on the water had vanished, replaced by huge banks of clouds to the south. The waves thrashed insistently at the seawall. The whole atmosphere pulsed in the sultry light.

After another moment, Danica solemnly turned back around to face the group and said, "We have to discuss life support and whether you want to continue him on it or stop."

Everyone was looking down, avoiding eye contact—at a loss for words. Each was desperate to have their family member wake up and be the man they once knew, yet each person knew it was not going to happen.

Mrs. Ruiz's eyes filled with a seemingly bottomless pain, as she composed herself as best she could and faced Danica squarely. A last glance at her husband in the bed convinced her. She clutched both of Danica's hands for support. "Thank you for everything you did for us, but it is time to let him go and ease him from this pain."

Danica's own eyes filled with tears, and she nodded mutely, unable to help but share in Mrs. Ruiz's agony, feeling the woman's pain and loss—the love of her life, the father of her children, her partner, and her most trusted friend.

The respiratory tech turned off the ventilation machine and extubated Mr. Ruiz as his nurse logged into the electronic medical record to put in final orders.

Do not resuscitate.

Do not intubate.

"Stay with him as long as you want," Danica said softly. "I am so sorry for your loss."

Danica emerged from the room on shaky legs and headed slowly down the corridor, pausing at the nurses' station. "What next?"

"Landfall in twenty-four hours they say now, unless it slows down again."

Huffing, Danica slammed her iPad on the counter, recomposing herself.

The nurse at the station looked away from the TV, surprised at Danica's expression. "Oh, you mean for you? Lemme look."

She ran her finger down a list. "Looks like you won the lottery," she said. "Jason Carter, prison wing."

Danica frowned. "Have I seen him before? The name isn't familiar."

"You're just going to inherit a patient from the infectious diseases service. Mr. Carter is an incarcerated forty-one-year-old male; day five for hospital-acquired pneumonia. He's been on IV vancomycin and piperacillin and tazobactam. He's doing better. His cultures grew methicillin-resistant staphylococcus aureus, which was sensitive to levofloxacin. His vitals are normal. Physical exam was notable for an improved lung exam with only mild expiratory wheezes. Plan for today is to wean him off oxygen, transition him to oral Levaquin, and send him back to his unit."

"Check." Danica nodded and swung toward the elevators that would lead her to the prison wing. As she crossed over from University Hospital to the Texas Department of Corrections, she couldn't help but be struck by the sharp contrast. Here, the walls were painted gray and white. It looked old and rundown with black stains on the floors and walls. A faint tinge of urine mixed with the heavy scent of antiseptic cleaner hung in the air. The hairs on her neck stood up, the echo of the clunking gates following her as she moved forward and presented her ID to the security guard to sign in. The barred gates opened and she climbed into the elevator to the fourth floor. As she entered, she forced herself to remember that prisoners were a vulnerable population and still needed to be treated as anyone else.

Outside her patient's room, a stone-faced guard stared blankly ahead of him as Danica approached.

"Can you open this room, please?" Danica asked.

The guard rose from his chair, went to the door, and unlocked it. He swung the clunky, heavy door all the way open, catching it on the magnetic stop inside the wall to hold the door in place. He waited outside, watching her closely.

Dylan Nguyen, a PA student who had been rotating with Dr. Diza, caught up with her just as the door caught on the magnetic stop. "Hi, Dr. Diza."

"Hi, Dylan." Danica motioned the younger man toward the door. "Be my guest. What are you still doing here? I thought you'd have evacuated by now."

"Just about," Dylan replied, turning back toward her as she entered. "I was working on the discharge summary for Mr. Carter. I just wanted to see if you needed anything before I checked out."

They strode over to the patient's bed. If Mr. Carter was touched by Nguyen's concern for his health even in the midst of a hurricane, he didn't show it. His massive, six-foot-plus frame lay huddled on the bed in the fetal position. The hospital gown, opened down the back, revealed an assortment of tattoos on his arms and back and an ugly-looking scar on his shoulder. The oxygen machine hissed in the corner.

Danica's heart went out to him. For all of his size, he looked terribly alone. And scared. After using the hand sanitizer provided, she strode to the bed. "Mr. Carter, are you awake?"

Annoyed, Jason opened his eyes and yanked the air tube from his nostrils. "What do you want? Can I get out of Dodge yet? How long is it going to take for you guys to get it together so I can leave?"

Dylan interrupted. "Mr. Carter, I apologize for the inconvenience, but we are working hard to get you out of here as fast as possible. We've started the oral medication that you will be discharged on. You can catch the last bus back to Huntsville today, but we just don't know when that will be. The Texas Department of Criminal Justice strictly forbids disclosing that information to you. It's up to them to decide when you will actually leave."

Jason, eyeing Dr. Diza skeptically, swung his long legs off the bed. "Fine. The sooner the better."

"This is Dr. Diza. She'll be overseeing you from now on," Dylan went on. "Thank you for allowing me to be a part of your care. This is the last time I'll be seeing you. Best of luck with everything."

Jason mumbled something without meeting anyone's eyes.

Danica checked his vitals and his breathing. "Where'd you get that scar on your shoulder?"

For the first time, Jason fully registered that she was in the room. He faced her full-on, his expression unreadable. "Iraq," he answered flatly. "Marines."

Danica opened her mouth to ask, "Then how did you wind up in prison?" but something in his eyes warned her away. So she merely nodded and backed off. "Those lungs sound pretty good! I'll be back in the afternoon to check on you in a few hours and we'll get you on the last bus to Huntsville."

Once they were past security, Danica couldn't contain her curiosity any longer. "Well, he sure seems in a hurry to leave. I mean, maybe the prison wing isn't great, but it's got to be better than a cell block, right? What do you know about Mr. Carter?"

Dylan volunteered. "I looked him up on the TDCJ offender search website to see what he was in for and found out he's doing time for armed robbery. He told me he was a veteran, though. From what I've seen of his overall affect,

PTSD could be a factor, especially after a couple of tours in Iraq. Not a happy guy."

"I don't like using that website," she told Dylan. "I would lose objectivity in treating patients if I knew they were a capital criminal."

"True, but gives you perspective as well," Dylan stated.

As Danica walked away, she glanced over her shoulder as to see the guard resume his seat. She had a feeling there was more to Jason Carter than anybody knew.

CHAPTER THREE

The National Biocontainment Lab, Galveston University Hospital

Twenty-four hours until Hurricane Beatrix makes landfall

Cory Finch headed toward Dr. Wong's office for his weekly lab meeting. Constant coverage of the storm was displayed on every TV in every room. For some reason, Cory felt on edge as the umpteenth blonde reporter stood in front of the cameras, reciting a litany of possibilities. The camera angle switched to a shot of shopkeepers and volunteers shoring up the seawall with bags of sand and boarding up windows. Less than twenty-four hours to go. Part of his mind couldn't help but think it was all somehow absurd. Faced with a powerful-enough hurricane, what difference would a few sandbags and some plywood actually make?

He knocked lightly on Dr. Wong's door. Hearing a "Come in," Cory took a seat across from Dr. Wong at his massive mahogany desk.

"Are all of your research samples secured per safety protocol?" asked Dr. Wong.

"Yes, Dr. Wong. I finished the last transfer and locked it in the freezer," Cory said, then hesitated. Deep down there was always a fear that he'd done something wrong. "Billy Andersen has some interesting ideas."

Dr. Wong cleared his throat. "Andersen has enough ideas to host talk radio or have a daytime TV show."

Cory nodded mutely. Dr. Wong had never given points for speculation.

Dr. Wong leaned on his desk and steepled his fingers. "After today, the lab will be closed in preparation for the storm. As with the rest of the hospital facilities, there will be a skeleton crew to ensure the safety of pathogens and to implement any necessary back-up safety protocols."

Cory nodded, gripping the arms of his chair with sweaty palms. He had a feeling he knew what was coming next.

Dr. Wong looked uncomfortable. "Cory, you were chosen at random to stay at the lab. I will be staying on with you as well. I'm sorry, son. Luck of the draw."

The room spun for a moment as Cory's heart sank in his chest. Part of him knew his selection was not at all random. He lived alone, had no family, and if anything happened to him, he would not be missed. It was unfair, but logical.

Dr. Wong eyed him sympathetically over the top of his glasses.

Despite his outward composure, Cory felt pale and shaken. "Thanks, Dr. Wong. Is there anything we need to do to get the lab ready?"

Abruptly, Dr. Wong's phone rang. He took it out of his pocket and answered. "Hi, honey. Did you pack everything?" He inhaled deeply. "No, honey, I can't leave. I have to stay here. How are the kids?" he went on in a low voice.

Even without the speakerphone, Cory could hear Dr. Wong's children screaming, "Daddy! Daddy!" in the background.

Amused, Dr. Wong replied, "Be good. Listen to your mom. I love you guys. Can I speak to your mother again?" There was a pause as he waited for his wife to come on the line. Now, he looked utterly miserable. "I love you, honey. Don't cry, please. It's going to be all right. Call me as soon as you reach your parents' house. Drive carefully." His voice cracked with emotion as he hung up.

Cory hung his head and stared at his palms. He couldn't imagine what Dr. Wong was going through.

After another moment, Dr. Wong spoke again. "Everything has already been done. We're as ready as we can be. Now we just wait. You should try to get some rest. Grab a meal. We can meet again in a few hours to run through the safety checks."

Cory brightened a little at the prospect. "Sounds good. I am sorry you're stuck here with me and can't be with your family, Dr. Wong."

The older man managed a wan smile. "Thanks. I guess you're stuck with me too."

***

When Cory departed, Dr. Wong spent a few more minutes staring at the ceiling as the endless stream of reporters danced across the muted TV screen in the office. *A few more hours*, he thought. *A day, maybe two. And this will all be over.* Then he could go home. Meanwhile, though, it was a good idea to take his own advice. Some rest, a hot meal.

Dr. Wong rose from his chair, grabbed the remote, and switched off his television. Grabbing his keys, he walked over toward the door. He switched off the overhead light, locked the door to his office, and headed down the hall. As he neared the elevator, he heard the sound of the elevator door, opening and closing and opening again, as if blocked by some unseen obstacle. Its interior light was casting crazy shadows in the darkened hall. Trying to see the problem, he moved forward, his hand already reaching for his phone.

There, curled up in the corner of the elevator, was Cory Finch, unconscious, his face and neck covered in blood, his back against the wall and right leg splayed out against the door's threshold, just enough to block the closing.

Frantically, Dr. Wong felt for a pulse.

It was faint, fluttering.

Cory was alive.

For now.

CHAPTER FOUR
Galveston University Hospital

The strong scent of cologne awoke Danica from her dreams, warm and pungent with a hint of sweetness. Next came the sound, a kind of unfamiliar roar, low, persistent, and faraway, like the approach of some thundering army, or the echo of one just passed. Then, a touch on her shoulder, pleasant and strong and reassuring, enough so that she reached up, almost involuntarily, to return the touch with her own hand. The sudden contact brought her fully awake, and she found herself sitting up on the couch in the residents' lounge, staring straight into the warm brown eyes of Dr. Shaka Sen.

"Good morning, sunshine" he said. "Time to rise and shine."

Danica shook the last of the sleep from her eyes. "Wow. I can't believe I fell asleep. After rounds I came here to write my notes. I guess I must have passed out."

Shaka smiled. "Barometric pressure. Some people feel the drops more than others. I let you sleep as long as I could. We're on the flip side now."

She stared at him blankly. "Flip side?"

"The hurricane. See, they swirl around in this big circle. In the center is the eye, where it's always calm. But all around the periphery are the winds. They're clocking at between one hundred and twenty and one hundred fifty miles per hour." He raised one arm in the air and made a circling motion. "As the wind circles out to sea, the pressure drops. As the circle comes back around, it rises again."

She grinned and tilted her head up at him as he rose from his chair. "Are you actually explaining a hurricane to me?"

He straightened up, unperturbed. "Can't help it. It fascinates me. Weather, the planet, climate change, everything. I mean, when you can feel what's happening outside in your own body, on an almost cellular level, it reminds you of how connected things are, you know?"

Danica nodded, looking at her hands and thinking of the Ruiz family. The drain of her own energy in the face of their loss.

"But you should be feeling better, anyhow," Shaka continued, making his way toward a table in the corner. "You were out for almost three hours. Now, look sharp, sweetheart. I have a surprise for you. Ta-da!"

"Don't you dare call me that—" she began, but then, seeing what he held out before her, she trailed off, astonished. "Oh my God, is that ... Starbucks? Real Starbucks?"

He nodded proudly. "One venti salted caramel macchiato latte with an extra shot of espresso and real whipped cream. Probably the last on Galveston Island. Thought we would share. C'mon, the caffeine will get you going, and the sugar will do you good."

He split the coffee into another cup and held it out to her.

"But how did you get these?" She took one of the cups and gulped gratefully. "I would have for sure thought all the Starbucks would have evacuated by now."

Shaka shrugged. "I did a crash C-section earlier since there aren't enough obstetricians left at the hospital. A National Guardsman's wife was in labor on the evacuation highway. Little tiny woman and a great big baby. Nine pounds, ten ounces. Beautiful kid. Anyway, it seemed like they were both in trouble, so he hauled them back here. Good thing too. I did the section, which I hadn't done since medical school, and he was so happy and grateful, he wanted to know if there was anything he could do for me. I couldn't blame him. I was pretty happy myself. There's nothing like a new baby, is there? Life renewing itself."

She nodded, not quite knowing what to make of the comment. "You never fail to surprise me, Dr. Sen. I wouldn't have thought a man like you would get soft over a baby."

Shaka cleared his throat. "Anyway, I was kidding when I mentioned Starbucks, but he took off like a bat out of hell and came back with this. Nice, huh? I don't know where he got it, but I wasn't about to question something that made my day—and apparently yours too."

Danica already felt the welcome surge of warmth and energy through her veins. Smiling for what felt like the first time that day, she raised her cup in salute. "To the hero of the hour, the formidable surgeon, Dr. Shaka Sen. We thank you."

Suddenly looking embarrassed, Shaka turned his head away. "Yeah, well. It's in my job description, isn't it? And just so you know, I had another emergency surgery today. I lost that one, so spare me the hero stuff, okay?"

Hearing the break in his voice, Danica tilted her head toward him. "Sorry. What happened?"

"Two maniacs got into a knife fight on one of the exit ramps. One of them didn't make it. Lacerated carotid artery. Nothing I could do by the time he got to us. The other is in custody. On his way to Huntsville on the last bus."

"A knife fight? With a freaking hurricane coming?"

Shaka shook his head sadly. "Desperate people do desperate things. And believe me, it's getting pretty wild out there. The National Guard closed every access road except one. People are scared. And we still have a good ten hours before landfall."

He observed her for a long moment. "Weird, though. How when you are scared to die, some people just get angry, but some guys would rather see somebody else dead first. And over what? Cutting in front of them in traffic? A fender bender?" He paused and shook his head. "The human condition, survival of the fittest, I guess.

"But drink up, Dr. Diza. This day's not over yet. You're needed in the ICU. We have a mystery case. Cory Finch. Post-doc fellow from the biocontainment lab, no less. His principal investigator, Dr. Wong, found him collapsed in the elevator. Massive nosebleed. Totally septic. He's unconscious, white cells through the roof, and a fever floating toward 105 degrees as of 1600 hours."

"Oh, Lord," Danica said, getting to her feet. "I'm there."

He smiled again as they headed into the hallway toward the elevator bank. "Knew you would be, doctor."

It wasn't until they were in the elevator, both sets of eyes inevitably raised to watch the floors ticking by, that Danica's heart dropped into her belly. Her eyes wide, she turned to her companion. "Did you say Huntsville? Something about the last bus to Hunstville? The prison?"

Shaka stepped aside to allow her to exit first as the elevator doors slid open. "Yeah," he answered. "The guy who shanked my patient won't be charged or arraigned for the crime until after the storm passes, so they took him into custody and shipped him up there to wait it out. Why?"

"Oh, crap!" she cried as she hustled down the hall. "That guy who I accepted on my service."

"Who?"

"Jason Carter from the prison wing, that's who. He was due to be released. I thought he'd be on that bus, but they never called to confirm and sign off on the release! Shit!"

CHAPTER FIVE

The National Biocontainment Lab, Galveston University Hospital

Dr. Wong headed back toward his office inside the lab building, after watching paramedics transport Cory to the main hospital. Alone in his office, Dr. Wong sat behind his broad desk. There was no need to alarm anybody unnecessarily, he told himself. Cory just had a nosebleed, right? Those could be caused by any number of things—high blood pressure, diabetes, a sinus infection, even allergies. With all the wind kicked up out there, who knew what was blowing around?

Another, more professional part of his mind answered him. *Yes, but a nosebleed shouldn't knock you unconscious, either.* For what seemed like the hundredth time, he opened Cory's latest research report file and scanned the contents, noted in Cory's own precise hand:

Crimean Congo Hemorrhagic Fever

Sudden onset, which can present in a variety of symptoms, including, but not limited to, joint and muscle pain, headache, vomiting, and diarrhea.

Dr. Wong frowned. It was true Cory had looked tired, but feverish? Ill? Dr. Wong couldn't remember. Dr. Wong had been so preoccupied with the phone call from his family that he hadn't paid much attention to Cory's appearance.

As the disease progresses from an initial incubation period of one to five days, symptoms may include subcutaneous hemorrhage, nosebleeds … .

Dr. Wong got up and paced the room restlessly. He should notify the ICU staff of every virus Cory might have been exposed to in the lab. But Cory's illness didn't make sense; this virus was transmitted by direct contact with bodily fluids. There hadn't been any breach of containment, and even at that, Cory was working with the attenuated strain, containing only twenty percent of the virulence associated with live specimens. With the HAZMAT suits and decontamination protocol, the chances were astronomically low that Cory had contracted something. Dr. Wong ran a tight ship; every member of his staff was well aware of the dangers associated with their work—how could something have gone wrong without his knowledge? And what about Cory's lab partner, Billy Andersen? He'd more than likely evacuated with the others, but could he have been exposed as well?

Dr. Wong's phone buzzed from his breast pocket. Another text from the kids. *Daddy! Grandma's house is so cool! You need to come and be with us!* To which his youngest had added a cat sticker and an emoji of a beating heart. Staring at the screen, Dr. Wong's eyes pooled with gratitude. They were safe, at least. His family was safe. After a quick text in return, he replaced his phone and stared miserably out the window, then texted the ICU for an update on Cory's condition. A message dinged back. *There has been no change.*

And that meant he had no choice. Anyone left in the hospital would be put on quarantine until further notice. They would have to be. If Cory had by some slim chance contracted CCHF, then others could have been exposed. Including himself. As much as his heart ached to rejoin his family in the wake of the storm, for their safety, he couldn't. Hurricane or no hurricane, they had to get Cory's full blood work to the CDC for testing ASAP. If they didn't, they might be looking at an outbreak of the deadliest virus on record. While he loathed to alarm anyone unnecessarily, he had to know for sure. But first, he wanted to check the lab for himself.

The wing that housed the biocontainment lab was eerily quiet, the lights in the corridors dimmed to conserve power. His footsteps echoed in the stairwell as he made his way down the three flights, his keys and pass card dangling in his hand. The unsettling stillness was punctuated only by the ceaseless, dull roar of the winds outside. His mind flooded with unanswerable questions, and it took all his concentration to fight back the terror of his own thoughts. *Have I been exposed too? My God, the death rate is what, forty to fifty percent? What happens then? What if I collapse, just like Cory did? How long would it take someone to find me? There is no cure, there is no cure, there is no cure … .*

His footsteps beat time to the mocking chants of his mind. At the door leading to the chamber where the HAZMAT suits were kept, he halted again. His pulse fluttered in his neck. *Don't be such a coward, Wong. That's why you went into research, isn't it? Because you don't like to get your hands dirty?*

C'mon, what about that kid down there in ICU? Doesn't his life count?

Inhaling deeply, Dr. Wong swiped his pass card and stepped in, careful not to touch anything more than was necessary. Step by step, he ran through the ritual for suiting up: street clothes off, shoes off, scrubs on, protective slippers on. Hands scrubbed and decontaminated, followed by the first pair of gloves. Suit zipped with first hood; taped seal around sleeves and inner glove. Second hood tied and tightened, followed by goggles and face mask. Second set of gloves and, finally, the hard plastic visor. With practice, a good lab worker could take five full minutes, but Dr. Wong was sadly out of practice. He took nearly fifteen. The heavy protective fabric of the clumsy suit crackled in his ears, as loud as wildfire. He was breathing hard and feeling more than a little claustrophobic as he sweated his way to the chamber where the lab samples were stored.

He peered through the narrow-paned window of the door that led to the lab proper, his gloved hand hovering over the entry access. At first glance, everything was as it should be: clean and orderly, nothing out of place. He punched the light switch to his left and caught his breath, then thumped the switch again. The lights inside maintained their dim twilight, neither fully extinguished nor entirely on. As with the rest of the wing, power had to be conserved in the event of a storm emergency. Impatiently, he snatched up his visor, trying to get a better look through his sweat-fogged goggles.

Then he spied it. There, on the far wall on the right side, stood the black freezer unit that contained the lab samples. It looked fully closed and seemingly secure. But something was off. He held his breath, one part of his mind knowing the answer, another part not daring to verbalize the thought into words.

He looked around one more time, trying to put the pieces of the puzzle together. His eyes snapped to the bright blue light that signaled the freezer unit was secure.

It wasn't blinking.

No blue light indicated that the whole refrigerator system had shut down.

Dr. Wong forgot all about trying to enter the lab. He didn't need to.

He inhaled sharply, frantically reviewing the past hours in his mind. He'd been notified of the power reduction to divert power to other areas, but had he notified his staff? Had he authorized a manual override for the computers that controlled the unit? *Dear God, could he have forgotten?*

He fought back a sudden hot wave of nausea. *Onset is sudden, symptoms may present as headache, vomiting … .* Dr. Wong's mind taunted him, his demons teasing out a host of possibilities. He turned from the doorway and broke into a clumsy run as he headed back toward the decontamination room. Dr. Wong stripped away the layers of suffocating gear. Inside the two-phase decontamination showers, he lifted his face to the spray and gratefully let it pound on his neck. The heat did nothing to loosen the painful grapefruit-sized knot of tension at the back of his neck. Exposure, quarantine, those things didn't matter, he told himself. No matter how much he loved his family, he couldn't afford the risk of joining them now. None of that was important at the moment. Freezing the test samples was their first and best line of defense against the spread of infection. The virus storage had failed. Whatever was inside that lab was a ticking time bomb until it could be disposed of.

He felt a bit braver as he pulled on his street clothes and made his way through a labyrinth of hallways out of the lab toward the ICU in the opposite building, dimly aware of the constant updates pouring from the TV monitors. Eight hours to landfall. Anything could happen. It might all amount to nothing, or it might mean the worst. But first, he had to know for sure what was wrong with Cory Finch.

CHAPTER SIX
Galveston University Hospital

nside the intensive care unit, over the patient's bed, Danica frowned at the monitors. The sheen of sweat on Cory's sickly pale skin only highlighted the rash of freckles on his arms and shoulders, and his red hair showed starkly against the clean white sheets. His vitals weren't good: temp was 104.5 degrees, blood pressure was 101/52, pulse was 107 with a respiratory rate of 26, and he remained unconscious. She ran over the existing notes on Cory's chart for the twentieth time.

The floor nurse hovered at her shoulder. "Looks like malaria or something, doesn't it? My dad had that. Came back from Vietnam with it. He looked just like that."

"Any similar condition looks like that," Danica answered, more sharply than she intended. "That's the problem. Until we know what it is, all we have is our surviving sepsis guidelines. That nosebleed worries me, though. When's his blood work due? Until we know more, I'm going to order broad spectrum antibiotics, fluids, and some pressors to keep his mean arterial pressures up."

"Thank you, doctor," a voice came from the threshold. "But it may be too late for that. Get this man quarantined and in an isolation room, stat. Everyone needs full HAZMAT suits. I'm taking full responsibility for Cory and further access by any staff will be severely limited until his blood work arrives. When it does, we need to notify CDC in Atlanta."

Startled at the tone of the orders, Danica looked up. "And just who the hell are you? Do you even have admitting privileges?"

"Yes, I do. I'm Dr. Wong. Director of the National Biocontainment Lab. There—we ... ." He paused, glancing around the room helplessly. "There might have been an event."

Danica, taken aback, raised a brow. "Might have been? What are we even dealing with?"

Dr. Wong stared at the floor while explaining that he believed Cory was exposed to a virus that causes a hemorrhagic fever. He finally found the courage to meet her eyes.

"I don't want to alarm anyone yet because this virus is normally transmitted by direct contact with bodily fluids, and I have no reason to believe my post-doc came into that type of contact with anybody here," he replied, lowering his voice. "But out of an abundance of caution, I think we need to add CCHF to your differential and get an expert opinion. Or at least some guidance from the outside, Dr. Diza."

The floor nurse piped up anxiously. "The blood work's not due back in ICU for another hour. We don't have much staff down there. And I don't know how you expect me to contact the CDC. With this storm, computers are blipping out all over the place as it is."

Suddenly furious, Dr. Wong faced her. "Do whatever you have to do, all right? My God, woman, we're a national lab! That makes this a matter of *national* security. And you're telling me you can't get through because of a computer? Call the National Guard if you have to—I don't want Galveston to be what Wuhan was in 2019. *Get it done!*"

Flushed with annoyance, the nurse turned back to Danica. "I'll set up isolation and bring up the personal protective equipment," she said.

Frantically Danica contemplated that the isolation rooms in the ED hadn't been used since the recent COVID-19 and Ebola outbreaks years ago. She turned her attention back to Dr. Wong, who was staring down at Cory Finch with a mixture of pity and terror.

"I'll order additional blood work on any caretakers and staff who may be at risk," she said, struggling to keep her voice steady. "If you think it's warranted."

Dr. Wong hung his head, backed away from the bedside, and, suddenly exhausted, sank into a nearby chair. When he looked at her again, his eyes were grave.

"Get suited up yourself first," he said. "You might as well come take mine too."

CHAPTER SEVEN
Galveston University Hospital

Mom, I promise you I'm safe. There's no way these buildings will come down. Besides, it's a hurricane, not an earthquake. Love to you and Dad. I'll be in touch as soon as I can.

Danica was desperately missing her family. She looked again at the text she was writing, realizing she hadn't been home in more than a year. The toll medical training takes on physicians is tough, she knew. Continuously having to sacrifice family time in order to advance in medicine is the norm. She promised herself that after all of this was over, she would go see her family.

Danica hit the send button from her phone as she rounded the corner to the prison wing and ran smack into Shaka, accompanied on either side by a floor nurse and an orderly from the ICU whose name she couldn't recall.

"Hey there, little lady! Didn't anyone ever tell you about the dangers of texting and driving?" He took her arm and pulled her to one side as he waved the others on.

The floor nurse shot Danica a questioning glance, tinged with just a hint of jealousy.

"It's Okay," Danica told them. "Sorry. Just clumsy, I guess." She glanced at Shaka, whose hand still lingered pleasantly on her arm. "Texting and driving," she said. "Very funny."

"Somebody has to keep spirits up around here," he replied. "I don't know if you've noticed, but fuses have been getting pretty short lately. Where are you off to?"

"Prison wing. This is my first chance to check in on Jason Carter. I still don't know how to explain how he got left behind." Danica glanced ahead anxiously.

"I'll come with you," Shaka said. "If he gets any ideas about causing trouble, he'll be less likely to try anything if you have a buddy with you."

"Because you're a big, strong man, you mean?" A hint of sarcasm crept into her tone.

"That," he answered undeterred, "and because I have to head over there anyway, to get some medical supplies. They decided to open up the biocontainment isolation unit that's in the ED. The one they used for the Ebola scare back a few years ago and COVID last year."

His expression turned suddenly serious. "They didn't tell me and I didn't ask. What's with all the hush-hush? You know anything?"

"Who's 'they'?"

"Dr. Wong and Dr. Stone. They called an informational meeting for later this afternoon, though. All available staff. Meanwhile, they asked me to get over there and oversee the isolation setup. I wasn't busy with anything else, so here I am. At your service. Any idea what's going on?"

Danica's hurried steps faltered and she glanced around to make sure they couldn't be overheard. "I don't know much," she admitted. "But Dr. Wong thinks the patient may have been exposed to something in the biocontainment lab. He's ordered Cory's blood work results to be sent to CDC for analysis, along with that of anyone directly exposed to Cory. I had to put on hazard gear just to take the samples."

Shaka's eyes suddenly grew dark with concern. "You were careful?"

Offended, she turned away and resumed her pace. "Of course, I was careful! You think I don't know how to take a blood sample? Must you patronize me?"

Shaka raced to catch up to her. "Wait a second!" He clamped a strong arm on her shoulder and turned her to face him. "You look a little flushed."

Danica's face grew hotter, more with annoyance than from his presence.

He placed his hand gently on her forehead.

Her veins felt as though they were filling with hot caramel syrup. She locked her knees to keep from falling into his embrace. To cover her response, she said, "Stop feeling my forehead. For heaven's sake, what if somebody sees?"

"I would tell them I'm checking you for a fever." He smiled then and dropped his hand to her neck. "Which I am. You looked a little flushed there for a second. Hold still. Let me get a pulse." He held her eyes for a long second.

Her breathing quickened.

Finally, he dropped his hand. "Hmph, a little bit fast, I'd say. Any idea what that might be about, doctor?" A wicked smile played at the corners of his mouth.

She turned away through the sheer force of will, trying to collect herself. "You never quit, do you? Probably too much caffeine."

"Touché!" He laughed out loud as he continued following her down the corridor.

Something about the sound of his joy made the worries of the day scatter in a great rush of relief. It was as if there were no hurricane, no patients in crisis, and no staff on edge. They might have been out on a date somewhere, out of the hospital, out of any possible danger. That alone was a real gift, one that had nothing to do with his looks or his obvious charm. There was something about Shaka Sen that could make you believe that whatever happened, it would all be all right. And she had sense enough to accept that gift for what it was. It was more than arrogance; he exuded a beautiful, naturally charming confidence that was more like faith.

She inhaled deeply as she paused at the door to Jason Carter's room. There was no guard in sight and the keys lay in plain sight on the chair nearby. Dr. Sen unlocked the door for her and stood back, allowing her to enter alone. "Go on," he whispered. "I'm here."

She could only wish for half his confidence.

Inside the room, Jason Carter lay on his bed, curled up in the fetal position as before, only this time dressed in a prison jumpsuit.

The never-ending coverage of the impending Hurricane Beatrix blasted from the TV screen in the corner as a rain-soaked reporter shouted above the winds: "Well, Nicole we have really seen the winds pick up here, enough to pull police and firefighters off the streets. You can see the debris now starting to blow into the streets. It is the first sign of what's in store for Galveston. And this is just the beginning. It's going to get worse. We're in a lull right now. But once those hurricane-force winds start in two or three hours, we're going to be facing winds of one hundred miles per hour, maybe more, for ten, eleven, maybe even twelve hours."

The cameras cut back to the studio, where a weary-looking anchor shuffled papers on his desk. He looked directly at the camera. "Yesterday, we saw some long lines of people trying to get into shelters. Has everyone found a place to ride out the storm?"

Nicole fumbled with her microphone and earbuds as she struggled to respond. "Well, we know that roughly fifty thousand people in the area have gone to shelters. Many of them filled up right away. There is only one that's still open. But road conditions have really deteriorated. So, at this point, if people aren't in evacuation shelters, police are saying they need to stay where they are. In fact, we have heard about a fatal accident between here and Houston as well as a fatal stabbing during an argument between motorists. That's why they want folks off the road. Tempers are short. Debris is flying off trees and buildings, and just a few minutes ago, we watched a transformer blow. So, wherever people are, they need to stay where they are at this point, because Beatrix is coming, and it's only going to get worse."

Back in the studio, the camera cut to a shot of the governor.

At that moment, Danica cleared her throat and picked up the remote, hitting the mute button before the patient could protest. "Mr. Carter? It's me, Dr. Diza. We met earlier."

He rolled over and sat up, his eyes assessing her coldly. "Yeah, I remember you," he replied. "You're the one who said I'd be on that last evacuation bus."

Ashamed, she glanced down at the floor. "Mr. Carter, I can't apologize enough. It's been a day of emergencies. The bus left early because they had to take a man into custody after a fatal stabbing out on the evac highway. There was no one left here in Galveston to keep him until he could be arraigned."

Jason waved his hand impatiently. "I know all about it. That son of a bitch guard told me. Right before he handcuffed me to this here bunk and ran himself."

Danica's jaw fell open in disbelief. "He did what? That's unconscionable!" She glanced frantically around the room. "Did he leave the key?"

"Maybe outside."

She rushed to the door where Shaka was already coming forward, holding up the ring with both the room and the handcuff key. He followed her as she grabbed them and strode to the bed, unlocking the cuff with one swift motion.

Jason rubbed his wrist appreciatively. "Thank you, ma'am," he said. "I was starting to wonder what I was going to do when I had to take a piss."

Danica was furious. She turned to Shaka, her voice shaking with outrage as she spoke. "Do you know what that prison guard did? He cuffed him to the bed and ran! Just to save himself! What if there had been an emergency? Have you ever heard of anything so completely irresponsible?"

Shaka shook his head, waiting for a moment to get a word in edgewise.

Danica snatched her phone from her pocket and began texting. "This will be documented in a full report, Mr. Carter. That guard is not going to get away with this. His actions were nothing short of cruel, and that is *not* how things are done at this hospital!"

Jason nodded. "I appreciate that, ma'am. But this was mild compared to some things I've seen a prison guard do.

Especially a scared one. I reckon you haven't spent much time in the prison system, have you?"

"No. I haven't. But that doesn't mean there's any excuse for—"

Shaka stepped forward. "Mr. Carter? I'm Dr. Shaka Sen, surgery. On board for the duration. Nice to meet you."

Jason rose and extended his hand. "Jason Carter. Somebody want to tell me what all the commotion was out in the hallway a while back?"

Shaka sighed heavily. "Unfortunately, it looks like we have to set up an isolation unit for full quarantine. We currently have a patient in intensive care with an unidentified infection. Until we know exactly what it is, he'll be put in the isolation unit and any attending staff will be severely limited. You will be moved to one of the open ED rooms as well, and we will close the whole prison hospital in the meantime."

Jason looked almost amused. "You sure about that, doctor? I'm a prisoner of the State of Texas, remember? Some of the higher-ups might not take too kindly to me mixing in."

Danica bit her lip in frustration. He had a point. She could just imagine Dr. Kirsten Stone's face when she applied for a room in an open ward. But what could she do? She couldn't leave Mr. Carter down here by himself, and she could hardly turn him out onto the street. She sought Shaka's warm brown eyes, looking for answers.

As if reading her mind, he stepped forward. "Mind if I ask what you're in for, Mr. Carter? Might make a difference."

"Armed robbery and felony assault. Ten years maybe, if I make parole. Served almost three years this October."

Shaka tilted his head and eyed him critically. "Did you do it?"

Jason didn't hesitate. "Yes, sir. I sure did. Got mixed up in a bad drug deal on the wrong side of a narc. Stupid. Guess you could say I was pretty crazy. Thought I needed the dope."

"You were hooked?" Shaka edged closer and sat on the bed.

"Bad hooked. Had a gruesome back injury from my tour in Iraq, which led me to an Oxy habit, just to ease the pain a little bit and allow me to function, eventually resulting in my addiction. Thought I could kick it on my own, but by then my wife had left me. No one wanted to hire me. I never finished school. I didn't have a job, and the VA wasn't no help. After enough trying, I just quit trying, that's all. I figured if nobody else gave a damn, why should I? No better way to get clean than serving prison time."

Shaka felt people deserved second chances. Early childhood had left an indelible impression on him when his uncle pleaded guilty to securities fraud and was sentenced to serve a seven-year prison sentence at the federal prison camp at Pensacola, Florida. His uncle, before he died in jail, had been a father figure to Shaka. Every weekend, Shaka and his mother had visited his uncle. But those visits instilled in Shaka a sympathy for the plight of prisoners in general.

Shaka continued his inquiry, gently probing like the surgeon he was, trying to determine the extent of the other man's wound. "Army?"

For the first time, Jason looked almost alarmed. "Hell no!" he said, rising to his feet. "Marine."

"Beg your pardon," Shaka replied evenly.

Jason nodded. "*Semper Fi.*"

"Thank you for your service." Shaka rose and shook Jason's hand once more. "I'll make sure the administrators know. It will definitely work in your favor. Just behave yourself until we can get this figured out, okay?"

"Yes, sir. Only a fool would try and make a break for it, anyways. Not now."

A flurry of activity in the hallway diverted their attention as nurses maneuvered carts full of HAZMAT suits, clean scrubs, and other equipment snaked out of the elevators toward the ED in the newly opened isolation unit.

Danica held up a hand to pause the conversation, then hurried after the nurses, returning in a moment with a fresh set of scrubs, which she handed to Jason. "I hope they fit. It's not much, but it's basically a disguised escape plan to help you blend in better."

"Thanks." Jason smiled for the first time. "I appreciate that, ma'am. I really do."

"You're welcome. Don't let me down. I've been burned before for being too trusting."

"Look," Shaka broke in. "I hate to break this up, but I'm supposed to be overseeing this setup, so I need to leave you for the moment. We're down to essential personnel. And some of them aren't quite sure what they're doing."

"Go," said Danica. "We'll be fine."

Just then, her phone buzzed with a new text message alert. Dr. Wong had collapsed.

"Shit!" Trying to get her mind around this new development, she glanced around the room, finally settling her gaze on Jason Carter. "Make that essential personnel minus one. Looks like we have another case of the mystery bug. Let's go quickly."

Jason got up to his feet and moved toward the door. "How many are left, ma'am? If I can ask?"

"Staff? I'm not sure. Around one hundred fifty?"

"Patients?"

"I think they said three hundred. Most of them are too sick to be moved. Why do you ask?"

Jason frowned. "No reason. Just that four hundred people make for a damn big quarantine, if it comes to that. You have enough food? Supplies?"

"Of course. I mean, I'm sure we do … . What's this about, Mr. Carter?"

He shrugged. "Nothing—yet. But the Marines teach you a lot of things. One of them is to prepare for the worst."

"I'm sorry, but we have to get moving," Danica insisted again.

Danica led Jason to the emergency department and checked with the charge nurse for an available room. Then, with him trailing behind, she took him to room 113.

"OK, Jason, stay here for now and one of the nurses will keep an eye on you," Danica stated. "Unfortunately, since we don't have guards or locks here, I am going to have to handcuff you to the bed until we get clearance. I am so sorry," she said with a hint of guilt.

He sat on the bed and extended his wrist. "Don't worry about it. You take care of what's going on."

Danica smiled sheepishly. "Thanks for understanding. Again, doing this goes against everything I believe as a human being."

Danica attached Jason's wrist to the bed rail. She turned to exit the room and swiftly walked out to the nurses' station. "Hey, Tommy, this is the TDCer who got left behind. Can you keep an eye on him?"

"Sure thing."

"Thanks, Tommy. Here are the handcuff keys in case you need them."

***

After she was gone, Jason Carter lay back on his bed, his free hand behind his head, staring at the ceiling and thinking hard. He'd had a real bad feeling about coming here, right from the first. He'd thought it was just about the hurricane. But now that feeling had morphed into a greater certainty. His mind drifted back to his tour of duty, and his memories resonated, filling him with a nameless apprehension. His concerns morphed into absolute dread.

Hurricane Beatrix wasn't the only troublemaker. Whatever was happening down that hall was a bigger threat.

He was sure of it.

Chapter Eight

Centers for Disease Control and Prevention, Atlanta, Georgia

Paula Davis hated traffic on a regular day, but the rain from the weather in the gulf made the commute twice as long. As she made her way to her job at the CDC, her blue Toyota Prius slowly inched toward the North Druid Hills exit off I-85. Despite her drive in bumper-to-bumper traffic every morning, Paula told herself she wanted this. She had dreamed of being an Epidemic Intelligence Service officer at the CDC since high school, when she first saw Kate Winslet play one in the movie *Contagion*. To that end, Paula put in the work, first by graduating *summa cum laude* with a bachelor's in microbiology from Columbia University, then publishing multiple first-author papers during graduate school, which positioned her to work as a post-doc in any academic department in the country. Yet she had taken a job as a microbiologist, calibrating tests and teaching students how to operate laboratory instruments at the CDC. It didn't matter to her. The *esprit de corps* of the CDC's EIS officers was contagious, and Paula loved it. Their unofficial motto, "A disease somewhere is a disease anywhere," made the monotonous work feel special—at least in the beginning.

At 9:20 a.m. Paula arrived at the threshold of a multi-story parking garage. *A two-hour-and-sixteen-minute commute*, she thought. *I'm wasting my life in this stupid car.* Paula lowered the automatic window and swiped her badge at the gate opener. After navigating through a maze of parked cars, she found her designated spot, B41. She turned off the ignition and let out an audible sigh. Paula knew she was lying to herself about her job, but she climbed out and prepared for another day. She fixed her tan slacks and red polka-dot blouse before putting on her long, white coat. She grabbed her cup of coffee and her laptop bag before making her way to the elevator to her office.

The CDC headquarters, located in central Atlanta, was an impressive structure with floor-to-ceiling glass windows lining the exterior. Paula got out of the empty elevator on the fourth floor. She slowly made her way to her desk, sat down, and began browsing her email inbox. A message from the Deputy Director for Infectious Diseases caught her eye. *Did I get it this time?* She held the cursor over the message and clicked. Paula read aloud, "After careful consideration, we regret to inform you that your application to the CDC's Epidemic Intelligence Service was not selected … " her words trailed off. Her heart sank in disappointment. Professionally speaking, she was stuck in a rut.

She didn't have time to ruminate over this right now, damn it. She needed to work to get her mind off of this latest disappointment. Paula made her way from the office to her bench, but not before donning a HAZMAT suit, following each step in careful procession.

Tapping her foot rhythmically against the floor, Paula sat on her stool, continuously checking the time until she could leave work, but it had only begun. She had been working for the CDC for seven years, yet she hadn't managed to get the position in the EIS program she had coveted. She had hoped this year would be different. So she applied three times and couldn't figure out why she didn't make the cut. She was a stellar scientist; she was sure of it.

Consumed by her thoughts, she didn't realize the timer had buzzed and that the latest sample had finished incubating. The sound of her intern's voice brought her back to reality.

"Dr. Davis, the sample is complete," her intern Mark said again.

Paula gave Mark a look of annoyance. "Yes, it would seem so. Why don't you get the plate from the incubator and examine the results?"

Strolling over to the incubator, he grabbed the microtiter plate and walked back to Paula, hovering over her. Mark was at least six feet tall. He was your typical science nerd, tall, lanky, with thick-rimmed glasses and the coveted pocket protector. He fit the bill as a lab intern, here to be trained in the different diagnostic techniques for running organic samples such as blood, tissue, CSF samples, etc.

Mark laid the plate on Paula's bench space.

"You see, in an enzyme-linked immunosorbent assay, or an ELISA, a positive sample will turn brown in color like it did in this well. If it hadn't, we might have had to incubate for a longer time," Paula explained. She then manually uploaded the positive results into the computer and hit the "send" button.

Paula glanced up at the clock again. Only ten minutes had gone by. She sighed and moved on to the next sample. "Okay, what's the next sample?"

She put on a new set of latex gloves and walked over to the table in the back to grab the next sample. She opened the bag with the test tubes. There were four tubes of blood with different colored tops.

Paula reached into the biohazard bag and twisted the red-topped tube in her hand to see the sticker. The requisition form read, "Finch, Cory DOB: 04/20/1990 RT-PCR for CCHF."

She turned to Mark and asked, "Can you tell me how RT-PCR works?"

Mark blurted out confidently, "The benefits of a PCR test is that, even with a small sample of DNA, we can detect the presence of a virus."

"Nice try, but this CCHF is an RNA virus. I'll give you a hint: it has to do with the RT part." Paula smiled. She secretly loved giving Mark a hard time.

Mark blushed. "Well, RT-PCR uses reverse transcriptase, so it takes the RNA copies of the virus, converts it to DNA, and amplifies to DNA strands so that we can detect them to confirm presence of this virus."

Paula beamed at him with pride. "Nice save!"

***

Two hours later, the alarm on the thermal cycler beeped. Mark got out of his chair, removed the samples from the chamber, and began to prepare them for the gel electrophoresis. Loading the DNA ladder into the well followed by his amplified sample was a tedious process.

After another few hours, Mark was finally ready to stain the gel. He placed it under a UV box. He looked puzzled and called for Paula's help.

"What is it?" asked Paula.

He glanced at her. "I don't understand these results. Look here. The first lane is my DNA ladder, the second is my positive control, the third my negative control, and the patient's sample is the last. The patient's run matches with the positive control—but why is there an extra 1500 base pair fragment?"

"Hmm. Maybe you just ran the sample incorrectly. Let's rerun the sample," Paula responded, scratching her chin.

They worked harmoniously to prepare the samples again to repeat the PCR. Paula hoped it was just a lab error and nothing more, but she couldn't turn off this nagging feeling that there was something else.

They waited quietly for what seemed like an eternity for the second gel to finish. Mark finally broke the silence. "What if this is a new strain? Have you ever seen this before?"

"I have not, but I have heard about something like this before. Let's hope this is not that." Paula answered.

Relieved at the sound of the buzzer, they both immediately got up, almost running into each other as they anxiously took the gel to the UV lightbox again.

Astonished and confused, they looked at one another, each thinking the same thing.

"We need to sequence this," Paula said with excitement.

Paula thought about the implications a bit more. She then looked up.

"This is very bizarre. It would make sense for a mutant strain to arise in an endemic area. Something fishy is going on in Texas."

"You think the strain has been altered by … being manipulated? That makes no sense. Why would they do that?" Mark asked.

"The only way to find out the answer to that is to sequence this virus. We need the director's permission. Let's go."

Once they had decontaminated, Paula and Mark headed to the office at the end of the floor that had the best view of the city. She knocked on the door and waited for a reply.

"Come in," Hale replied.

Paula entered with Mark closely behind. "We need to show you something, sir."

Hale looked up. "Paula this better be good. I was just heading out."

Paula handed Hale the results and waited as he went through it. Hale had been at the CDC for more than twenty years and the head of epidemiology for eight years. He was a stubby man whose thinning hair showed more white than black.

He looked up and pushed his glasses back. "This can't be right."

"We ran this twice, sir. It's accurate!" Paula evened her voice. "We need access to the next generation sequencer."

Taken aback, Hale stared at her. He knew the implications. "You think someone created this?"

"It's imperative we find out who created it right now." Paula urged. "We could be running out of time."

CHAPTER NINE
Galveston University Hospital
Hurricane Beatrix makes landfall

After checking on Cory Finch and Dr. Wong, Danica stood in the decontamination shower. As she removed her HAZMAT suit, she was again aware of the sounds of the hurricane. She hadn't realized how well the suit had insulated her against noises. The wind was white noise, a dull roar that permeated the atmosphere, as thick as humidity. Ceaseless and unrelenting, it hovered at the very edge of Danica's hearing, like the rumble of never-ending subway trains, deep underground. *Landfall.* She allowed the water to pound her tired muscles. *The hurricane must have made landfall by now.* There was no special emotion associated with the realization, just acceptance. She was too tired to feel anything more.

Yet another part of her mind continued working, as ceaseless as the wind outside. Exhausted as she was, she relentlessly reviewed the signs and symptoms displayed by Dr. Wong and Cory, weighing their cases carefully against her experience. There must be an answer; there had to be. Cory had taken a turn for the worse. She'd been called away from her evening rounds to the isolation unit when he'd begun to vomit blood. His current white cell count was off the charts. As far as she'd gathered from Dr. Wong's notes and her own research, everything pointed to CCHF, but without a confirmation from the CDC, she couldn't be sure.

Crimean Congo Hemorrhagic Fever.

The words played like a chant in her mind as she scrubbed herself nearly raw. She recalled the evidence on the young man's back as they'd examined him. Nearly purple blood pooled beneath his fair skin. But even a confirmation could only go so far as there was no vaccine and no cure. The best they had to offer was supportive care: fluids, platelets, plasma, Vitamin K, and respiratory support. Dr. Wong was doing better, but not by much. Then again, he'd been the last to show symptoms. Maybe he'd worsen with time. All she could do was wait.

After her shower, she donned clean navy blue scrubs and a lab coat, pulling her hair into its customary ponytail as she headed out to complete her evening rounds. She nodded at an orderly as she passed into the adjoining wing and he unplugged his earbuds long enough to give her an unhappy nod.

"Are you anybody?" he asked petulantly. "'Cause if you are, you need to know that I don't get paid for passing out no damn dinner trays. That ain't my wheelhouse, okay? I'm janitorial. I don't need to be going around making small talk with no sick folks like some damn waitress. You got me?"

She tried not to smile. "Sorry, we're pretty shorthanded, uhh …" She peered at his ID. "Booker, is it?"

He stuck out his thumb and pointed to his chest. "That's me. Booker F. Johnson. Janitorial, mechanics division, apprentice. I fix these machines around here, and I'm damn good at it too. You tell them that!"

Danica smiled. "Don't worry. I'll tell them."

Suddenly aware that she was ravenous, she eyed the meal cart hungrily. "You don't have a spare sandwich on that cart somewhere, do you? I haven't eaten since, well, I don't remember."

The young man's expression softened. "You take whatever you want," he said. "All they done told me in the kitchen was to pass out these trays until I ran out; then come back for more. Ain't nothing on there but sandwiches, anyway. They turned off the stoves till after the storm passes."

Gratefully, she grabbed a sandwich and a bag of chips and unwrapped them on her way down the hall, eating it so fast she wasn't even sure what kind of sandwich it was. It didn't matter; it had carbs and that was all that counted.

Chapter Ten

Centers for Disease Control and Prevention, Atlanta, Georgia

Paula walked into Hale's office with a yellow Manila folder, with Mark following close by.

"We need to get in touch with the principal investigator of this lab in Galveston, a Dr. Wong," Paula stated without missing a beat.

Paula showed Hale the results from the next generation she and Mark had sequenced. He quickly scanned through each page of the fifteen-page report with color-coded letters above the peaks of the chromatogram. He could see that a 1500 nucleotide sequence had been neatly inserted in between the usual segments.

Hale nodded as he dialed the number on the original requisition sheet, put the call on speaker, and waited for an answer.

A bleak voice answered. "Dr. Wong speaking."

"Dr. Wong, this is Conner Hale from the CDC. Listen, we have received a sample from the University Hospital in Galveston, Texas that we aren't sure about. We understand that the patient was exposed to a virus while working in your BSL level-four lab. What kind of pathogens has he handled?"

Hale was an excellent poker player and didn't want to reveal what he had already surmised. For all he knew, Dr. Wong may be the bad actor.

"Dr. Finch was working with an attenuated strain of the Crimean Congo Hemorrhagic Fever." Dr. Wong paused, took a deep breath, and continued weakly, "It was part of a study that we recently had funded by the Department of Defense."

Hale could tell by the concern in Dr. Wong's voice that he was genuinely worried. Wong wasn't the bad actor. Hale decided to spit out his news.

"Listen, this isn't easy for me to say, but your post-doc has CCHF. We've confirmed it with two RT-PCRs. What we don't understand is, why was a protein inserted to allow for aerosolized transmission of the virus?"

Dr. Wong's breaking voice answered, "Pardon my confusion Dr. Hale, but I assure you my lab has not engaged in creating any recombinant pathogens. What we get from the DoD are attenuated strains of a virus."

"Look, I'm not accusing you of anything," Hale replied, drawing in a breath. "Do you know where your substrate sample is coming from? Are you getting this from the DoD?"

Dr. Wong continued, "Yes, we are getting it from the Dugway Life Science Test Facility in Utah."

Hale started to worry about Dr. Wong. He didn't sound right. "Dr. Wong, are you feeling all right?"

"No, Dr. Hale. I was infected with the pathogen as well. Exposed most likely from Dr. Finch. The CDC should have received my blood samples as well."

"I am sorry to hear that, Dr. Wong. Hang in there. We are going to get an EIS officer to speak to Dugway and get more answers."

"Thank you, Dr. Hale. Please keep me updated," Dr. Wong responded, and the line went silent.

Hale slammed the receiver down, then turned to Paula and said, "This wouldn't be the first time Dugway has done something incredibly stupid. You might not remember this, but in 2015, Dugway mistakenly shipped live anthrax spores to dozens of labs across the country. At least no one got hurt then."

Hale remembered his contact from that 2015 incident was a General Drucker. Hale remembered him being a no-nonsense career military officer with a thin skin. Hale would need to choose his words carefully, otherwise he'd get nowhere. Hale picked up his cellphone, called him, and hit speaker.

"Drucker here."

"General, this is Hale. You remember me from the CDC?"

"How could I forget? We've been under a microscope since your team finished their investigation. No hard feelings. What can I do for you today?" Drucker replied.

"Well, sir, it seems like there's been an outbreak at the Galveston lab, in the midst of Hurricane Beatrix. The CDC evaluated their blood samples and the results were remarkable. I was hoping you could help me identify where a novel strain of the Crimean Congo Hemorrhagic Virus came from."

Drucker remained silent for what seemed like an eternity over the phone. His standard reply about national security wouldn't work on Hale, owing to the CDC director's own security clearance. Finally, he stated, "Hypothetically, let us say that the military knew about this. What do you propose we do?"

"We need to contain this immediately. Under no circumstance can we have another incident like the SARS-CoV-2 of 2019. That was a global catastrophe, crippling the global economy, burdening the healthcare systems, with an enormous global death count. I don't need to remind you that we still have not fully recovered," Hale replied solemnly.

Drucker held his tone. "I agree. I am open to suggestions for containment," he replied.

Hale leveled his voice. "The CCHF is a highly contagious virus with a high mortality rate as it is. Depending on how it was altered, it could be even more infectious and deadly."

"I understand your concern. We do lots of research with the civilian world. I have no idea about this one particular project. If your concern is containment, the National Biocontainment Lab was built on Galveston Island for a reason. We can cut off the entire island from the mainland easily, as there are only three points of access to and from," Drucker responded.

Hale sputtered angrily, "We are not there yet! We need to get ahead of this and create the narrative before the media take a hold of it and write a disastrous one for us, painting the military and the CDC in a not-so-flattering light. Come clean and tell me what you know about this virus."

Paula and Mark shifted nervously next to Hale.

Drucker laughed. "I have no idea what you are talking about. We didn't have any hand in creating this virus. You're wasting your time coming up with conspiracy theories. I am giving you practical advice. Which do you prefer?

Containing it now? Or letting it become a global pandemic and scrambling later?"

"Contain it immediately," Hale responded. "And you better pray we come out on the other side unscathed."

Hale hung up the phone, defeated. He looked up from his desk to see Paula and Mark still in the room, their faces shocked.

Paula broke the tension first. "Sir, are you going to do it? Quarantine unsuspecting Americans in the middle of a hurricane?"

"Paula, we aren't making that decision. It's been made for them already when the DoD helped build that lab. What does concern us is what happens next. All samples that come from Galveston, Texas need to go through me. Make sure we have enough kits and solutions to run the tests. As of now, these samples are top priority. Keep it discreet. The fewer people who know about this incident, the better. You are running point on this. You will update me every day with numbers. This is a need-to-know basis, effective immediately. Do you understand?"

Hale waited for a response.

"Y-y-yes, sir," Paula managed to stutter.

"It is in both of your mutual interests that neither of you discuss any matters regarding this situation with anyone. Nothing said here today leaves my office. Is that clear?"

Finding his voice, Mark answered, "Crystal."

Standing from his mahogany desk, Hale ushered Paula and Mark through the door.

"Now get out of my office, and get back to work. I need to notify Dr. Singh," he said sternly, as he slammed the office door shut.

CHAPTER ELEVEN

National Guard Headquarters, Field Office, Galveston Island

Colonel Henry Wilson didn't take kindly to having his nap interrupted. He sat behind a makeshift desk with his feet up, hoping to catch a few Zs before something else demanded his attention. That was the thing about commanding a guard unit—good men and women, most of them. Hell, most of his folks had been out there sandbagging for seventy-two hours straight already. Willing and able to serve, but at the end of the day, they were a volunteer army. And in the colonel's mind, "volunteer" translated to just one word: "amateurs."

A young corporal came in and saluted, a piece of paper fluttering in her other hand. "Sir. Corporal Katie Mendoza, communications office."

"Yeah!" he barked. "What is it now?"

"We had something come through I thought you should see."

She laid a rain-spattered telex message on the colonel's desk.

The colonel fumbled for his reading glasses. "For Chrissake, they still have telex machines? Would somebody mention to Washington that those things went out in the fifties?"

The corporal retreated two steps. "Respectfully, sir, cell coverage is down. Satellite phones are unavailable due to the overcast conditions. We have two-way radio and telex."

"What the fuck is this?" Colonel Wilson peered at the few lines of text in front of him.

"A general from Dugway Proving Grounds in Utah is asking us to enforce a quarantine due to an outbreak of Crimean Congo Hemorrhagic Fever in Galveston," said Mendoza.

"Crimean Congo Hemorrhagic Fever? Never heard of it," retorted Wilson.

"Me neither. I had to look it up, but it has no known cure or vaccine. It's found primarily in Europe, Russia, and the Middle East."

Wilson stared at her. "How the hell does somebody catch something like that in Texas?"

Corporal Mendoza swallowed hard. "There are a number of possibilities, sir. The bio hazard lab may have been compromised. Or—"

"Never mind that!" thundered the colonel. "How bad could this get?"

"Very bad, sir. Fatality rates have been recorded at forty percent."

"Forty per—sweet Jesus. If so much as a word of this gets around, there's going to be a panic. Not to mention what could happen when folks start coming back after the blasted storm's over. We will send supplies and food, but as of *now* Galveston is completely quarantined until further notice!"

Wilson stood up. "Get me that general from Dugway on the phone. And don't tell me you can't. We have to nip this thing in the bud or all hell is gonna break loose."

Corporal Mendoza saluted once more and turned to leave.

Wilson called out after her. "And find me whoever's in charge of the bridge detail to Texas City. I want him in my office in five minutes!"

CHAPTER TWELVE
Galveston University Hospital

Danica rounded the corner into the west wing and made her way into the last room on the right. Inside, ninety-two-year-old Gloria Chavez lay in her bed, dozing, her fingers lightly clutching the rosary beads around her neck. A candle burned on her bedside table, throwing a soft golden light against the shadows. The monitors blipped her vitals from above.

Danica checked her charts. No change. Mrs. Chavez was in progressive congestive heart failure and her DNR and DNI orders were clear. At her age, it was unlikely that she could survive a resuscitation, and CPR compressions to her chest to revive the heart would likely shatter her fragile bones, doing more harm than good. Her family had already evacuated at her own insistence, and Gloria had spent the ensuing hours resting, dreaming, and drifting in and out of consciousness, somewhere between this world and the one that awaited her.

"How are we doing today, Mrs. Chavez?" Danica asked softly as she reached for the candle.

"Leave it." Gloria stopped Danica with a surprisingly strong grip on Danica's arm. "I know it's against the rules, but I enjoy the scent. It's peony. My niece made it for me." She pressed the button on her bed to sit up a little farther and blinked rapidly. "*Dios mio*, for a moment, I thought you were one of my spirits."

Danica placed her stethoscope gently against the old woman's skinny chest and listened. Still beating. "Spirits?"

"Oh, yes." Gloria smiled faintly. "I see them quite a lot now. They're waiting for me. My Hector, *mi abuela*, all the others. *Mis angelitos*. Some I don't even know; they have to introduce themselves. But they're waiting, too. Over on the other side."

Danica studied her. "Mrs. Chavez, I hope the storm isn't upsetting you, is it? Because we're safe here. You know that, right?"

Gloria straightened up even further and met her gaze, her eyes shining. "Don't be silly. I've lived through more hurricanes than you can even think about, and believe me, the weather is not going to kill anybody unless they're so stupid they think they can fight it. My third husband did that. Had himself a brand-new shiny black truck. He was so proud of it, he thought he could drive it through a storm like this, back in '87. Well, he hit a wash and that was all she wrote. The police found that truck, but they never did find him." She shook her head. "Nothing so vain as a man who thinks he can defy nature, eh?"

Danica hid her smile. "Well, Mrs. Chavez. You seem to be holding your own just fine here. Is there anything you need?"

At that moment, the wind howled past, rattling the windows and making them both jump. Danica hurried over to the window and struggled to see anything, but visibility was next to nil, just a greenish haze of wind and water. She drew the blinds. "It'll help keep the noise out."

"Child, I am far too old to be frightened by a few rattled windows. But sit with me a while, if you can. It's pretty quiet around here, since the family left. But they're safe, and that's a blessing."

"Yes, ma'am."

The old woman peered more closely at her. "You ever had your cards read?"

Danica reflexively pulled her phone from her pocket, then checked her pager. No new messages. "My fortune, you mean?" She indicated a stack of *Loteria* cards on the tray table. "Is that what these are for?"

"Sometimes," the old woman answered. "I learned from my mother. I use them to talk to my spirits and they show me through the cards."

With that, she picked up the deck in her gnarled fingers, shuffled them expertly, and spread them out in a fan shape in Danica's direction. "Pick three," she directed.

Hesitating only a little, Danica did as she was directed.

"Ah." Mrs. Chavez moved the candle closer. "This is you, the lady. It speaks of your grace, your ability to handle whatever difficulties come your way."

Danica smiled. "I sure hope so."

"This next one." The old woman turned over a second card. "This is the card of the recent past, the rooster, *El Gallo*. He's warning you, sending out an alarm or alert. There is danger in the vicinity, but then, we already knew that, right?"

She chuckled.

When she turned over the third card, her expression changed. "*El Apache.*" She breathed in sharply and shook her head. She glanced up at Danica, her eyes concerned. "There is something else. A problem. I don't think it's the storm. It's serious, though. Very serious."

Without so much as looking down, she shuffled the remaining cards once more. "Pick again."

"Mrs. Chavez," Danica protested gently. "Please don't upset yourself. I'm sure—"

"Pick!" Gloria insisted.

Not sure of what else to do, Danica chose three more cards. Turning over one, then another, Mrs. Chavez studied them closely, fingering the rosary beads around her neck. "*El Valiente.* There is a hero nearby, a man of great courage. Or possibly, the spirits speak of your own courage. And this one—" Mrs. Chavez pointed a bony finger. "The cactus. Some things that are most beautiful to you can also sting. Pay attention."

Another blast of wind howled around the corner of the building, and Danica could have sworn she heard the whole structure groan. Not wanting to disturb her patient further, she asked, "What about the last one?"

Gloria turned it over with trembling fingers, then made the sign of the cross as the image was revealed. "*El Muerte.*"

Danica blinked but quickly recovered herself, knowing she couldn't afford to let herself be distracted by an old woman's superstitions or getting fixated on an ominous grim reaper card. This was a parlor game to pass the time, nothing more.

Suddenly fatigued, the old woman leaned back against her pillows and closed her eyes. After a moment, she spoke again. "I understand," she murmured. She reached out then, and patted Danica's hand. "I think I will sleep a while now."

As Danica rose to her feet, Gloria added, "Thank you for sitting with me. And have no fears about old *El Muerte*. Heroes all around you, and you are strong. Should he come for you or somebody you love, you look him in the eye and tell him, 'No. Not today.' You hear?"

Danica smiled weakly. "Don't you worry, Mrs. Chavez. I will. That's kind of what doctors do every day, isn't it?"

A sleepy smile was her answer. "*Buenas noches*, then."

Danica waited until the old woman's breathing regulated, light and shallow, then, with a last glance at the monitors, still holding steady, she grabbed the candle and blew it out before placing it back on the table. "Sweet dreams, Mrs. Chavez," she whispered, and she closed the door on her way out.

CHAPTER THIRTEEN
Galveston Island

Dylan loved the unmistakable growl of his red Honda CBX as he barreled down Harborside Drive. The CBX was the fastest production bike when it was first introduced in 1978. The Formula 1-like racecar sound that the 1,047-cc, inline-6 engine made was symphonic to his ears and lessened the pain of maintaining it. Dylan had bought the bike two years ago, used, on Craigslist for a thousand bucks, and he'd easily poured double that amount into rebuilding it.

As he approached the right turn onto I-45, he glanced down at the gauge cluster to match his RPMs on the tachymeter. The rain and wind obscured his forward visibility, but this drive had become second nature. He pulled on the clutch, rolled back on the throttle, downshifted, and let the clutch drop into the second gear as he made the turn. The tires slipped but regained traction as he completed the turn.

The on-ramp ahead of him was blocked. The faint, orange, capital letters of the electronic TxDOT sign read, "HURRICANE WARNING TEXAS COAST."

"No shit, Sherlock," Dylan muttered to himself.

He had two choices: he could shelter somewhere on the island, or he could get back to the mainland. He punched it. The telescopic fork suspension shortened as he climbed onto the on-ramp of the causeway. He had never seen a deserted stretch of I-45 like this before. Exhilaration came over Dylan as he changed into third gear. The pouring rain and wind made him feel like his bike would hydroplane at any moment. He slipped into fifth gear.

Suddenly a gust of strong wind knocked him over. He hit the concrete barrier of the bridge with crippling force. Screaming in pain, face down, he laid there on the pavement, limp.

I'm alive.

Dylan tested each limb. He could feel all his fingers and toes. As the shock and adrenaline surge subsided, he tried to lift himself by putting one leg against his chest and using it to stand up, trying to push against the strong winds. Unable to see more than six inches ahead of him, he searched wildly with his hands for the bike, inching his way toward where he thought it might have landed. When he finally felt the cool of metal, he tried to pick up the bike, but he failed to push it upright against the gusts. Unable to abandon his bike, he maneuvered his body at an angle to get underneath it. He pushed up with all of his strength, getting the bike off the ground. The wind threatened to topple him over with each step, but he walked slowly back off the bridge toward the island. At this point, there was no getting off. He had missed his window. All he could do now was to ride out the storm.

When Dylan got off the causeway to a point where the sheer forces weren't as bad, he swung his leg over the bike. The engine sputtered and then roared to life as he headed back. Every second he thought he was going to slip and die, but it gave him an unbelievable high from being alive. Dylan slowly rode down Harborside and turned toward the hospital garage. He swiped his badge at the barrier, releasing the parking gate open. Then, he drove his bike to the top of the multi-story parking structure, hoping it wouldn't flood or get damaged by any flying debris.

He turned the key and removed it from the ignition. Soaking wet and shivering from the cold, Dylan made his way down the stairs and back toward The Prince Apartments, two blocks away. The ominous sounds of the wind mixing with thunder and lightning were deafening. He had never experienced this before.

Dylan was exhausted. Every breath sent a sharp pain down his flank. He figured he had probably fractured a rib or two, but no matter. He just needed shelter. When he finally reached the complex, he climbed the stairs using the railing like a mountaineer's belay. He opened the door, walked over to his medicine cabinet, and took some oxycodone. He stared at the bottle, looking at the dispensary date. It read "2017," the last time he had wiped out this badly and ended up in the emergency room. He could already sense the bruises and knew his body would ache tomorrow. He took off his jacket and threw himself on the couch.

Twigs from a large tree next to the apartment complex broke and bounced off the window outside Dylan's unit. He could see the faint outline of its branches whipping in the wind against the street light.

Try to get some rest, Dylan thought to himself.

Around 12:30 a.m., the street light went out, and the winds got louder. One minute it sounded like a wolf howling, and then another like a freight train. The winds were probably between eighty-to-ninety miles an hour by that time, he figured. It was relentless, hours of pounding. The crackling of the lightning intensified with each rip. He heard the loud thuds of debris flying and becoming projectiles. In the next second he saw a blinding light race across the sky, followed by a loud boom. Windows cracked, as the boards ripped off of a nearby building. Water was running off the roof like he was living under Niagara Falls. Dylan was terrified, more frightened than he had ever been before.

Around 2:00 a.m., Dylan got a text alert. "Beatrice makes landfall," he read aloud.

Dylan realized he didn't have enough food or supplies to survive in his apartment. He had to go back to the hospital. He quickly gathered his belongings into a duffle bag and put on his raincoat. He knew he couldn't save everything, but at least he had put his most important possessions and documents in a waterproof folder. He grabbed the folder from his room and made his way out the front door. The first floor was already halfway under water. He got into the water slowly. As he got deeper into the water, he felt the icy coldness all over his body. Dylan knew he had to get out of there before his body went into hypothermia.

Chapter Fourteen
Galveston University Hospital

The power was holding, and that much was good. Inside his room in the ED, Jason Carter listened carefully to the pattern of the winds as they punished the perimeters of the building. Nothing unusual, but the dinner cart was late. And that wasn't good. Not that he cared so much for the hospital fare, but more because he knew from experience that in a crisis like this one was shaping up to be, variations in routine always meant something big. With his senses on alert, he sat up at the sound of hurried footsteps in the hall. In less than a minute, Shaka's face appeared in the doorway. "You hanging in there all right, Mr. Carter?"

"I could use a meal, but that don't mean nothing. Thought you might be that lady doctor."

Shaka approached his bedside. "Yeah, I was looking for her myself. Sorry about the room service, we're pretty shorthanded. And, well ..." he trailed off. "There's a—situation upstairs. The admins are all in a huddle, trying to figure out how to deal with it."

Jason raised an eyebrow. "What kind of situation?"

Shaka sighed heavily and rubbed his eyes. "There's no point in keeping it from you, since you're going to be here for the duration. You're not prone to panic, are you?"

Jason almost laughed aloud. "Panic? No sir. Escapism, denial, sometimes acting like a damn fool. Maybe even that. But not panic."

Shaka lowered his voice. "This is just between us, okay? We've got two, possibly three cases over in the isolation unit. Unknown virus. At least until we sent the blood work over to the CDC. Now, we know what it is, but there's very little we can do to treat it. The whole hospital is under quarantine until further notice. That's why the admins are freaking out. They're trying to figure out how to announce it without causing a full-scale panic."

Jason nodded. "I hear that. On top of this hurricane, that's bad. What is it? The sickness, I mean."

Shaka glanced again at his phone, then looked up. "Crimean Congo Hemorrhagic Fever. That's a mouthful, isn't it? CCHF for short. No vaccine, no cure."

Jason's eyes grew wide with sudden comprehension. "Doc, you gotta let me up from this here bed. *Now!*"

Shaka backed away, looking startled by Jason's sudden change of tone. "What's wrong? Don't even think about running, Jason. There's nowhere to go."

"I'm not thinking about anything like that!" Jason jerked his arm impatiently, jangling the handcuff that held him in place. "You gotta let me up. I can help you with them folks. I had that fever back when I was deployed in Iraq."

"What? Are you sure?"

Jason's eyes grew suddenly distant, remembering. "It was a village outside Baghdad. My line company was doing a routine patrol. One day, couple of the men picked up this shepherd and brought him to the field hospital. Said they found him just lying on the road. He was covered in what looked like bruises, all red and purple, and just burning up with fever. When we got him undressed and into a bed, all the locals ran. They'd seen that sickness before, but even the ones who were helping us wouldn't touch him. They told us to just let him die. But we were Marines, understand? Marines don't play that."

Shaka nodded.

"So our docs went to work and took some blood and did what they could. But it was just a field hospital. And the patient was just an old villager. He died pretty quick, but he died awful hard. It wasn't until the two guys who'd brought him in got sick, too, that the command got serious about learning what it was."

Jason paused and inhaled deeply. "Anyways, maybe thirty percent of our unit took sick. Before it was over, about half of 'em died. I didn't. The thing was, though, CCHF don't always act by the book, you know what I'm saying?"

"How do you mean?"

"They took all the usual precautions. They kept us as cool as they could, gave us the fluids and such, some kind of drugs, I guess. They said the old dude probably got infected from the ticks on his animals. Only there weren't any animals around that field hospital. Some that got infected caught it from the patient, but some that swore they weren't ever exposed got it too. And some never got it at all. They couldn't figure it out. I took a whole shitload of tests afterwards. But all they told me was that I had …" Jason paused again, frowning. "What do you call 'em?"

"Antibodies," Shaka said, as he reached into his pockets for the key to the handcuffs. He then shoved the key in Jason's direction. "And I'm going to need some blood from you."

"Sure. I know you have to make sure I'm telling the truth, but I can help. Depending on how bad it spreads, you're gonna need the manpower, and I ain't gonna go down."

Shaka finished up a text to Dr. Kirsten Stone and hit "Send."

"Let yourself loose and come with me."

Jason unlocked the cuff and rose from the bed, stretching gratefully. "Where we going?"

Shaka grinned and clapped him on the shoulder. "To our chief medical officer. If I'm not mistaken, Mr. Carter, you just talked yourself into a job."

CHAPTER FIFTEEN

Lakeland Linder
International Airport, Florida

3:58 AM

After he finished the pre-briefing and reviewing the flight logs of the P-3 Orion that had a communication call sign National Oceanic and Atmospheric Association 42, First officer Kai Tsai stared at his OMEGA Speedmaster wrist watch. The black bezel etched with white lettering reminded him of the time he had practiced timed turns while studying for his instrument flight rules certification in flight school on numerous aircrafts. The P-3 Orion was a rugged surveillance aircraft initially developed for the Navy to be used for antisubmarine warfare, but due to its indestructibility, it became the preferred aircraft for flying into hurricanes.

Kai had come a long way since then. He turned his attention from his watch and walked onto the tarmac, knowing with confidence that the engines had recently been overhauled with less than fifty hours on them.

"Good morning, Kai," said Captain Aadit Decenzo, handing Kai a heavy black flashlight.

"Sir," said Kai.

Both were reservists in the US Air Force and had been acquainted with one another from prior seasons. They had met up in May during previous years, but usually by November, at the end of hurricane season, they went their separate ways. Kai flew a freighter variant of the Boeing 777 for Primera Air, a new subsidiary of the retail giant Rainforest. Captain Decenzo, who would be the pilot in command for this flight, flew an Airbus A330 for Pacific Airlines. Each had logged over one thousand five hundred hours in the aircraft individually and were probably the most experienced pilots on the P-3 in the country. The two conducted a brief exterior inspection of the aircraft under the humid darkness. As they searched for any obvious leaks or open panels, their flashlights illuminated the aircraft, occasionally projecting an outline of the propellers onto the fuselage like dancing shadow puppets.

When the pilots, along with their crew of twelve, climbed aboard the stairs leading to the rear entrance of the hulking Orion, they felt like they were stepping back in time. The airframe itself was older than her pilots, but she was tough. Aside from the Lockheed C-130 Hercules, no other plane could withstand the punishment the Orion endured during her grueling eight- to ten-hour missions flying through the eyewalls of hurricanes. The pair made their way forward—past the rows of computer screens displaying information from the rear-facing doppler radar, the galley, and the dropsonde station—and settled into the cockpit. As Kai donned his David Clark headsets, he turned to Captain Decenzo and said, "Nothing else beats flying into a hurricane, huh?"

"You bet," said Captain Decenzo with a twinkle in his eye.

"It still boggles my mind that, despite all the advances in radars, satellite tech, and supercomputers, there's still no better way to get information about what's going on inside a storm than to go right through it," said Kai. This was the last stick-and-rudder, fly-by-the-seat-of-your-pants assignment left in the Air Force. The pilots themselves were proud to carry on a tradition of hurricane hunting that hadn't changed conceptually since 1943, when Colonel Joseph Duckworth of the US Army Air Corp flew an AT-6 Texan from Galveston into a storm.

"Job security," replied Ellie Willis, the flight engineer, over the coms. "I ain't complaining."

Kai then continued, "Ground control, this is NOAA 42 requesting permission for engine start."

"NOAA 42, you have clearance to begin engine start procedures, over," crackled air controller Zay's voice over the radio.

Captain Decenzo then selected the engine start switch and pushed the "on" button for engine one. The slow whine of the energizing solenoids could still be heard through the headsets as the aircraft came to life. After completing the remaining items on the checklist, Captain Decenzo finally called the tower, "NOAA 42 requesting permission to taxi, over."

"NOAA 42, taxi to runway two seven via Charlie and hold," replied air controller Zay.

A few moments later, the tower controller's voice crackled over the headset. "Cleared for take-off."

Captain Decenzo lowered his microphone to his lips as the aircraft idled at the threshold of the runway. "Nothing like a little storm chasing to get the day going, but safety is a priority. So all malfunctions need to be called out by engine number. Capiche?"

Mumbles of affirmation were heard throughout the aircraft.

Smiling, Captain Decenzo reached for the throttle. "Great. Let's rock and roll."

Captain Decenzo and Kai pushed the throttle levers forward, slowly lurching the aircraft forward from a crawl and then to a gallop.

With his eye on the airspeed indicator, First Officer Kai then called out, "One hundred fifteen knots, rotate."

Captain Decenzo pulled the yoke, lifting the front gear off the runway.

Air traffic control was nearly inaudible over the roar of four turboprops at max power, hurtling the aircraft skywards into the dawn. "NOAA 42, climb and maintain flight level one zero."

Surveillance missions like this one could be as frequent as twice a day when the storm was forecasted to make landfall within twenty-four hours. They were grueling for man and machine. The Department of Commerce and US Air Force would stagger missions hours apart with one another to maintain more time inside the storm, using a C-130 Hercules from the 53rd Weather Reconnaissance Squadron at Kessler Air Force Base in Biloxi, Mississippi. Captain Decenzo and Kai would fly a standard alpha pattern outlined by the National Hurricane Operations Plan, starting at a point northeast of the hurricane eye at 1,500 feet above sea level.

Flying low was dangerous, but it was the only way to gain valuable observations about surface wind speed. No satellite, drone, or surface vessel could do it. This information was also the most relevant since it directly informed residents and businesses in the path of the oncoming storms what actual weather conditions would be.

Each leg of the triangular pattern would be one hundred and five nautical miles. A vertical dropsonde observation was required at each turn point. These dropsondes contained sensors to measure windspeed, wind direction, humidity, and atmospheric pressure. Additionally, each time they crossed into the inner edge of the eyewall, they would take additional soundings. Captain Decenzo and Kai would do their best to maintain tasked altitude while maintaining 210 knots indicated air speed. This was absolutely critical—if too high, the G loads or the gravitational force would exceed design limits of the aircraft and the aircraft could disintegrate, and if too low, the plane would stall and fall out of the sky.

"Twelve kilometers out from the eyewall," called out the meteorologist on board, Zaylen Phoenix.

"Fasten your seat belts and secure all the equipment," said Captain Decenzo over the comms.

The crew stowed away loose items and strapped themselves into their safety harnesses.

As the aircraft approached the ominous towering cumulonimbus clouds, Kai felt a growing pit in his stomach. He thought back to the third flight he had been on investigating a super typhoon. He had become petrified by the roaring sound of the wing shattering from the turbulence. Subsequently the crew had to abandon the aircraft and use life preservers, plunging into freezing waters with limited visibility. He would never forget the feeling of being stabbed by icy shards as he hit the water with tremendous force. Kai had remained in the water for six hours until he was rescued, fighting hypothermia while barely conscious. In his head, he had replayed the line from Gary Allen's song, "Every Storm Runs Out of Rain," the message of which gave Kai a grim sense of hope. His crew had been scattered across the trail of the storm. Ultimately, five survived; the rest of the bodies were never recovered. No matter how many times Kai had done this, at the back of his mind, he knew each flight was a calculated risk.

Within moments, bright skies turned dark. Ellie, herself a veteran of twenty missions, smiled and said, "It feels like riding a roller coaster in a carwash, every time."

The wings of the Orion began to buffet.

Violent up- and downdrafts shook the crew and their equipment.

Though the visibility outside the aircraft was nil, Ellie saw the prop pump warning light on the number four engine was illuminated. "We've got a warning light illuminated on number four," announced Ellie calmly over the comms.

Kai looked at the instrument cluster and noticed the propeller over speeding. His concern grew as he executed the overspeed procedures without any avail.

Wham! A massive explosion jolted the aircraft.

Captain Decenzo looked out of the left window at his position and saw a cloud of black smoke.

CHAPTER SIXTEEN
Galveston University Hospital

Shaka, accompanied by Jason Cater, stood before Dr. Kirsten Stone's office. He tapped lightly on the door. "Enter," she called out.

Shaka went first, followed closely by Jason Carter. Up here, the wind outside was infinitely louder. Even though Dr. Stone had lowered all the blinds and pulled the drapes, it still whistled around the building's corners and shrieked incessantly against the window glass, like a symphony of souls let loose from somewhere beyond.

She glanced up briefly from her computer when they walked in. Jason's eyebrows rose as an especially loud gust of wind howled nearby.

Noting his expression, she managed a thin smile before looking back at her computer monitor. "Noisy, isn't it? Last time I lobby hard for the corner office. Sit down, gentlemen, please."

Shaka took a chair, while behind him, Jason assumed a soldier's "at ease" posture with legs apart, eyes ahead, hands clasped in back. Shaka glanced around appreciatively. For an administrator, Dr. Stone's office was unexpectedly tasteful, even elegant. Fine brown leather club chairs blended beautifully with low Japanese tables inlaid with abalone and mother of pearl. The walls were adorned with a variety of colorful contemporary art. One framed print in particular caught his eye. If it were genuine, it had to have cost a fortune. The question was past his lips before he could stop himself. "Is that a real Rauschenberg?"

She shook her head. "Nope. Jasper Johns, but you were close. And no again. It's a litho reproduction I picked up at auction many years ago. But a good one, I think." She paused. "But as much as I love to talk about art, doctor, that's a discussion for another day. I take it this is Mr. Carter?"

Jason took two steps forward. "That's right, ma'am."

Shaka interrupted. "Two words: convalescent plasma. I was reading an article in the *New England Journal* previously during the Ebola and during the COVID-19 scares—"

"I think Mr. Carter can speak for himself." Dr. Stone rose, came around, and perched on the edge of her desk as if to get a closer look. "Tell me about these qualifications, Mr. Carter. And keep it short. As you can imagine, I have quite a lot on my plate just now." She sighed a little and passed a hand over her tired eyes.

Jason revealed his history with the Corps, as well as his personal experience as a survivor of the virus.

Shaka watched Dr. Stone closely as her expression changed from weary impatience to genuine interest.

Jason explained he might be especially useful—and not just for his antibodies. In the aftermath of the hurricane's landfall, University Hospital might well be operating in an environment that more closely resembled a field hospital.

"You're gonna have to plan for that," he said. "Work out some logistics ahead of time."

"Such as?" Dr. Stone reached around for her phone, ready to take notes.

"Have the back-up generators been checked recently?"

"As far as I know."

"You're going to want somebody to go over the batteries, too, and measure the charge. You can't afford a lapse when we lose the grid."

Dr. Stone began tapping texts into her phone. "Quite right. I hadn't thought that far ahead."

Jason faced her squarely. "You got a morgue here?"

She nodded, frowning. "Of course. On the lower level."

"Well, we're gonna have to move it. Set it up some place higher, where you can keep it cold. We set the bodies out on the mountain to keep 'em frozen. But if that seawall out there gives way, or the storm surge that comes after the hurricane disperses gets too bad, the lower levels are gonna flood. Since we can be pretty sure to lose people to the fever, you can't have virus-contaminated corpses out there floating around till the waters recede. There'd be hell to pay, no doubt."

Dr. Stone texted furiously. "What else?"

Jason cleared his throat. "Quarantine lasts how long?"

The two physicians exchanged glances.

"I'm not sure yet," Dr. Stone answered. "We have to monitor the existing fever patients and track any new cases through CDC before we get an all-clear. But about two weeks at the outside, I should think, barring a widespread outbreak. We're taking every possible precaution against that."

Jason shifted his weight and looked to the ceiling, making calculations. "Back-up generators for a facility like this hospital here are usually good for about ninety-six hours. They'll probably have the power back on by then, but it depends on the storm surge."

"I've cut power to conserve energy systems all over the hospital," Dr. Stone answered. "The only things fully operative are food refrigeration, life support, and essential lighting in the operating rooms."

"Air conditioning? The fever victims need as much cold as we can give them."

Dr. Stone looked momentarily annoyed. "I'm aware of the course of treatment, Mr. Carter. Unlike other parts of the building, the ICU is being kept steady at sixty-eight degrees."

Jason shook his head. "Colder," he said. "You got ice machines down in the kitchen areas?"

"I suppose so—"

"And big floor fans?"

Dr. Stone went back to her phone. "I'll check with maintenance."

"We can bring some of the ice machines upstairs and keep 'em going till the power goes down, using the fans to cool the rooms even more. That way, even when the ice starts to melt, we can keep the fans blowing, and use some sheets to sop up the ice water and wrap the patients. It won't work forever, but it will buy us some time."

Dr. Stone nearly smiled. "Ingenious. Did you learn that in the Marines?"

Jason flashed his teeth and slowly shook his head. "No, ma'am, I grew up on the Mississippi delta. We didn't have air conditioning."

Dr. Stone rose to her feet. "Very well, Mr. Carter. You'll report to the ICU along with Dr. Sen here, for a blood sample. Sen, we need to send it for an IgM antibody test for the CCHF virus and get a type and cross on him."

"Don't you mean IgG, Dr. Stone?" replied Dr. Sen. "Since IgG tests for evidence of a past infection, and IgM tests for a current one."

"Yes, thank you, Dr. Sen," replied Dr. Stone as she rolled her eyes in annoyance. "After that, I want you to report to Mr. Hodges of the maintenance staff down on the third floor. He's been instructed to give you whatever manpower you need to start moving equipment around. We may not need it, but it doesn't hurt to be prepared."

Jason's eyebrows rose again. "Ma'am?"

Dr. Stone sighed and riffled through some papers on her desk. "I've had some communication from the National Guard unit headquartered on the island; they're aware of the quarantine, but have assured me they'll be commencing rescue operations in conjunction with the Coast Guard as soon after the storm passes as is feasible."

Jason's expression turned doubtful.

"Is there a problem, Mr. Carter? With the presence of the military, I should think you'd be relieved."

"Yes, ma'am. I am. But my time in the Corps taught me a few things about the chain of command when it comes to logistics. And one of them is that 'feasible' is the kind of word that can mean a lot of things to a lot of different people. I don't want to borrow trouble, but sometimes the orders get mixed up a bit, especially in a joint operation."

She nodded abruptly. "I understand. Meanwhile, we'll just have to do the best we can. Now please excuse me, gentlemen. I'm going to find an empty office without quite so many windows."

CHAPTER SEVENTEEN
NOAA 42, Gulf of Mexico

As the dark smoke cleared, to his utter dismay, meteorologist Phoenix saw the number four prop missing and the reduction gear box on fire.

"Engine four is on fire," shouted Phoenix in a panic.

"Shut down the number four engine," called out Kai.

All of a sudden, the instrument cluster went dark due to a total loss of electrical power. Shaking his head, Captain Decenzo said, "You've got to be fucking kidding me."

Kai directed Ellie to pull the hydraulic boost handles and start the auxiliary power unit to get back-up power.

"It keeps flaming out and malfunctioning," shouted Ellie.

Things looked bad for the crew of the NOAA 42, Kai thought. When the boost handles were pulled, the aircraft should have switched from the hydraulic to the mechanical cable controls. For some reason that didn't happen.

Kai and Captain Decenzo looked at one another, with a horrible gut-wrenching feeling that this was going to be the end for everyone aboard.

The aircraft began to roll uncontrollably, banking at a ninety-degree angle, leaving a fiery, smoky red blaze in its wake.

Suddenly, the control columns unlocked at two hundred fifty feet above sea level. Captain Decenzo added power and banked hard to the left. The wings leveled, and the crew suddenly emerged into the relative safety of the hurricane's eye.

The turbulence ceased, and outside the aircraft the crew could see a majestic stadium of clouds surrounding their aircraft in a 360-degree fashion. The spiraled, puffy white haze was massive, looking like cotton candy from afar. It was a devastatingly beautiful sight to behold. The storm clouds themselves rose to almost fifty-five thousand feet. Blue skies were visible for the first time since they entered the eyewall. Kai estimated the eye was at least thirty-six nautical miles in diameter.

Kai glanced back and watched as the crew took a moment to collect themselves. He thought they had managed to survive the inbound leg of the mission, but the exit would be something else—especially on the remaining three engines.

Flight director Shiv Patel finally took the comms: "Holy shit! That was a rough ride, but we're here on a mission. Might as well complete it and start hunting for the center."

Kai took control of the aircraft and began to fly a standard triangular pattern around the suspected center of the storm, observing for any changes in wind shift. Finally, when the wind speed outside the aircraft had dropped to zero miles per hour, Shiv identified the center. Latitude and longitude were transmitted via satellite communications.

Kai gazed out in fascination, taking in the tranquil oasis within a vortex of uncontrolled fury. Scientifically extraordinary and catastrophically ferocious.

"This has got to be one of the biggest storms I have ever seen," he said, in genuine awe. "A true, unique beauty of mother nature."

Captain Decenzo leaned over to Kai and said, "That's great and all, but how do we get out?"

Kai thought aloud, "Maybe we can wait for the Air Force guys from Kessler to guide us out. But we'd have to wait another hour or so."

"If we divert to a closer airport than Lakeland, that just might work," said Captain Decenzo.

CHAPTER EIGHTEEN

National Guard Armory, La Marque, Texas

Twenty-four hours after Hurricane Beatrix made landfall

Colonel Wilson leaned back in his chair and closed his eyes against the relentless sound of the wind. They'd downgraded the hurricane to a category four as it neared land. That was good, he reassured himself. Well, maybe not good, but definitely better than nothing.

The governor had just issued a state of emergency. The next set of orders came directly from the US Army Chemical, Biological, and Radiological Weapons School director, General Drucker, at Dugway: do what had to be done. He recoiled at what followed. He'd been in this kind of command situation only once before, and the recollection itched in his memory like a fresh scar.

A light tap on the door roused him. That would be Corporal Mendoza. He could tell by her knock. He couldn't say why it irritated him exactly; certainly, he had nothing against women in the Guard. It was only that she always seemed so willing to question his authority. He couldn't afford that, least of all today.

She entered and saluted with her usual efficiency. Following closely was their local disaster planning expert, Sergeant Sam Alvarez, a native-born Texan, as was Wilson. They had shared the bond of having seen a few campaigns together, something a young woman like Corporal Mendoza would never understand. But that was women in general, Wilson supposed. Always wanting explanations for everything.

"Sam," he said, rising to his feet and coming around the desk to shake the other man's hand. "We all set?"

Sam grinned. "Ready as we'll ever be, I reckon. Just waiting on the eye to detonate. Too much earlier and the air pressure could set off enough spark to torch the oil refinery there." He paused and shook his head. "Can't afford another scene like '05, can we?"

"Oh, hell no," Colonel Wilson replied. "Though the corporal here was probably still in grade school back then."

Corporal Mendoza stood at ease, blushing. "If you're referring to the British Petroleum refinery fire, sir, then I'm well aware. It killed my father and fourteen others. And with hundreds of others critically injured."

A brief, uncomfortable silence followed.

"Well, let's just hope the new owners take better care of the safety protocols than the last bunch," the colonel went on. "Marathon's advised total evacuation. But in case it does blow, taking out the bridges to the island is the only way to prevent an even bigger disaster."

Sam nodded. "How 'bout you, Henry? You and your unit ready to bend over and kiss your butts to kingdom come?"

"Not likely. Not just yet, anyhow. I have another detail for you and your team."

"Yeah?"

"University Hospital is now under full quarantine until further notice. Orders from Washington and the CDC. They have an outbreak of some kind of fever."

"Crimean Congo Hemorrhagic Fever," the corporal put in. "There is no known cure. And only a fifty percent survival rate."

Sam's expression turned serious. "Never rains but it pours, I guess. What do you need from my team?"

Wilson drew a deep breath. "Rig the causeway to Galveston Island to blow in case this virus gets out of hand. Another team is working on the Bluewater Highway. If that happens, we're only going to have one access road—the one we're on. Anyone wanting access or escape is going to have to come through us first. Whatever disease they got spreading up there is going to stay there until I get the all-clear."

Sam nodded. "So, you want to contain a possible outbreak, same way you contain a fire? I guess I follow that, except—"

"Except what about the people?" Corporal Mendoza piped up. "What about the patients and the hospital personnel? We can't just cut them off without anything and leave them to die!"

Colonel Wilson struggled to control himself and his temper. His eyes flickered over to her, then back to Sam.

"First of all, this is worst-case scenario. There is a reason the National Biocontainment Lab was built on an island; it's easy to cut off. Secondly, I can and will do whatever is called for to contain a possible pandemic, corporal," he answered carefully. "My orders are clear and directly from a General Drucker at Dugway Proving Grounds. If this fever's what they claim it is, then forty percent of them are going to die anyway."

"But—"

"Corporal, you are excused. See if we can send in one last shipment of resources to the hospital before the eye hits."

Mendoza hesitated, looking fierce, then offered a perfunctory salute before she left, closing the door behind her.

Wilson sighed heavily and sank back down into his desk chair.

Sam maintained a respectful silence for a moment. Then, he said, "I figure we have two hours before the eye. Have you been in contact with the hospital folks?"

"Of course. I was the one who passed along the quarantine order."

"So, what did you tell them?" Sam continued.

Wilson glanced up at the sergeant with a dark, unreadable expression. "I told 'em to hang in, Sam. What the hell do you think I said? I told them we had their backs."

Sam winced and placed his hat back on his head as he turned to go. "Better get to it then. I'll let the corporal know when the bridges are ready. I know it's a tough decision, but you have done your best, Henry. Maybe it's better to let them think the cavalry's coming with aid, until they are able to figure out how bad their situation is."

The colonel watched him glumly as he turned to go. "Sam?" he called the moment before the sergeant closed the door. "You be careful out there, okay? You and your team. Wear your goddamn raincoat."

When he was gone, the colonel resumed his former posture, leaning back in his chair and closing his eyes, hearing only the howling of the wind as the day darkened to something like twilight, and the water in the harbors grew black with rage.

CHAPTER NINETEEN
Galveston University Hospital

I t was midafternoon by the time Danica could make her way back to the ICU. Crossing from the other side of the hospital where she'd been making the rest of her rounds, she was dimly aware that something had changed but couldn't put her finger on it. She passed the great glass wall, now bathed in an eerie, yellowish-green light, almost as if the sun were pressing hard on the cloud cover that whirled above, trying to break through. Outside, the winds had calmed to a degree, and as she peered curiously through the rain-spattered panes, she blinked uncomprehendingly. Upended yachts were thrown sideways across the seawall highway, and the palm trees littered the landscape like a handful of children's plastic toys. Her eyes darted frantically around as she tried to assess the damage. The roof was gone on a nearby shopping complex, its Spanish tiles scattered and broken over the parking lot. The high, white sand dunes near the beach were also gone, blown inland onto the streets of the city or swallowed whole in the relentless maw of the still-pounding surf. But from what she could see, most of Galveston was holding on, and the rows of sturdy adobe houses, hillside beach mansions, and seaside hotels were still intact, lined up like soldiers stoically awaiting the hurricane's next lash.

"At least the power's holding," she said to herself as she rounded the corner to enter the chamber to suit up for isolation. Just then, her text alert and pager went off, almost simultaneously.

She fumbled in her pocket and saw the message from the floor nurse: *Dr. Diza: We just lost Cory Finch. I'll need you to sign off on the paperwork.*

"Dammit," she said, struggling with the layers of her HAZMAT gear. She felt the sweat creep down from her armpits in the sweltering heat. At Dr. Wong's insistence, any attending ICU staff had to switch from the usual protective gear to full HAZMAT precautions, and she was still somewhat clumsy with the additional layers required. Under most circumstances, hospital personnel would don and doff the gear in teams of two, but operating on a skeleton crew, the monitor system was the best they'd been able to do. When she finally mounted the protective shield over her face mask and hood, tightened the drawstring, and double-checked for any exposed skin, she glanced at the camera and flashed a thumbs-up sign. The door lock released and the door swung inward.

The curtains were drawn around what had been Cory's bed. Dr. Wong was next to it, and a quick check on the other side revealed yet another patient. Danica started; it was the same young intern she'd saved from a tongue-lashing by Dr. Hardy on rounds the other day. What was her name? It seemed like eons ago.

A quick glance at her chart, however, confirmed it. Her name was Beth. Beth Windsor. Danica quickly scanned the details. After collapsing while on duty in the lab, Beth had been admitted to the ICU just hours earlier.

Danica drew closer to Beth's bedside and patted her hand somewhat clumsily through her two layers of rubber gloves. Beth was conscious but covered with an unhealthy sheen of sweat, breathing shallowly through her oxygen mask. Danica tried to smile with her eyes. "I guess I should say we have to stop meeting like this."

Peering at her closely, Beth's face revealed a spark of recognition. She struggled to sit up straighter until Danica found the control button to raise the bed and placed it in her hand.

"Oh, God," she whispered. "Do I have it? The fever? I should have turned myself in yesterday! I knew something was wrong; I was dizzy all the time and I had the worst headache! But I was just trying to do my job, you know? Oh, God, how could I be so stupid?"

Danica reached over and squeezed Beth's hand through her two layers of rubber gloves. "It's all right, Beth. It's all right. Do you … can you … remember anything that might have exposed you? A needle stick? Anything like that?"

Beth hazily struggled to focus. "Not that I remember. I tried to be careful. They brought him—Cory—in and he was delirious most of the time. At least, when he was conscious. When I came on duty the next day, the floor nurse told me to try to keep him calm while she changed his IV."

"What did you do?" Danica asked gently.

Beth turned away, her eyes filling with tears. "I asked him if there was somebody we could call. Bad question to ask. He kept shouting that he was all alone, no family. That he was scared and nobody would even care if he died. I just tried to comfort him somehow. We didn't know what he had at first, so we only had the protective suit. Not like what you've got on. Maybe I patted his hand or something. I don't know. He looked so awful; these hemorrhages were breaking out all over, underneath his skin."

"Don't think about that now," Danica reassured her.

"Anyway, I couldn't sleep after my shift yesterday. I kept thinking about him, all alone up here. About how it would be awful to be so sick and maybe even die like that. So, I came back up here and put on all the protective gear again and just—sat with him—until the shift changed. Talked to him a little. Just so he wouldn't be afraid. I don't even know if he knew I was there." Beth's eyes met Danica's, pleading for understanding. "I just wanted to be a good doctor, you know?"

Danica smiled behind her mask and patted her hand once more. "And you will be, Beth. I promise you that. But first we have to get you well, okay? You concentrate on that. Get some rest."

She double-checked the patient's white blood cell counts and vitals. So far, the young intern was holding her own, and her fever had even dropped a degree. Danica made a note on her chart to up Beth's dose of ribavarin. Until they got her lab results back, it was the best they could do.

Danica turned and made her way to the far side of the ward near the window where a single bed was occupied. Dr. Wong lay listlessly on his side, eyes closed, with the first brutal traces of petechial rash showing darkly purple against the golden tones of his skin.

"Who is it?" he asked, without opening his eyes.

"It's Danica, here for my rounds. How are you, Dr. Wong.?"

He sighed deeply. "Worse, I think. Weaker. Tachycardia. Localized pain to the upper right abdominal quadrant. Discernible liver enlargement. I'm going to need another transfusion."

Danica made a note. There was nothing like a doctor determined to dictate his own treatment.

"My eyes aren't bleeding yet," he went on. "But it shouldn't be too long." He sighed again and closed them against the light. "This is so fucking rotten … ."

"Dr. Wong," she said gently. "I know how hard this must be for you. But you can't give up hope. You have to hang on. We've got every pair of hands we can get on this one, including the CDC. There is even a survivor on the premises, Jason Carter. He got the fever while on tour in Iraq with the Marines. We've got the lab screening him for antibodies now. Maybe we can work up something that will help."

As he slowly absorbed this information, Dr. Wong pulled himself to a painful sitting position. His breath came more rapidly as he stared at her. "Antibodies?" He clutched her arm so hard it made her jump and back out of his reach.

"Yes, I don't know what they intend to do, but—"

"My phone." Dr. Wong breathed hard. "You have to find my phone."

"Dr. Wong, please lie down. Don't overexert yourself. I told you, we're doing everything we can."

"No! You need to call my wife; text her—something. Her number's in my phone. You need to tell her and my kids that

I'm doing fine, all right? Lie your head off if you have to, but tell her! Promise me!"

Danica nodded. "I will. I don't know what the cell service is doing; it keeps going in and out, but I'll tell her."

Dr. Wong fell back against the pillow. "Then you need to find that kid—Billy Andersen. He worked with Cory in the biocontainment lab. His number's also in my phone somewhere, or I have it upstairs in the lab. But find him, wherever he is. Get him back here."

"But we're under quarantine," Danica protested. "Nobody gets in. Or out. I'm not sure I can—"

"You don't get it. The DoD played us." Dr. Wong paused for a long moment, trying to catch his breath. "But I think in all this, they had Andersen unwittingly working on a vaccine for this strain of CCHF. We could invoke an animal efficacy rule with what he knows about the vaccine and go straight to human trials so you won't be starting from scratch."

Her mind went into a tailspin. *What the hell? What do you mean "this strain?" They were testing this strain on animals already?*

She composed herself after a moment. "I'll do everything I can, Dr. Wong. I promise."

"Do that," he answered. "And while you're at it, order me some oxygen. I don't want to die from this shit if I can help it."

For the first time, Danica allowed herself a smile. "I will. But it's your turn to promise me something."

"What's that?"

"That you'll keep on reminding yourself that a good virus isn't supposed to kill off its host. You've got a lot to live for. Remember that."

After she doffed her HAZMAT suit and decontaminated, she managed to locate Dr. Wong's phone at the nurses' station outside the isolation ward. The nurses had it packed up with his wallet and other personal effects, duly labeled and placed in a storage locker. Gingerly, she took the plastic bag in her newly gloved fingers.

"Have these been through decontamination?" She asked.

It wasn't that she was especially concerned about contagion at that point, as viruses such as this one didn't normally survive outside a host for more than a few hours, but under the circumstances, it didn't pay to take unnecessary chances either. She carried the phone over to a nearby container and wiped it down carefully with sanitizer, praying that it wouldn't be locked or password protected.

Mercifully, it was still charged at least, showing three bars of power. She waved at the head nurse on her way out. "I'll have this back in half an hour."

The nurse shrugged. "Whatever."

She took the stairs to the lower level, heading to the residents' lounge for a moment of quiet. She needed time to think of what she would say to Dr. Wong's family. She paused at the entrance to the hospital chapel, where an assortment of patients and staff had gathered to pray. Above the altar, a Mexican-style crucifix displayed a figure of Jesus that was unlike any other she had ever seen. No longer a figure of suffering and death, it showed a moment of genuine healing, of grace, almost as though the very soul of the statue was about to take flight.

The chaplain glanced up and beckoned her forward.

She demurred and headed to the next flight of stairs. On the way down, she suddenly became conscious of the sounds of the ocean once more. The winds had calmed in the eye of the storm, but the waves had not. But even she was unprepared for what she saw as she crossed the glass-walled corridor that led to the adjoining wing. Mesmerized by the horror outside, she moved toward the windows, her errand momentarily forgotten.

Thirty-foot waves crashed ceaselessly over the seventeen-foot-high seawall that separated the hospital complex and the rest of the city from the roar of the ocean. The boulevard, still visible two hours ago, had disappeared entirely and rivers of water reached into the city streets, watery tentacles seeking their prey. The dunes were gone, the beach was gone, and in their place was a wall of debris, composed of trees and cars and boats and the ruins of buildings, all being pushed inexorably forward by the relentless, pounding surf. And with each break of the waves, the whole building—the earth itself—moaned in protest.

Unable to move, even to run, she began to shake uncontrollably. Unbidden, Beth's words came echoing back to her: *It must be so awful. To die like that—all alone.* Fumbling for her own phone, she tried with trembling fingers to tap out a text to the only person she could think of who was stuck here with her.

Shaka? Where are you?

No response. Another mighty wall of water and ruin surged forward with a deafening roar. Danica backed away involuntarily. She put her hands over her ears and tried hard not to scream as the world outside the glass turned to water and foam.

Then she was on her hands and knees, struggling to get to her feet, when a tiny ding signaled a message though the din:

O.R. They just brought in a Guard guy from south of Jamaica Beach. Pretty much blew his arm off setting explosives. I'll come find you later.

For some reason, even those words calmed her enough to stand, and she resumed her journey to the opposite wing, step by shaking step. She heard the blast a split moment before it sent her hurtling against the far wall, smacking her hard against the concrete. She only saw that in the next instant the world outside the windows turned to fire, as a blazing column of flames shot up from the earth and boiled away the water in its wake.

Dazed, Danica stared uncomprehendingly as another blast shattered from the right. No longer sure if she was awake or dreaming and unable to move, she watched with a kind of wonder as the first threadlike cracks appeared in the safety glass, far above her head, glistening like jewels.

And then all was darkness once more.

CHAPTER TWENTY
Galveston University Hospital

Danica opened her eyes slowly, aware of a dim pounding in her head and the utilitarian firmness of a hospital bed mattress underneath her. Though the room was all but dark, a sideways glance through the open doorway revealed a dim light coming from somewhere down the hall.

What happened? Frustrated, she tried to piece together events through a painful fog, even as she mentally assessed her own physical condition, moving her fingers and toes, then lifting an arm to check for an IV. Nothing there. Whatever the damage, it couldn't be too serious. She fumbled for the call button on her bed, then raised herself slowly to a more upright position, fighting the uncomfortable little flashes of light at the edge of her peripheral vision. Though her shoes had been removed, she was still in the same set of scrubs rather than a hospital gown. Whomever had put her in this room had clearly been in something of a hurry.

Though it hurt to breathe, she sat up a little further and swung one leg over the side of the bed, meaning to get up and go investigate.

"You stop right there!"

The voice made her jump, but even that didn't surprise her as much as the face that peered around the doorjamb.

"Dylan Nguyen! What on earth? What are you doing here? I thought you evacuated days ago!"

The young man came forward and took her hand, blushing. "Glad to see you awake, doc," he said. "Mind if I have a look?" He reached in his pocket and shone a light into her right eye, then the left. The brightness made her wince.

"Looking good," he went on. "Your pupils are the same size. How's the pain? You got quite a knock on the head."

Danica reached up gingerly and fingered the lump on the back of her head. "Throbbing pretty bad, but bearable."

"Let me know if you need any acetaminophen. Any nausea?"

"No. Saw a few stars when I sat up, but that's it."

He smiled. "That's good. Looks like you lucked out with a mild concussion."

She frowned at him, momentarily confused. "But what happened? How did you get here? I thought you were on your way off the island."

He shot her an embarrassed glance. "Long story short, I never made it off the island. When I signed off the other day, I had my motorcycle, so I figured it would be fastest to stay off I-45 and the main roads and head for one of the old causeways so I could circle around and back north once the worst of the storm was over."

Danica frowned at him. "On a motorcycle?"

He hung his head. "I know, bad idea, right? Especially when I found out every access road was blocked by the National Guard except for I-45, and by the time I turned back, they'd even shut *that* down. Anyway, I was out there on the road when I got the text about the quarantine here at the hospital. I knew I wasn't supposed to break it, but it was either die out there in the storm or come back here. So, I came back here. I managed to sneak in one of the basement entrances they hadn't locked yet, headed for the sub-basement where they store the supplies, and eventually I made my way up. I figured if anybody caught me, I'd get fired for sure, so I just hung out down there for the past couple of days until the water started coming into the basement a few hours ago."

Danica nodded as much as her throbbing head would allow.

"I wasn't really scared. I just didn't know what else to do. But then, the lights went out, the generators hadn't kicked in yet, and all of a sudden, here comes Jason Carter, that prisoner I'd treated for pneumonia. And I was like, what the hell, dude? How did *you* get down here?" Dylan paused and chuckled. "Believe me, he didn't waste a lot of time explaining. He just hooked me up with these two other guys he had with him and said we had to clear out the sub-basements and the food storage units and haul it all upstairs before the flooding took hold. He knew what he was talking about too. The water was already ankle-deep in some places."

"So, then what? Is the power back on?"

Dylan shook his head. "We're on the back-up generators. From what they told me, we should be good for about ninety-six hours."

Danica frowned. "What? That's only four days!"

"Take it easy, doc. By then, the storm will have cleared out completely. Worst possible case, the National Guard should be able to get in here and refill the diesel tank by then."

"If you say so." She fell back against her pillows, struggling to recall something that tickled at the edge of her memory, just out of reach. Something important.

"Hey, you think you could eat something?" Dylan asked. "That's what I was doing when I passed here and saw you were awake. Delivering dinner."

He reached over and swung her meal tray in front of her, locking it in place. He headed into the hallway and returned with a lidded microwave bowl, plastic eating utensils, and a small pitcher of water.

A heavenly aroma arose from the bowl when he removed the lid, and Danica inhaled deeply, instantly ravenous for whatever was inside. She unwrapped her spoon and fork, examining the contents. Thick brown noodles and an assortment of colorful vegetables floated in a clear broth, all topped by a perfectly poached egg.

"My udon fusion noodles. Specialty of the house," he announced with a little flourish. "Sorry about the no chopsticks."

She stared at him. "You made this?"

"Of course! Well, the chicken broth was canned and the veggies were mostly frozen, but use 'em or lose 'em, as they say. I added a spoonful of sriracha for the heat too. And those udon noodles? Made of buckwheat and gluten-free, if that's your thing."

After a few minutes, she slurped up the last spoonful and sighed, feeling instantly revived.

Dylan smiled approvingly. "Good?"

"Beyond good," she said.

"Wait till you taste my Vietnamese mole."

"But I still don't understand; they had all these supplies in the sub-basement? And how in the world do you know so much about food?"

He laughed. "My folks own a small chain of noodle houses in San Antonio. Until I was thirteen or so, I thought I was going to grow up to be a chef. But Mom and Dad, they had other ambitions for their number one son, you know?"

She nodded understandingly. The American Dream was serious business for so many families and their kids.

"Anyhow, last year I worked here in the hospital cafeteria to help pay my tuition. I even had my own noodle concession a couple of days a week. But I couldn't keep up with the schoolwork and the job too. And I had to graduate. Best thing was, some of my supplies were still stored downstairs, so when I saw them, I jumped on 'em. Mr. Carter and the other guys had to cap off all the gas lines to the grills and stoves in the main kitchens for safety, so I figured I could work from the microwave stations on each floor and at least get people a hot meal every once in a while. That's where we were headed when we found you out cold by the glass wall. I yelled for Mr. Carter and the other guys.

"Man, that Mr. Carter is something else. Once I made sure nothing was broken, he just picked you up, slung you over his shoulder like a sack of potatoes, and carried supplies with his other hand. Listen, if you're okay, I have to get back to passing out food. Can't have it getting cold."

She had begun to wave him out of the room when the memory of what she'd forgotten hit her full force. Her hand flew to her mouth. "Oh my God! The phones! Dylan, where's my lab coat?"

He stared at her curiously. "Just right over here in the locker. I hung it up here when we found you this room."

"Are there phones in there? In the pocket? Give them to me."

He reached in and withdrew two phones, turning them both on for her. "You have a charger?" he asked. "That one is pretty low. You're down to one bar."

She glanced down at Dr. Wong's phone and turned it off immediately. "Damn it, no, I don't."

Dylan shoved a hand in his pocket. "Use mine. Portable. Don't even need an outlet. But I don't see the hurry. I doubt there's a working cell tower within a hundred miles."

Danica frowned and fumbled to connect the device. "Wait, how long have I been out? What time is it? Doesn't matter. I promised Dr. Wong." She glanced up suddenly, her eyes full of fear, searching his face. "Is he … he isn't … " she trailed off, loathe to even say the word aloud.

"Dead? Not as far as I know, and you have been out for a few hours. They won't let me in the isolation unit, though. Told me I'd be more useful if I wasn't exposed."

"That makes sense. Have there been … others?"

"One orderly who was a first responder. He's stable. But we lost an intern. Beth Windsor. They set up a temporary morgue in the old prison wing. I couldn't believe it when they told me her name. I took classes with her back in college doing pre-med. But she went fast, less than twenty-four hours. Passed in her sleep."

Danica's eyes filled with unexpected tears. "She was so young. Anybody else?"

"Not that I know of. But I heard this morning that another patient, a Mrs. Chavez, wasn't long for this world. But it's not because of the virus."

Danica glanced down at her phone and blinked back still more tears. Struggling to control herself, she forced herself to ask the question that was stuck in her throat.

"Have you … have you seen Dr. Sen?"

Dylan's worried face brightened. "Yes! Yes, I did! And he told me if I saw you, he'd come to see you when his latest blood work was clear."

"Blood work?"

"Dr. Stone's orders. Any personnel exposed to CCHF and those in isolation get blood drawn every twenty-four hours for testing. She figures the sooner we can track it and isolate, the sooner we can administer ribavirin as a prophylactic. They'll probably be by for another sample from you pretty soon."

"Yeah," Danica murmured. "That makes as much sense as anything." Feeling her short burst of energy abate, she leaned back against her pillow once more.

"Listen, I gotta go. But don't stress yourself, okay? Just get some rest. We can handle it till you're back on your feet, all right?"

She nodded and tried to smile. "Thank you, Dylan. For everything. I'll be okay."

But when he had gone, she shifted herself up and stared hard at the screen of Dr. Wong's phone. She turned it on and scrolled until she found the number she sought. With clumsy, trembling fingers she composed a text.

Dear Mrs. Wong, your husband asked me to get in touch and let you know we at the hospital are safe and to tell you and your children how very much he loves and misses you … .

CHAPTER TWENTY-ONE
Galveston University Hospital

Sweat dripped down Shaka's forehead as he irrigated the burn wound with sterile saline. The operating rooms in the burn unit were kept at a sweltering ninety degrees Fahrenheit to combat the hypothermia that would otherwise set in—burn patients are poikilotherms and can't thermoregulate. Shaka was becoming irritated and uncomfortable in the gown with all the heat from the surgical light glaring down his neck. Condensation accumulated on his visor, limiting his vision. The putrid smell of burnt human flesh only added to this discomfort.

The patient on the table was also a cause of annoyance as he was the guardsman who blew up the Bluewater bridge, essentially stranding the medical staff on the island.

"Need a ten-blade that can cut. People, let's go. Anesthesia, keep those IVs wide open. This guy will need plenty of fluids post-op," he confidently announced.

The surgical tech passed him the blade and Shaka continued to debride the wound. He made his way through the layers of dead, charred, leathery flesh, cutting through one layer at a time.

Shaka hated burn surgery.

It didn't require any technical skill or mastery of anatomy. It made him feel akin to a butcher, hacking off dead tissue to reach a margin of healthy tissue underneath, and then stapling split thickness skin grafts. It was a mindless monotonous surgery with the only critical thinking occurring when one decided whether an amputation was required. Shaka wished he at least had a medical student to teach something to.

Drained after finishing the debridement, Shaka stepped out of the OR and went straight to the nurses' station in the burn unit. He naturally gravitated toward a petite brunette nurse in form-fitting scrubs, but in that moment, he felt no spark as he took her in. She was, nonetheless, a welcome sight after staring at burned eschar in the OR.

"Kelly," he said after scanning her chest for an ID badge, "Let's continue hydrating the patient based on the Parkland formula."

She turned to Shaka and looked at him with confusion. "Don't we use the Galveston formula around here?"

"I take it you haven't worked in the burn unit before. That formula is for pediatric patients," Shaka said, grinning from ear to ear. He usually loved nothing more than to correct someone, but he saw a wave of embarrassment overcome Kelly.

"No, I'm usually in labor and delivery. I've never worked with burn patients," she admitted sheepishly.

Exhausted, Shaka sat down on the chair and gave her a sympathetic look before diving in.

"Sorry, it has been a long time for me too. I haven't been on the burn unit in a few years myself, since I was an intern. Fluid resuscitation for burn patients is based on weight and total body surface burned. Our patient is at a forty-seven percent, thanks to his botched stunt. So according to that, you can use the Parkland Formula and calculate the rate of his fluid replacement. After a burn, the blood capillaries are more permeable, which means they are leaky and will result in rapid fluid loss, and we have to compensate for that loss to maintain perfusion and to prevent organs from shutting down," he stated matter-of-factly.

Shaka waited for Kelly to finish writing her notes before he continued. "The patient is also going to remain intubated and sedated for now."

Kelly looked at him with admiration. "Thank you for taking the time to explain that to me. Not many people would do that, especially at a time like this."

"If we are going to make it out of this thing, we need to start treating each other better, trusting one another, and learning from each other. Otherwise, we are all doomed. Page me overhead if you have issues or call me if there is cell service. Good thing we are at a state-of-the-art burn center." He turned and scribbled down his cell phone number.

The nurse mused, "I hope I never have to work on burn patients after this. It is too grim for me. I prefer pregnant women and babies."

Shaka managed a nod of reassurance. He got up, then walked past room two hundred and one, the first bed in the burn unit. His mind wandered back to a memory from his intern year. He remembered a patient flown in from Mexico. A bipolar sixteen-year-old teenager who had stopped taking his medications and gotten into an argument with his girlfriend. The ensuing break-up led him to isolate himself inside his room and to immolate himself using lighter fluid.

His poor parents had to take an ax to break the door down and put out the fire, but by the time emergency services arrived, he was barely breathing. They were air-flighted to Shriner's. He came in with ninety-eight percent total body surface area burn, the worst Shaka had ever seen. Shaka could still remember the parents' grim faces, full of sadness and fear. The teen's parents had no idea what was happening in his life, as they had been working double shifts to provide for their kids and to give them the best life possible. They had to get the history from the younger sister. Shaka felt for the parents. It was heartbreaking. They thought they were doing the best they could for their kids. That rotation helped Shaka decide against becoming a burn surgeon, and he vowed to be present in his children's lives—in a way his own parents weren't—no matter how demanding his work schedule.

Unknowingly, he found his way to the one person he wanted to be near after a brutal day. Her calming presence made all his worries and fears dissipate. He wanted to be with her, close to her, and in her presence at all times. He would do anything to make her smile. For the first time in his life, he was happier being with a person than in his sanctuary, which was the operating room. He couldn't get her out of his mind, and he was afraid of what that meant. He let that thought linger for a moment as he watched her dream. He made his way to the recliner next to her bed, and he fell apart in it, wrapping himself in the hospital-issued blanket, allowing sleep to come quickly.

CHAPTER TWENTY-TWO
Galveston University Hospital

Two hours later, after checking in vain as to whether she had any cell service and catching another short nap, Danica awoke in an empty room to a light tap on her door. Hastily, she sat up and ran a hand through her unruly hair, still painfully conscious of the bump on the back of her head and the dull ache causing her head to spin. No convenient ponytails for her for a couple of days.

"Come in," she called, half-hoping to see Shaka at last.

Instead, it was Jason Carter, standing somewhat sheepishly in the doorway, holding, of all things, a huge bouquet of flowers. He marched toward her bedside, holding the flowers out awkwardly.

"What in the world?" Danica gaped at him in astonishment. "Mr. Carter, I swear, you're full of more surprises than a magic show!"

She took the flowers, an odd assortment of carnations, chrysanthemums, roses, and gladioli, and sniffed appreciatively. "You didn't have to—" she began.

He held up a hand in protest, blushing furiously. "I found them down in the gift shop on the first floor. They're kind of beat up and the worse for wear, what with all the water. But I thought they might cheer you up a little. I wasn't sure. It's been a long time since I brought a woman flowers, to tell you the truth. But they weren't doing anybody any good down there. Besides, we needed the refrigeration unit."

She continued to look at him, genuinely touched. "Thank you. It's sweet of you to think of me." There was a slightly uncomfortable pause as she considered the implications. "But I'm the one who ought to be bringing you tributes. Dylan Nguyen told me you're the one who picked me up and got me out of there before the glass wall—wait, did it collapse? There was an explosion, maybe even two of them. I'm sure of it. I saw fire … ."

Jason shook his head, frowning. "So far, only nine of the windows are compromised. But they're leaking bad. Turns out, one of the maintenance guys had a whole bunch of windshield repair kits in his locker. I can't say why unless he had a side hustle he was working in the parking garage, but I wasn't about to ask too many questions, either. I figured it was the hand of God, plain and simple. I got a few of my crew up on the ladders now, using them to reinforce the safety glass. I don't expect it'll hold for long. But it may buy us some time, anyhow."

He scowled for a moment. "That fire you saw probably came from the refinery over at Texas City Petrochemical. Still belching black to the east. You can see it once you get back on your feet. I guess the fools over at the National Guard thought they could contain it by blowing up the bridges between Galveston and them. Dumbasses. Fire like that can swim. Just like an oil spill can. Bad as the smoke is now, I don't think they could medivac us out of here by air if they wanted to."

Danica rolled her eyes. "Great, can't catch a break. What else will go wrong?"

Jason continued, "Well, I was going to check it out, but you all have been keeping me pretty busy. Good thing I ain't afraid of needles. I've been stuck so many times I feel like my grandma's pincushion. Dr. Dunn upstairs told me I got the antibodies all right, but they need to wait until I'm clear of the medicine I was on for the pneumonia before they can use me."

Danica looked up at Jason meaningfully. "In all honesty, thank you, though. You really are a hero."

He shook his head, and glanced around the room, refusing to meet her eyes. "Don't be talking like that, ma'am. I know all about heroes. Seen plenty of 'em, decorated, too. Men who didn't do nothing but step on a land mine or get toked up and take after a whole village with an M-16. It's bullshit. There ain't no glory in that, just ugliness."

"But, Jason, you've got to give yourself some credit ... look at all you've done for this hospital, for me. You should be proud. Maybe missing that bus was a blessing in disguise."

He met her eyes full then, full of emotions she could not name.

"What about you, doc? You give yourself credit? I bet not. Yet you save lives every day. That's what I mean. Look, the Corps taught me a lot of technical know-how and I'm grateful for that. But mostly, they taught me to serve, same as my grandma did. Working as a housekeeper, Grandma raised me and my brother after our mama lit out. Yeah, we were poor, but she taught us to use what we had, to respect ourselves and others. And that, when you get right down to it, there wasn't a dime's worth of difference between us and the folks whose houses she cleaned. Hell, ain't nobody gets through a life without needing help sometime, do they?"

Danica smiled. "You're right about that, for sure."

"So, I don't ever think about being a hero or nothing like that, any more than you do. I just try to do the right thing and serve folks the best I can. Like they say in the Corps, '*Semper fi.*' You know what that means, ma'am?"

"Sorry, Latin wasn't my subject."

"Means 'always faithful.' Might be to God, or to your job, or to the Marine Corps. But mostly, it means you got to stay faithful to yourself. You reminded me of that, for the first time since I got sent to prison. You gave me a chance at being the man I used to be. And I'm always going to be grateful to you for that. Always."

Danica's eyes filled with tears. As she struggled to make some response, they were interrupted by a light tap at the door. The floor nurse came in, wearing full precautionary gear, and pointed to the clock. "Time for another blood sample."

Danica nodded as Jason Carter slipped quietly out the door. At the last moment, he turned and pointed to his raised forearm with the *"Semper fi"* tattoo emblazoned in blue. He nodded at her, then he was gone.

The nurse saw the array of flowers on Danica's bed tray and raised a curious eyebrow. Glancing from Danica to the doorway and back again, she asked, a little snidely, "Hmm. Flowers, eh? Something going on here I should know about?" She tied the tourniquet around Danica's arm and inserted the catheter to draw blood.

"Nothing," Danica snapped, surprised at the sharpness of her tone. She watched her blood fill the small glass tube and sighed deeply. "Sorry. I didn't mean to snap."

"None of my business," the nurse replied. "But even if there was something going on, who could blame you? Or anybody else in this godforsaken place? Half the staff is bedding down with the other half any chance they get, from what I hear. If they're not fighting, that is." She gathered her supplies while backing out of the room. "I'll let you know the results as soon as I get them. So far, you're clear from the virus, but who knows with this thing? I expect you'll be cleared to be up and around later today."

Danica reached for a few bunches of flowers and thrust them in the woman's direction. "Here. Take these to the nurses' station. You all need cheering up as much as anybody else around here. Maybe even more so."

The nurse's eyes smiled behind her mask. "Hey, thanks! That's real sweet!" She clutched the bouquet close.

As she turned to go, Danica couldn't resist a last question. "Half the staff? Seriously?"

The nurse shrugged. "Well, maybe not that much. But who could blame 'em? For all we know, we're all gonna be dead in another two weeks. And you know what they say, 'sex is the opposite of death.'"

When she was gone, Danica lay back on the pillows, trying to sort her circling thoughts and the churn of emotions that roiled inside her. What if it were true? What if they didn't make it? It wasn't that she feared dying; she'd seen it too often to be afraid. But what about living? What about all those things she'd put off or missed entirely in favor of becoming a doctor and pursuing a career?

Danica's parents were immigrants who didn't even have a college degree. They'd had an arranged marriage, meeting for the first time on their wedding day at the altar. Back in those days, the word of a parent was considered final, and it was the child's duty to follow. Danica's mother was forced to get married to whom her father had chosen for her without being able to refuse or having the option to experience life first before settling down. Then her mother had Danica when she was a teen, living below the poverty level. Her parents resided like two friends dwelling under the same roof. They grew old together and had children together, but there was little love. Danica's mother couldn't leave because she didn't know how—and for the sake of her children. Danica saw her mother trapped every day, just putting up with the union for Danica and her brothers' sake. Her mother always encouraged Danica and her two younger brothers to get an education above all else, something her mother hadn't had the luxury of seeking.

God, she could barely recall what the inside of her own apartment looked like, much less the last time she'd gone on a date. Hell, she didn't even have a cat. Was that what she was becoming? A series of might-have-beens? Danica had blown off dates and put off romance to become a successful professional, the first in her family. She wanted to make her family proud, particularly her mother who had given up so much. She wanted to finish training before settling down, but now she was questioning that decision. Medicine was brutal, especially for females.

Outside the window, the shadows gathered as the last of the wan daylight filtered through the clouds. She turned, unable to stop the hot tears that trickled slowly down her cheeks, suddenly recalling Beth Windsor, the old woman with her cards and her candles, and thinking of Cory Finch. All gone. All alone. Just as she was. "No," she said to no one. "The opposite of death isn't sex … it's love."

***

Her face was still damp with tears when she awakened, startled out of sleep by the sound of the wind. A voice spoke to her softly out of the shadows. "Hey, hey—it's okay. You're safe, Danica. Go back to sleep."

She fumbled for the nightlight by the side of her bed, switching it on; when she saw who had spoken, she jumped up and threw her arms around his neck.

"Shaka? Oh my God, I'm so glad to see you! Where have you been? Why didn't you text me?" She hung on his neck, her tears starting afresh.

He reached up to loosen her grip and faced her, his black eyes shining through the dark, and drew a thumb across her damp cheeks. "What's this? Tears?"

She sat back a little, burying her face in her hands. "Nothing. I'm sorry."

"Tears are never about nothing," he reminded her gently. "What's going on?"

Danica drew a deep breath, struggling to compose herself. "I'm sorry," she said. "I'm ashamed of myself. It's just that I hadn't heard from you and I didn't know where you were, and I was afraid maybe you'd gotten sick and—oh God, I'm so scared. Of everything. The storm. The virus. We could all die!"

"All perfect reasons to be frightened, if you ask me. We're all scared, every one of us. Whether we show it or not." He placed his warm surgeon's hands on her neck and shoulders and massaged gently.

She visibly relaxed, as though the warmth of his fingertips might somehow chase the chill from around her heart.

She turned to him. "But we're not supposed to be frightened. We're doctors!"

Shaka suppressed a little smile. "I don't know about you, lady, but I didn't get that particular memo. I was a human being long before I became a doctor. That didn't come with some superhuman license. Even when we're arrogant enough to think it does. If anything, we should be humbled."

She struggled to corral her thoughts, her body distracted by the heat he emanated, as though he could transfer his energy directly into her veins, his warmth spreading over her like a comforting blanket. "I just meant—"

"I know what you meant," he interrupted. "Take a deep breath. Good. Now another one. Better?"

She nodded sheepishly.

"Look, Danica, feeling vulnerable is perfectly normal. You're allowed, okay? You got a bad knock on the head. We're in the middle of a damn hurricane and facing what could very well turn out to be some sort of pandemic. That's pressure, all right? And I'm not talking about barometric pressure, either. Everybody's feeling it. Nobody's immortal. We just can't afford to panic, is all."

"I was okay—I honestly thought I was okay. But then I texted you, and I didn't know where you were or what happened to you. That scared me more than anything, I think."

He tipped her chin up to face him and she saw that he was smiling, his teeth glowing white in his caramel-colored skin, his eyes alive in his face, burning with an unmistakable longing. "No cell phones, remember? And since you're so curious, for the past couple of nights, I've been right here. With you. As much as I could manage, anyhow. Dr. Dunn and I have been playing tag team to cover rounds."

She gaped at him. "What? Here? But why?"

Now he hesitated. He backed away, momentarily nonplussed. Then he nodded toward the remaining flowers near her bedside. "What's this? You have some sort of a secret admirer or something?"

She propped herself up on her knees. "Don't change the subject! And no, at least I don't think so. Jason Carter brought them up from the gift shop. He said they were just going to get flooded, and besides, he needed the refrigeration unit."

She paused, her emotions running high once more. "And just in case it's any of your business, I'm honored to be his friend. He was the one who picked me up after the explosions, so if you have anything bad to say about that, you'd better say it to somebody else."

Shaka held out his hands, palms up, surprised at her vehemence. "Sorry," he said sincerely.

"You didn't answer my question," she continued. "What made you come here?"

Suddenly uncomfortable, Shaka's eyes flickered around the room. "I have to keep an eye on my patients, don't I?"

"Not all night, you don't." Danica threw a leg over one side of the bed and stood in front of him, once again feeling the incredible warmth that rose from his skin.

"I like to watch you sleep, and I didn't want you to be alone," he murmured softly.

Their eyes met and he ran his index finger softly down her nose, lingering for just a moment around the fullness of her lips, taking his time before tracing down the pulse on one side of her neck. Her breath came faster now; she could feel her heart's insistent pounding in her chest. Without thinking, she reached up and grabbed his hand, clutching it in her own like someone drowning.

"You're beautiful when you sleep, do you know that?"

She laughed softly, pressing his hand to her cheek. "Thanks, but whoever sees themselves asleep?"

For a moment, they fell silent, basking in the powerful currents of energy that ran between them like an electrical charge, communicating in an ancient language that needed no words.

He spoke again, his voice thick with emotion and desire. "But I didn't come just because you're beautiful—you are—or because your hair smells like flowers, not a hospital. I can't explain it, exactly. But sitting here with you? It made me feel safe."

Danica stared upward, deep into his bottomless brown eyes. "Safe?" she whispered.

"Like we were the only two people in the world. And there wasn't any storm or fever or danger. There was just … peace. I could turn off all the chatter in my head and just—be. Because it was just us, I could believe, even for a little while, that this thing is going to turn out—somehow. It's different with you. You ground me in a way no one else has before."

She leaned her head back against his powerful arm, her lips already parted, awaiting his kiss. It came softly at first, then harder and more insistent. And when his probing tongue met hers, he tasted somehow of chocolate and spice and the kind of sweetness that set her nerves on fire, making her tremble and draw him still closer, knowing she could never have enough.

CHAPTER TWENTY-THREE
National Guard Headquarters, Field Office, Galveston Island
Forty-eight hours after Hurricane Beatrix made landfall

Colonel Wilson stared out grimly at the wall of debris piling up around the field office and the team of exhausted men working constantly to clear it. A senseless jumble of unmoored boats and fallen buildings, of trees and drowned animals and detritus, it pushed over the roadways and parking lots, urged by the never-ending waves into a wall of destruction, moving ever inland, crushing and absorbing all in its path—fifteen feet high in some places, and spreading as far as the eye could see along the fallen seawall on either side. The sky was bathed in sickly yellow-gray light, and the winds still battered tortured palms into eerie contortions in some dark ballet of pain.

But they had weathered the worst of it, anyway. Only two of his team lost, not counting the fool who'd botched the explosives set under the Bluewater highway bridge and nearly taken off his own arm. As far as the colonel knew, that man was still alive, along with the two others who'd brought him to the hospital, but even that didn't count for much. They would have to remain in quarantine along with the rest, and in less than an hour, his unit would be pulling out, blowing up the last bridge to the mainland and leaving the rest behind.

He didn't like it; he didn't like any of it. But the colonel had enough experience to know that serving your country sometimes meant making a deal with the devil. And this was surely one of those times.

He stabbed at a button on his desk. "Mendoza!"

As if by magic, the slim, young corporal appeared from the adjoining office, a clipboard in her hand. "Sir?"

"That load of supplies and diesel ready for the hospital?"

"Yes, sir. Food and water, only. The refuel tank for the back-up generator system was faulty and leaked everywhere, so we couldn't transport it. And basic medications. All we had, anyhow. As well as all the ice we still had on hand, and the emergency radio units."

"Even without the tank, it should buy them a few extra days, anyhow. That and a Hail Mary or two," the colonel muttered, more to himself than anyone.

"Sir?"

"Order all the available portable generators over there too. From what they're saying up in Houston, we're not going to need them on the mainland. They got part of the grid back up already. Besides, I want those folks over at the hospital to believe we got their backs for as long as possible. If they survive the storm surge, maybe it'll be some comfort."

He glanced up at her then, meeting her eyes for the first time. "You got that? Get it done, Corporal! We have an hour at most. Then we pull out and await orders."

He rose from behind his desk. "I'll be leaving sooner rather than later. Lock up behind me, will you? If you have any questions, you know where to find the sergeant."

Corporal Mendoza looked horrified. "So we're just leaving them … to die?" she asked. "There have to be three hundred people left in that hospital."

Wilson sucked in a slow breath. "I remind you: they are under quarantine and highly contagious with a fever that has no cure. If we can't contain it, then we risk the possibility of a pandemic, especially under current conditions. Hospital personnel and patients are not to be rescued until the CDC lifts that quarantine. The military has done their best by offering aid for as long as possible. And maybe, just maybe, they'll be able to survive long enough for FEMA or the 1st Army to move in. I don't know the future, Corporal. I'm only following orders. God himself is going to have to do the rest. Now, go do your job. Finish getting whatever we can over there. Then await instructions. Understand?"

On his way out, he paused and glanced around his makeshift office, his mouth a grim line, his shoulders back, not sparing the corporal so much as a glance. "Oh, fuck it," he said. And was gone.

***

Corporal Mendoza headed back to her desk in a kind of trance, shocked and numbed to the enormity of the crime she had no choice but to commit. Three hundred people, possibly doomed to this island like lepers, cast aside with a few meager supplies to help aid, or prolong, their suffering. And an army, helpless against nature's fury, able to do nothing more than sacrifice them for the greater good.

She managed to order and dispatch the additional generators and verified their time of departure, as the remnants of the unit departed Galveston Island for the last time.

Chapter Twenty-Four
Galveston University Hospital

Jason Carter stood on the loading dock, hands on his hips, sniffing the wind at the sharp scent of salt and musk of death in the air. The rain had stopped pouring, but the water level hadn't receded yet. The storm surge was far from over.

He looked at the havoc that ripped through the city. Old buildings ripped apart into pieces, roofs missing, cars still submerged under water. To the left, in the periphery of his vision, he watched a bright red flare light up the sky on the other side of the city.

At first, he thought his mind was playing tricks on him. Why would there be a flare? Who lit it? A few minutes later a second scorching red flare illuminated the sky. He got a better sense of direction of where the signal came from. In that moment, he knew what it meant.

Jason turned back on the loading dock toward the hospital, shoulders hunched. "Son of a bitch," he said under his breath.

Jason squared his aching shoulders and climbed the last flight of stairs toward the isolation unit in search of Dr. Stone. He figured she needed to be the first to know they'd seen all the help they were going to get from the National Guard, and it was his duty to be the messenger of that particular piece of bad news.

But she sure as hell wasn't going to like it.

He found Dr. Stone coming out of one of the isolation rooms.

She greeted Jason with a meek smile as she took off the gown and gloves. Black bags were forming under her eyes. She looked visibly spent. "Why do you look like you saw a ghost?"

He looked at her right in the eyes. "I saw a signal flare across the city. Have you received any messages from the CDC or National Guard?

"No, not recently. Last I heard, they were working on getting us supplies to help us ride out the quarantine and storm."

"Well, looks like it has arrived—halfway across the city."

Her jaw dropped in anger. "How are we going to retrieve that? Why the hell wouldn't they try to bring the supplies closer to us? They think we don't have enough to worry about? Now we have to figure a way to send people out there to retrieve supplies we desperately need. The water level hasn't even receded yet. We don't even know how safe it is. We can't go out there. I will not risk the safety of the people remaining."

Jason rubbed his temple to ease the tension that was forming. "I can start putting together a team working out logistics. But we are going to have to try as we are running low on essentials."

"Do what you need to," she agreed as she stormed off in frustration.

CHAPTER TWENTY-FIVE
Galveston University Hospital

Since Danica's two days of bedrest after her concussion, three more beds, all occupied by fever victims, were lined up by the windows. Huge floor fans arranged over the ice makers Jason's team had brought up from the kitchen blew slowly back and forth, circulating the heavy air. Danica heard the hissing of her own breath inside her HAZMAT suit as she struggled to concentrate in the course of her rounds. At least it was cooler here. In the rest of the building, the AC had been shut down entirely, and humidity permeated the thick, sultry air in a heady mix of smells from the hospital, diesel fumes, and fish.

But it wasn't the air that made Danica dizzy this morning; it was the memory of Shaka as he'd held her close last night, their bodies intertwining again and again in a riot of lovemaking.

His touch had left an imprint on her very flesh, sending flutters of renewed desire up from deep in her solar plexus, shaking her to her core. She'd risen before dawn to slip from the bed, shower, and change silently, careful not to awaken him as he snored contentedly on. She'd lingered just for a moment, watching his chest rise and fall as the shadows played against his warm bronze skin, her mind and heart churning and crashing like the waves against the shore.

She tried to convince herself it hadn't been love so much as desperation. The thought of love terrified her. She didn't know anyone around her truly in love. Even Danica's own past relationships were one train wreck after another filled with cheaters, liars, and one particular fellow who had a proclivity for swinging.

She heard the nurse's words echo again in her mind. *Half the staff is bedding down with the other half from what I can tell, and who would blame them?*

The ghost of his smile flashed across her mind, causing a surge of lust in her veins that shot through her like a drug, making her weak in the knees. His reputation preceded him. She was sure he was just using her as he had half the hospital before. He had broken so many hearts before. What made hers different? She didn't have time for a heartbreak. Whatever this was between them, she had to stop it; she knew that now, in the hard light of the morning, in the ravaged faces and bodies of her patients in their beds as they fought to stay alive. Her duty was to them, not her own pleasure. She couldn't afford to let her attention lapse for so much as an instant. Neither of them could. Whatever they had begun, she had to end it. She couldn't afford a distraction or a broken heart.

"Dr. Diza, did you hear me?" Dr. Kirsten Stone's voice cut sharply through the tumult of Danica's thoughts. Dr. Stone, in her own HAZMAT suit, stood next to Danica, studying a chart—that of the hospital chaplain, newly stricken with the virus. He lay silently in the bed before them, his skin an ashy, grayish color against his sandy blond hair, purple blotches already surfacing on his hands and forearms.

Danica glanced at her guiltily. "Doctor? I'm sorry, could you repeat that?"

Dr. Stone's icy blue eyes studied Danica from behind her mask. "Are you all right? No ill effects from your concussion, I hope?"

Danica shook her head. "No. Yes. I mean, I'm fine. Just momentarily distracted."

"Good. What I said was, they discovered the chaplain collapsed on the altar. Apparently, he lost consciousness shortly after a service he held during the eye of the storm. You didn't happen to attend that service, did you?"

"No, I didn't."

"I see. Well, as you complete your rounds outside the isolation unit this morning, I need you to interview every single patient you can find who did."

Danica stared at her curiously. "But why?" Ordinarily, a patient's religious beliefs fell outside a physician's purview, even in a strongly Christian community like this one.

Dr. Stone sighed heavily. "If he was passing out Communion, then I need to know if he was personally placing the hosts in their mouths or if the individuals each took one for themselves. The tradition varies from church to church, and I'm not familiar with the chaplain's particular denomination." She paused and glanced again at the bed. "I can't believe he would be so foolhardy as to do it himself even as an act of worship. But if he did, he risked contagion for everyone who received Communion, you understand? That would mean we'd have a much bigger problem than we do already."

"Oh God," Danica murmured. "I didn't even think of that!"

Dr. Stone managed a wan smile. "Neither did I until the idea woke me out of a sound sleep. No matter. If we're going to contain this thing, we have to follow up every possible lead. Even men of God make some pretty big mistakes. Especially if he didn't quite have his wits about him and was already infected."

"I'll find out anything I can and report to you immediately."

"Good. Now, for some brighter news, I hope."

Danica followed her to the bedside of Dr. Wong.

"How's our star patient?" Dr. Stone asked, a little too brightly.

She turned back to Danica, lowering her voice. "His fever broke early, Dr. Diza. More so than any of our others. That's always a good sign."

Dr. Wong turned to face them, his face an implacable mask. "Hanging in there," he said.

Dr. Stone rattled off his current stats enthusiastically. "You're five days out, David. You have to know how encouraging that is. We're still pending the PCR of your latest viral titers, but five more days like this and I might just be able to give you the all-clear. You a drinking man, Dr. Wong?"

He shook his head and managed a weak smile. "Not before," he said. "But if I come out of this alive, I might just start."

"You'll make it, David. You're too much of a fighter not to."

Danica had to admit it was true. Dr. Wong still looked weak and miserable, but the purple blotches over his chest and face seemed less vivid than they had, and it was clear he was consciously tracking their conversation.

"Just keep on doing whatever you're doing, David. You know as well as I do, attitude is everything." Dr. Stone paused. "Well, maybe not everything, but it helps. Besides, we need you up and around. Truth is, we're not making much progress on a vaccine. We need your expertise. We've got plenty of pathogens to isolate from existing patients, and Mr. Carter's been more than cooperative, but his antibodies are five years out. So far, we haven't had a lot of success trying passive immunity using his plasma on volunteers."

He peered at her, thinking hard. "Did you ever locate Billy Andersen?" he asked in a raspy voice.

"We're trying, David, but it's difficult. They're only just now beginning to restore the grid in Houston. All communications have been down. I've reached out to the CDC and the National Guard here on the island, but so far, no luck."

"Damn it," Dr. Wong answered. "He's the man you need."

Seeing his obvious agitation reflected in his monitor readings, Danica stepped forward. "Don't stress yourself, Dr. Wong. You need your rest," she said soothingly. She held enormous respect for Dr. Kirsten Stone's administrative abilities, but her bedside manner could get a bit aggressive. Especially with so much at stake.

As if reading her mind, Dr. Stone took two steps backward. "Dr. Diza's right. All you need to do right now is recover, David," she said, softening her tone. "And in a few days' time, we'll be around to see you for some of those nice, fresh antibodies of yours."

Once more, he managed a thin smile. "It's a deal, doctors."

Back inside the decontamination unit, Danica saw Dr. Stone eyeing her curiously. Known for her unremitting professionalism, Dr. Stone rarely let down her guard, so Danica was surprised when she said, "Thanks for reining me in back there. I know better than to upset a patient. It's just that we need his help so badly."

"I know," Danica agreed. "He does too. But he has to fully recover or he'll be no use at all. The rest of the surviving victims in the ICU are just too early to call. Remember if we can save one, the odds are pretty good we can save more of them. You have to remember that."

Wearily, Dr. Stone leaned her back against the wall, stretching the tension from her neck, then looked at Danica again, the same curious expression in her eyes. "You're sure you're all right, after your accident?"

"Of course, I am. Why do you ask?"

Dr. Stone shrugged. "I don't know. You seem different somehow."

Danica hoped Dr. Stone couldn't see the guilty blush that crept up her neck as the two of them headed into the hall and Danica prepared to continue her evening rounds.

"Well," Dr. Stone acknowledged, "I don't know how any of us can go through something like this and not be changed, at least a little bit. And we're not through it yet."

They rounded the corner by their usual route, hoping to cross into the west wing via the breezeway and its towering glass wall. But at the end of the hallway, before they made the turn, they were met by the orderly, Booker Johnson, his beefy arms crossed over his chest.

"Sorry, doctors, this route's off limits. You're going to have to go around."

"Nonsense!" Dr. Stone insisted. "That will take three times as long. Let me through!"

Booker Johnson reached out and grabbed one of Dr. Stone's arms, even as Danica placed a restraining hand on the other.

Dr. Stone inched around trying to get a better look. "What's wrong?"

Booker let go of Dr. Stone's arm. "The glass wall. It held through the storm all right. But they clocked the surge at thirty-four feet. Now, some of it held, but mostly it's gone. Jason and the boys are down there at both ends with sandbags and plywood. No access till further notice. Unless you're aiming to drown."

The women froze in place, looking first to him, then to one another. After a long moment, the air left Danica's lungs from a breath she didn't even realize she'd been holding, the implications washing over her like another monster wave.

Dr. Stone barked out a question. "And the rest of the structure? Will it stand?"

Booker's eyes were sad and serious. "Can't say, ma'am. Too soon to tell how long it will hold. Lower levels are already flooded. It would take an engineer to tell you for sure. We're just doing the best we can."

Danica bowed her head. The hand that had been holding Dr. Stone's arm slid to and clutched her hand in some involuntary gesture of supplication. "God help us," she whispered.

Dr. Stone squeezed her fingers in return.

"Amen."

Chapter Twenty-Six
Galveston University Hospital

Completing her rounds for the day, Danica quietly closed the door to the obstetrical patient's room on the third floor of the east wing. This was the same woman, the National Guardsman's wife, Shaka had performed a C-section on the day he'd brought Danica Starbucks. That seemed like a lifetime ago. Though the child was thriving, the combination of the surgery and the trauma of the storm had taken its toll on the petite young mother, and her milk production was less than ideal. Danica frowned over her chart, making a note that while mother and baby were both doing well, she should begin supplementing with formula as soon as possible.

Danica's eyes had filled with tears when she saw they had named the baby Shaka in Dr. Sen's honor, a bittersweet reminder of just how much it meant when a doctor did his duty in the world. Especially a world as ravaged as this one. She wondered if he knew. He would be very proud.

But at the same time, that knowledge only served to strengthen her resolve. Whatever she and Shaka had shared, whatever they had between them, there was no time for that now. Now, duty was all that mattered, all that *could* matter; she needed to focus on those who remained, needed to battle the fever that raged so carelessly among them, snatching up lives and futures with horrifying indifference to those who lived or died. Two more had fallen ill in the last two days: a floor nurse from the west wing and poor Dylan Nguyen, for whom his family held such high hopes. Danica's eyes again welled up with tears at the thought of him and how he had saved her. If only he had left the island when he was supposed to. She tried not to think of his prognosis—or anyone else's, for that matter. For all her compassion, her own fears for the future had a way of creeping in, and she could ill afford that emotion. No matter how terrible it was to feel so helpless, she couldn't let it show. Fear, she knew, was as contagious as the virus itself.

The young mother had teared up, too, when Danica made some gentle inquiries as to her state of mind and if she'd been experiencing anything by way of postpartum depression. She laughed a little through her tears. "With all this going on, how could you tell?"

Yet in the next moment, she broke down entirely. "Why are we even here? We should be out there with my husband. Should have run while we had the chance."

Danica tried hard to reassure her. "I know how you must feel, but you're as safe as you can be. You and the baby. Besides, if you'd chosen to run, you wouldn't have gotten far. After your surgery, you could barely bend down to tie your own shoes."

Yet for all her confusion, the young mother had been clear on one thing. She hadn't been at the chaplain's last service before he collapsed, which was good news. Out of the thirty patients Danica had seen that day, only seven of them had attended, and each recalled removing their Communion host themselves. At least that lessened the possibility of hand-to-mouth contact from the infected chaplain.

She nearly jumped out of her skin when she rounded a corner and almost ran right into Shaka. His nearness was once again intoxicating, his warmth washing over her like a drug. She forced herself to back away, avoiding his eyes and the well-muscled arms that reached to embrace her.

"I've been searching all day for you!" he cried. "Guess what I saw!"

Danica scowled, suddenly aware of the scent coming off him, a mixture of dirt, sweat, basements, and something like rotten food. She waved her hand in front of her face.

Embarrassed, he stepped back. "Sorry," he said. "I'm filthy. I spent most of the day with the crew downstairs, working the sump pumps and sandbagging to alleviate the flooding in the lower floors."

"You're pretty ripe, I'll give you that."

"But you'll never guess what I saw!"

She stared at him, frowning. "Look, Shaka, I don't want to be rude, but it's been one hell of a long day. And I'm way too tired for guessing games. Can we do this later?" She turned abruptly, and it was all she could do not to break into a run. She steeled herself, clutching her clipboard closer to her chest as he hurried to catch up with her.

He stopped her with a hand on her arm. "What's going on?" His warm brown eyes held a trace of hurt.

Danica shrugged in a gesture far more casual than the storm of emotions burning through her. "Nothing," she lied. "I need to get something to eat."

He dropped his hand but continued to peer at her, trying to read her mind. "I wouldn't have figured you for the sort of woman who sneaks out before breakfast. Not after last night, anyhow." His voice dropped slightly, low and seductive.

She blushed furiously, angry with herself for betraying her emotions, but felt determined nonetheless. "Well," she replied, turning once again to head down the hall. "Maybe you don't know me as well as you thought."

Shaka drew back as though he'd been slapped. "Look, whatever it is, I'm sorry. If I said or did something to offend you, tell me what it is! I thought last night was—"

"Fun," she said sharply. "It was fun, okay? And you needn't worry about your prowess in bed, either. You certainly live up to your, shall we say, naughty reputation? But that's all it was, okay? A one-night stand. Just sex. Last night was a lapse of judgment. We were both vulnerable, needing a distraction. But it ends here. Now."

Shaka made a helpless little gesture with his hands. "I don't get it. Why? Why does it have to end?"

Danica uttered a short, painful little laugh. "Why? Wow, I knew you were arrogant Dr. Sen, but how could you possibly be so self-absorbed? I don't do relationships. I need to focus on myself and my career. Don't you see what's going on around you? People are dying from a disease we know almost nothing about. We don't have any staff; we can't risk infecting other patients, most of whom were already too ill to evacuate. The convalescent plasma has been hit or miss and the CDC isn't much help. We're running low on supplies too. I don't know about you, but that means I have to do everything I can, with every drop of strength I've got, to be a doctor, get it? I don't have time to be distracted to role-play a hot little skank in your make-believe TV drama."

Shaka's face darkened. "Please don't insult me, Dr. Diza. I get your drift. You're so fucking terrified of feeling anything for anybody, you build walls and shut them out."

She stared at him, incredulous. "Scared? Of course, I'm scared! And if you weren't so selfish, you'd have the sense to be scared too."

He backed off then, his mouth lifting in that all-too-familiar sardonic sneer. His devil-may-care mask. "Pardon me for getting in the way of your path to sainthood, doctor. Let me know how it works out for you." He paused, shaking his head ruefully. "You want to know what's funny? I was so excited to see you today because I was outside on the loading docks and I looked out over the bay and saw the gulls. They've come back. You know what that means? The storm, the surge, and the wildlife coming back. We're through the worst of it. And yet here we are, still alive. It filled me with such hope. Like there really is a God, and he's looking out for us. Like we really will make it through this, and the only person I wanted to share that with was with you. Excuse the hell out of me."

Danica turned to face the wall, anything to get away from the pain in his eyes. She spoke louder than she needed to, sure that he could hear the sound of her heart breaking in her chest. "Gulls are scavengers," she replied coldly. "There's a lot of death out there. They should eat very well."

His low chuckle sounded hollowly between them. "Play the cynic if you wish, Danica. Shower your patients with compassion; ease their suffering. I won't stop you. Just be sure you don't get addicted." With that, he turned and slowly walked away.

"Addicted? What's that supposed to mean?" she called out before she could stop herself.

Shaka didn't bother turning around. "I think you know," he said. "When people are dying, it's easier sometimes. You can be all-powerful—even heroic. You don't have to think about how much courage it takes to dwell among the living, to fight for your own life. Lots of caregivers get addicted that way. Doctors, nurses, even hospice workers. But trust me, Danica, it's just another ego trip."

Rage surged through her then, and she shouted after him, not caring who heard. "Why, you arrogant—"

Again, that spooky, hollow chuckle. "You should take a chance for a future together. Instead, you throw it away with both hands. Just so you can be safe and devoted to medicine. And you call me arrogant … ."

And then he was gone. Even the lingering scent of his labors, even the last traces of his warmth. All gone, replaced only by a cold, hard pain that gnawed at her from every cell, like peeling away her living skin. Every movement was agony, every breath a kind of sob. Worst of all, she had done it herself with no real idea of how quickly hurting him would come back, engulfing her in a wave of terrible remorse.

After what seemed like an hour, she managed to make it to an empty room, reeling from her emotions. She sprawled across the newly-made bed, one waiting, no doubt, for the next patient, the next victim, the next corpse.

Why did I do that? Why do I self-sabotage my own life and my happiness? What am I scared of?

She stared mindlessly at the ceiling, her exhausted thoughts unable to focus, until shock, grief, and guilt, mixed in with regret, gathered in her throat. She began to sob hoarsely, choking back her tears until they, too, began to flow, hot and unceasing until she finally fell asleep, too spent to even hear the muffled sound of a series of explosions, somewhere in the distance.

Chapter Twenty-Seven

National Guard Armory, La Marque, Texas

Seventy-two hours after Hurricane Beatrix made landfall

Corporal Mendoza impatiently awaited orders in the small office space, struggling with the idea of abandoning the whole island and everyone on it. She knew when the time came, she would either break rank or be the person she'd told herself she'd never become.

A sharp knock on the door startled her out of her reverie.

"Look sharp, Corporal," spat Sergeant Sam Alvarez. "The last delivery to the hospital completed?"

Katie only nodded.

"Is the last truck of the convoy back?" Alvarez asked.

"Barely, sir. Winds over the causeway were more than twenty knots. One trailer almost tipped over on the way back."

Alvarez dug through his pockets and handed Katie an envelope. With pity in his eyes, he said, "Here are your orders. Sorry it played out this way. We'll monitor the explosions and meet you for the last boat out. You've got ten minutes." He awkwardly patted her shoulder and walked out.

Katie barely heard him. Her eyes filled with sorrow as she stared at the envelope. She trembled as she turned it over and ever so slightly tore open the back, still hoping for the best. Horrified, she looked at the page, reading and rereading the words in disbelief. Tears poured down her face as she struggled to make sense of the words.

Unable to evacuate. Initiate total lockdown. 1700 hours.

She grabbed her few belongings, packed in her duffel, and headed out, locking the door behind her. Outside, the pale afternoon light had given way to a sharp band of rosy gold as the sun prepared to set along the horizon. The air reeked of decay and explosives as she took her kayak out of her Humvee, leading it as close to the water as she could. A mountain of garbage and debris was piled along the edge of the shore. She kayaked as fast as she could, putting much distance between herself and the causeway, inching closer and closer to the glass sanctuary. In the distance, the wounded façade of the University Hospital, the shattered remains of its proud glass wall staring blindly out to sea, rose above the garbage. The last bridge to the mainland swayed crazily in the breeze like some giant broken limb.

Breathing heavily, she glanced at her watch. The detonator in her hand seemed to take on a life of its own as her trembling fingers punched in a code. She closed her eyes and waited for the sounds that would signal their doom. Her duffel hung heavy on her shoulder, but heavier still was the weight of her conscience as she surveyed the chaos. Nature had done its part, and she had facilitated the destruction.

Corporal Mendoza couldn't have pinpointed the moment when she made her decision. It came all at once, without conscious thought or struggle. Roughly calculating the distance between herself and the hospital complex, she reckoned that, barring injury, with any luck, she could hike through the debris and make it there by dark. She reached into her duffel and withdrew her Beretta pistol, securing it in the holster slung across her hip. After filling the pockets of her cargo shorts with cartridges, she started walking, her footsteps echoing spookily along the broken pavement, the humidity clinging to her like a filthy blanket as the stench of death grew stronger. Above her, she knew that high-altitude drones would be circling overhead, piercing the cloud cover with their synthetic aperture radars to document the destruction she had perpetrated. She had no idea what she would find when she got to University Hospital or if the Guard might come after her. She doubted the Guard would, and the people at the hospital needed whatever help she could give them.

Court-martial be damned. Come what may, she had to try. For the survivors. For herself.

CHAPTER TWENTY-EIGHT
Exurban Houston, Texas

Now that the worst of the storm was over, boredom itched at Billy like a rash. Try as he did to fill his days repairing the roof and cleaning up the yard, the quiet suburb where his mother lived held all the charm of a penitentiary.

Billy smacked down another fistful of microwave popcorn, followed by a long draught of Shiner Bock. His mother sat off to his left, working her endless crochet through a basket of afghan squares, sighing heavily from time to time. From the kitchen came the familiar scent of collard greens with bacon and fresh-made biscuits as the twilight gathered in the corners of the room.

"Billy," she said softly. "Get your feet off the coffee table. I raised you better than that, didn't I?"

The slight whine in her voice raked across his nerves, and he fought the urge to shout at her. He loved her, he truly did, but after more than a week cooped up in her house, it was all too apparent to Billy Andersen that he was far too old to be living with his mother.

While most of Houston's grid had been restored, the cable was still out. After Billy ran through the house selection of VHS rom-com movies and Broadway musicals, he had MacGyver-ed a makeshift antenna for the old TV. The TV managed only spotty reception, but it was better than nothing. They flipped through a tired selection of TV reruns from the food channel, the shopping channel, and whatever fitful footage the local news station managed to find. And his mom seemed to have a real thing for Guy Fieri. Go figure.

So when the television flickered, and the broadcast was interrupted by the local news, he stared at the static like a sign from heaven.

"Holy shit, Ma!" he cried. "The Guard just closed off Galveston from the mainland. Under full isolation until further notice." He leapt up from the sagging sofa, his mind moving at a thousand miles an hour.

"Don't cuss, Billy. I raised you better than that." She admonished him for what seemed like the millionth time.

He stared at her, running a hand through his short-cropped hair. "There's only one reason why the Guard would do that. I gotta get back there, Ma."

"What?" she cried, thoroughly alarmed. "What do they need you for?"

He raced to the bedroom, which had remained virtually unchanged since he graduated high school, yanked his backpack from under the bed, and began packing.

"But Billy," she said, reaching out and grabbing his arm. "Stop! Tell me right now!"

He paused momentarily, reached down and pinched her cheek. "Ma, it's top secret. I can't tell you what I know or how I know it. Just know I'll be okay. I'm one of the good guys, remember? I'll head south through the old oil fields to beat the traffic."

"Let me make you a sandwich first."

"Not hungry, Ma. Thanks anyhow. I gotta go. Dr. Wong needs me."

Her voice rose to the point of hysteria. "But Billy! How will you even get to the island? They've blown up the causeway. You said so yourself!"

He slung his backpack over his shoulder and bent down to kiss her cheek. "Don't worry. I'll figure out something. I'll call you as soon as I can."

She waved at him from the front porch, her eyes filling with tears.

Billy fired up the engine of his beat-up car and wheeled out of the driveway, blaring "Bad Moon Rising" from the radio.

For the first time in what felt like forever, he wasn't a cynical post-doc. He could be the hero that, deep down, he always wanted to be.

Chapter Twenty-Nine
Galveston University Hospital

Jason Carter stood alone on the dock, watching the darkness fall. He was smoking one of the last contraband cigarettes. It amazed him, how quickly night came. Most of the island's electricity was still down, and, devoid of the familiar glow of streetlights and neon, the sky shimmered with stars, brighter than he would have believed possible. It spread out above him, indifferent to human suffering, moving in the sky like some fine lady in a party dress, dancing her way till dawn.

He was tired to his bones, but somehow the sheer physical fatigue satisfied him too. For the first time, he knew with certainty, he was doing something that was actually helping the people around him. It was a feeling he'd never experienced as a Marine.

Jason had joined the Marines after dropping out of school. His mama found out and gave him an ultimatum: get a job or join the military. Jason found a Marine recruiter the next day, who offered a free T-shirt. Within months, Jason was on board a C-5 Galaxy deploying to Iraq.

His first memory of that country was disappointment. He landed in the middle of summer at the Baghdad International Airport and was picked up in a Humvee by a corporal. The US was in the midst of fighting an insurgency after the invasion and downfall of Saddam Hussein. His superior officers led Jason to believe that the Iraqi civilians would welcome US military personnel with open arms. He had seen the footage on CNN of Iraqi civilians pulling down a twelve-meter-tall statue of Saddam in Firdos Square back when he was still in the States. It had made sense at the time. After all, Iraqis had been under an oppressive regime of Saddam Hussein for the past twenty-four years. He was a brutal dictator who gassed his own people. Jason had expected a warm welcome.

But that's not what Jason experienced when he got there. He remembered feeling invisible, as if he didn't exist. The Iraqis living in small huts, essentially. They were nothing like him. They didn't smile, and they didn't greet the Americans. Americans weren't wanted there.

Jason thought more about his time in Iraq as he took another drag on his cigarette. He remembered early in his first tour when he was sent to meet a bunch of "detainees." Since they weren't enemy fighters or combatants, the military classified all civilians in their custody as detainees. It was a euphemism to make the job easier. Jason remembered seeing a whole bunch of Iraqi civilians on the roof of an armored personnel carrier as it pulled into his forward operating base for processing. As Jason looked closer, he saw that many of them had their heads covered in burlap sacks. Their hands and feet were bound with cable ties. The Marines began hurling these people off the roof of the APC about six to eight feet to the ground. These "detainees" had no way of breaking their fall. They were old men, women, and children. He couldn't believe the Marines were treating people this way.

Jason remembered turning to his commanding officer and asking, "Aren't we supposed to be helping these people?"

The officer gave him a stern look and said, "Carter, keep your mouth shut until you know what's really going on."

It went downhill from there. As time passed, it became clear that the enemy lurked among the very people Jason saw on a daily basis around Baghdad. He couldn't tell friend from foe. Day after day, Jason remembered his patrols would run into snipers and improvised explosive devices. Snipers and IEDs. Snipers and IEDs.

One month he was there, he remembered seeing five armed Iraqi militia, yet his battalion experienced fifty-four casualties, half of whom died. Jason began to think all the Iraqis were the enemy. It was a vicious cycle. He would go on patrol and get sniped at. He'd call in an airstrike, then sweep the neighborhood looking for weapons, only to find none—solely the bodies of dead women or, worse, children.

The notion he'd had before joining the Marines was that Saddam's former Ba'athists were terrorizing the population. Looking back, he now realized that Saddam's men didn't need to do that. They just need the Marines to sweep through a neighborhood. Jason understood only years later why he'd been hated. But it didn't change the fact that every day his friends had been getting killed. It was a self-perpetuating mechanism. This is what had created the insurgency and, later, ISIS.

Jason just wanted to get out, fly away, and forget the whole thing. It wasn't that easy. His last six months in Iraq, he ceased to think. His sole purpose was just to stay alive. Everyday questions presented themselves with ugly answers—answers he couldn't deal with.

Jason reflected as he took another drag of his cigarette. He could not have made sense of what he was doing because he didn't have a full deck. He was expected to play this game with twenty-one cards and not fifty-two. He didn't have any understanding of the political realities—he just knew the situation was nuts. This notion of defending people from invaders was wrong. The Iraqis had hated him. People wouldn't say good morning because they had every reason to hate the Jason Carters of the world. He had destroyed their homes, their fields, their culture—why should they like him? He saw CNN and Fox reporting about what a difference they were making, but in reality, the circumstances were worse than before the US had gotten involved. What a shame to blindly justify the military's actions and orders bestowed upon soldiers only to realize it was all a sham.

He could envision the war continuing on day after day with no end in sight. When Jason left Iraq, it was in the midst of a surge. He and what remained of his company were exchanging fire with insurgents when a Humvee came up. A corporal sought him out and said, "Carter, your orders are in. Let's go."

Right there in the middle of a firefight, Jason stripped off his gear, distributed it to the other guys there, and left. He didn't feel any guilt leaving those men as he got onto an Army Blackhawk to the airport. He was just glad it was over.

He'd never had the sense, as he did here in Galveston, that he'd done any real good. So, now, he watched the stars and smelled the ocean breeze that brought the first wafts of something fresh, the scent of it rising once again above the stench of destruction that had settled over everything, mixing with the comforting, familiar tobacco smoke in the air. He probably shouldn't, since he was still getting over pneumonia, but given the circumstances, pondering the ill effects of smoking seemed a little beside the point. And a few puffs of pleasure here and there weren't likely to make a difference in the end, anyway.

Out of the inky blackness, a pinpoint of light shone in the corner of his eye; yet when he turned his head, there was nothing, only the stars above and the orange coal of his cigarette here on the ground. He shook his head; perhaps it was a flash of metal or glass reflecting the starlight, or maybe he was more tired than he thought and had begun to imagine things. In the next instant, though, he caught the faint, yet discernible crunch of something like a footstep on the pile of rubble to his left. He ground out his cigarette and crouched near the wall, not wanting to give away his location on the dock to some stray looter or one of the many starving dogs and cats that roamed the city, searching for food in the wreckage.

Squinting through the dark, Jason saw it again, that pinpoint of light, larger and closer this time, moving rhythmically through the murk. Side to side and down, side to side and down, like some disembodied spirit orb seeking its way. At the same time, the crunching grew louder. He crouched low, his weariness forgotten and his adrenaline on fire, ready to spring back inside or confront a threat, whatever emerged from the gloom.

"What the …?" he whispered.

The silhouette of a lone woman, tall and slim, emerged, slowly picking her way up and over the last mound of debris between her and the dock near the harbor, using her phone's pinpoint flashlight to navigate the treacherous terrain. In her last pass of the otherwise empty dock, the light caught Jason's boots, then bounced back again, to travel slowly up his legs.

"Halt!" she cried. "Hands up. Come out where I can see you. I'm armed, so don't get any ideas."

Jason knew better than to try any fast moves, so he did as he was told. When he was in full view, the woman extended her hand for a boost up to the dock, her other hand brandishing a Beretta M9 pistol.

She was filthy, drenched, and disheveled. Both knees were bleeding from tumbles she'd doubtless taken scrambling through the detritus. Clearly, whatever had brought her had involved far more than a casual evening stroll. Yet she was also military, that much he could see from the stripes on her sleeves.

Breathing hard, she glanced only briefly at him as she gazed around her, weak with relief at having arrived at what she hoped was her destination. "Is this Galveston University Hospital?"

Hands still up, Jason stared at her like she was an apparition. "Yes ma'am, it is. But I can't let you in there. We're under quarantine."

For the first time, she turned to really look at him, taking him in with a glance that seemed to swallow him whole. "You in charge here?"

Jason smiled in spite of himself. "Not hardly. I just boss around the muscle, mostly. Try to keep things going. Or at least from getting any worse."

Straightening her spine, she looked straight at him. "Corporal Katie Mendoza. Reporting for duty."

He raised an eyebrow. "That mean I can put my hands down now? You ain't gonna shoot me?"

She glanced down at the weapon dangling from her hand as if just remembering it was still there. She clicked on the safety and lowered her gun, a little embarrassed. "No offense," she said. "It's not exactly safe out there."

Jason smiled. "None taken. But where in the world did you come from, corporal? Guard units pulled out hours ago, notifying us in style by red flares."

Through the darkness, he saw an unexpected flash of agony cross her face. "I felt my place was here," she stammered. "It was horrible … what they did. Blowing up the bridges. Leaving you all here to—to—"

The unspoken word hung between them. Jason inhaled deeply. He couldn't imagine what had driven her here, but he knew now was not the time to go into it. She was already trembling like a leaf in the wind and whatever the wound she carried, he knew better than to probe it while it was still so fresh.

A few more moments passed while her breathing grew less ragged and her shoulders straightened once again.

"You AWOL then?" he asked softly.

"Yes, sir," she said, looking him straight in the eye. But there was no shame in her expression.

Jason tilted his head, thinking hard. He had no way of knowing what had brought her here, but one thing was for sure. She had some fire to her. He sighed and glanced upward, toward the stars. "Well, I don't reckon that matters too much at the moment."

He paused again. "You know the danger? I let you inside, you got maybe a fifty-fifty chance of catching this virus, and a fifty-percent chance of surviving if you do. And I'll do my best to keep you as far away from those who are infected as I can, but there's no guarantee. I had it already, back in Iraq. I figure that's the reason the Good Lord put me here now. So I could help these folks as they figure it out. You made rank though, and that's a plus. You have a specialty?"

"Communications officer," she answered. "That's how I knew about the quarantine. The orders for the shutdown came through me after they dropped off remaining supplies."

"Well, I guess that confirms that it was supplies they dropped off. We haven't been able to get them, though, since the surge hasn't gone down yet and it's across the city." He swung open the door that led off the dock and held it for her. "I don't reckon we'll have much need for communications. At least, not until them bastards get some kind of grid back up and running."

"I don't care. I'll do anything I can to make myself useful. I also know exactly where the rations are."

Jason Carter glanced once more at the stars in the heavens and smiled, thankful once more for the few minutes of beauty before reality settled over his shoulders like a stone.

Inside, their heavy footsteps echoed in the empty hallways as he spelled out the specifics of staff, patients, and locations.

Katie nodded mutely, memorizing as much as she could.

As they passed a makeshift kitchen stocked with whatever they had left, Jason had a sudden inspiration.

"Corporal Mendoza," he said, "I don't suppose by any chance you can cook? I've been trying my hand at some of the things, but I ain't got the knack. And we can't afford to be burning up supplies. Not even rice."

She shook her head and snatched an apron off a nearby hook. "Let me wash up, first."

He led her to a sink through piles of unopened bags of rice, canned goods, and other sundries. She ran the water and scrubbed furiously, anxious to remove any remaining reek of the rot outside.

He waited patiently, his face a mixture of anxiety, anticipation, and admiration.

Tying her apron more securely about her waist, she smiled for the first time. "Nothing like using cooking as a therapeutic distraction at times like this."

Jason pointed to one of a half-dozen industrial-sized cookers lined up on the counter. "It's this contraption that's got me stumped," he said. "Tried the setting for rice three times and burned it up every time."

Katie studied the array of settings on the control panel and whistled through her teeth. "Well, what do you know? I guess you are in luck that I came when I did."

At his confused expression, she explained, "They're multi-cookers, you know, pressure cookers. Not only can you cook things in a fraction of the time it usually takes, but they use less energy. That means you won't be burning up your back-up power as fast." She glanced up at him. "When's the next meal due?"

"Whenever we get it to 'em, ma'am," Jason answered solemnly. "We had a boy down here cooking for us for a while, but he came down with the fever. His folks are in the restaurant business, so he knew his way around. Not sure if he'll even make it. Damn shame too. He's just a kid. Since then, we've just been passing out canned soup and peanut butter sandwiches."

For the next few hours, working in tandem, Jason marveled as Corporal Mendoza went to work, cooking vat after vat of rice and beans, keeping those warm; managing a pile of fluffy scrambled eggs from the unappetizing, government-issued powdered stuff; and even producing, with Jason's help, a mountain of handmade, fresh tortillas, grilled on a small hot plate and kept warm on the top of the cookers. They had finished off the remaining stockpile, but figured their efforts should last a few days.

She worked, for the most part, silently, focused on the tasks at hand with a singular sort of concentration that said *do not disturb.*

Jason Carter was nonetheless fascinated and couldn't help from asking a question or two. "Don't tell me," he interjected at one point. "Your folks in the restaurant business too?"

"Ha! Not likely. My grandfather, my dad, and his brothers were all wildcatters back in the day, and it was the women's job to keep them fed. I was making tortillas by the time I was four. My mom and my aunts would be up before dawn most days, cooking for the crew. We had a big old Buick station wagon we'd load up at lunchtime so we could drive to the newest oil field and serve it all up out of the tailgate, every day during the summertime and beyond that, sometimes too. Hell, until I was nine or ten, I think I spent more time in a kitchen than I did in school."

"I feel that," he answered, wanting to keep the conversation going. "Only in my case, back in Mississippi, the oil fields didn't keep me out of school—it was cotton fields."

She nodded, pulling up a stool to rest a minute while she flipped tortillas. "Sometimes a well would come in and we'd all be rich for a little while. Or so we thought, anyway. And we'd fill up that old Buick with real beef and beer, sometimes even a whole side of pork, and set up the barbecues right in the fields. And there'd be carnitas and tacos and raspado. Man, that was fun. That's what you call a real Texas barbecue."

"So how did you come to enlist?" Jason prodded, anxious to know more.

She shrugged and rose to release the pressure valve on the last of the giant cookers, sending another blast of heaven-scented steam into the air.

Jason's stomach growled in anticipation. "How does anybody?" she asked. "Down here in Texas, wildcatting all but fell apart when the big corporations moved in, and my dad and his brothers couldn't see a way to beat them, so they joined them. It wasn't a great living, but it kept us off welfare. Say, now that I think about it, you got any of that awful government cheese?"

Jason rose and examined one of the higher shelves, where a series of boxes roughly half the size of a two-by-four were stacked against the wall. He tossed her one.

She caught it easily. "That's the stuff. Good old processed cheese food."

"More like glue food," he muttered.

Katie set to work, dicing the orange bricks into bite-sized pieces. "Doesn't matter now," she told him. "It's got fat, protein, and calories. And that's what's going to keep us going."

Out in the corridor, drawn by the tantalizing scents of a hot meal, a few members of the staff had gathered among the food carts, awaiting what was to come. When Katie appeared on the threshold, spatula in hand, many stared at her curiously, but no one questioned her presence as she began barking out orders like she'd been doing it all her life.

"Okay, people. Today we got the house specialty. Katie Mendoza's Breakfast Burritos. We're going to do this assembly-line style, two tortillas, two scoops of rice and beans from the next pot down, one scoop of scrambled eggs, topped by a handful of diced cheese. Feed yourselves first, then load up the carts and get rolling."

Katie and Jason moved to a far corner of the space, to allow the staff to pass through. Jason happily munched on his own portion, feeling the weight of reality that had settled on his shoulders lighten with every bite. "Man, this is good. Thank you, Corporal, from the bottom of my heart."

She turned to the sink and started rinsing. "Better to do these dishes by hand to save energy. Then, thanks to those pots over there, we can sterilize them afterward. And save the water we used to do that. Depending on how long this thing lasts, we may need it."

"Man," he replied. "Are you always thinking two steps ahead of everybody else?"

She looked at him oddly. "Don't you? And another thing. When you get a moment, put some of your crew to work, building a barbecue pit out on the loading dock. It's solid concrete, so you're not going to burn anything down. And if the generators quit, there will still be something to cook on."

"And just what are you planning to cook? In case you haven't noticed, we're not exactly rolling in supplies here. Most of the meat went bad when the refrigeration units went."

If she heard the hint of sarcasm in his tone, she didn't flinch. "I thought about that. But there were a couple of grocery stores inland, within a mile or so. I know A&M was strictly local. They bought their meat directly from the slaughterhouses and kept a huge meat locker in the back so they could butcher it themselves. Sub-zero. Even if the power went out, it would take more than a week to thaw a side of beef, especially if no one's opened the locker door. And they would have moved all the dry goods too. To the upper shelves, in case of flooding. Shit! Now that I think about it, they even had a pharmacy. They must have left medicines behind too."

She turned to him, her eyes shining with excitement. "How soon can we get a recon team over there? And, when the water has receded a bit more, we need to get out there and retrieve the rest of the supplies. There are portable generators and diesel tanks for the generators, along with medicine and food. Pretty soon we'll be able to fish the bay again, depending on how much longer we are stuck here. There will be flounder, grouper, redfish, drum, maybe even shark!"

Even while he was smiling, Jason held his hands out in front of him in protest. "Slow down, woman, slow down. You sure you're just a corporal, not a general? Didn't you forget something?"

She whirled to face him, her thoughts racing with possibilities. "What?"

"We're under a damn quarantine! Nobody leaves the hospital, got it?"

There was a long pause, and when she spoke again, it was almost gentle. Her dark eyes shone with a bottomless sadness and her voice held not a trace of sarcasm. "Maybe you didn't get the memo, Mr. Carter, but there isn't anybody here but us. They left us all here to die, got it? I saw the orders myself. I—I—" she broke off, unsure of how to continue.

How could she tell him she herself had pushed the button? She inhaled deeply, gathered herself, and went on. "Until the CDC or the Red Cross decides to send in some relief at some unnamed time in the future, we have nobody left to save but each other. So, if that means we leave the hospital and forage whatever we can to stay alive, that's what it means, okay?"

She still had a smudge of flour on her cheek and it was everything Jason Carter could do not to reach up and brush it softly away from her cheek. Her eyes were shining with unshed tears and with a passion he hadn't seen in anyone, anywhere before.

"Okay," he answered softly. "But first I'm going to get you upstairs to clear it with the admin. I have a feeling Dr. Kirsten Stone is going to be right fond of your way of thinking."

"Let's go then," she replied. "I'm ready."

He opened the door and followed her into the corridor, realizing he was dangerously close to having an emotional reaction toward her. Though, hell, he couldn't be sure of his own emotions anymore. Maybe he'd been in prison too long. But one thing at least was certain.

That woman had fire.

CHAPTER THIRTY
Galveston University Hospital

till reeling from Danica's rejection, Shaka moved away from Danica like a sleepwalker, too numb from the shock of her sudden dismissal to feel much of anything. He moved with no real sense of where he was going, his baffled, exhausted brain unable to process what had happened. How could he have been so wrong? Had he only dreamed the connection they had the night before?

He wandered for what seemed like an eternity through the maze of hallways, now and again passing people who seemed like shadows to him, staffers who stared at him curiously as he hurried by, barely acknowledging their greetings. Then, by degrees, the pain set in, beginning with a dull, throbbing headache taking shape behind his eyes, and a strange, disoriented sensation, as though he was somehow floating just outside his own body and couldn't quite get back in. Haloes appeared around the dim lights in the corridors, and the painted numbers and arrows on the walls that indicated east or west hospital wings only contributed to his sense of unreality. Now and again, distant voices echoed over the PA system, calling to him like ghosts in a forsaken castle.

Danica. Even hours later, he replayed the scene in his tired mind. Her words hit him with the force of a sucker punch. He saw again the coldness in her eyes, heard the flat, unfeeling cruelty of her voice as she'd simply dismissed him. "Fun," she'd called it. Nothing more. And then she was gone.

And he had no choice but to let her go. What was that saying? "If you love someone, set them free"? He wasn't sure if he was in love or not, but it seemed to fit the moment. A brush-off like that never did anyone's ego any good, but accept it he must. Yet, at the same time, she'd hurt far more than his pride. She'd taken some vital part of him with her, like an organ or a limb, leaving him weakened and helpless in her wake. He would never again feel that sense of peace settle over him as he watched the rise and fall of her breath while she slept. She would never make him feel safe again. There would be only this awful, phantom pain in place of the amputation. The thought so terrified him he broke into a run at one point, jogging aimlessly around the hallways and up and down the stairs, not sure of what pursued him, only sure that he needed to escape.

"Pull yourself together, man," he muttered when he could run no more.

He paused to lean against a nearby wall, all the time fighting a dizzying sense of unreality. He was sweating profusely, uncomfortable, as though his very skin had suddenly become too small. And yet he kept moving, relentlessly. He couldn't afford to fall apart here, not anywhere. Not now. He struggled through a few deep breaths, wondering what was happening, a whirl of emotions expanding in his chest. He strangled back a sob—the hoarse, choked sound of a man unused to tears. He was no stranger to women, he reminded himself. And while he was not always the gentleman, he wasn't a total cad, either. He trusted himself to do right by them, even when it wasn't always pleasant. So, how was it possible? How could you follow your heart so completely, only to learn it had lied? Or had the strain of the storm so distorted things and stirred emotions to the point where people clung to each other like pieces of driftwood, trying to save themselves from drowning? If that were the case, was everything else just an illusion too? Some big hallucination? He was overcome by a dull rage and a sense of utter futility. As though he could put his own fist through the wall, only to have the wall dissolve in front of him. Maybe he was crazy, but he no longer cared. He, like all of them, was just dreaming, moving through some universe of grief.

He reached out a hand to steady himself, and as if by some cosmic response, he was suddenly made keenly aware of his own stink. He had not yet showered or changed since working with the team on the loading dock earlier that day, and the scent of the decomposition outside permeated his every pore. His mind fought to stay organized; he had to find a shower, clean scrubs, a bed. Sleep—that was all he needed now. Not women. Not Danica. Not even to be a doctor. Just to feel clean again. And the sweet, dark oblivion of sleep.

Chapter Thirty-One
Galveston University Hospital

Ninety-six hours after Hurricane Beatrix made landfall

Shortly after eight the following morning, Danica dragged herself to the nurses' station nearest the isolation unit and prepared to complete her rounds on the critical care ward. The rest of her rounds had gone smoothly enough, and of the patients in her caseload, everyone was doing as well as could be expected, at least medically. Their anxiety, on the other hand, was palpable; everywhere she went, those able to communicate plagued her with questions.

"Now that the storm is over, how long before we can get out of here?"

"When's the cavalry coming, doc?"

"When they gonna turn the AC back on?"

"Are the phones working yet?"

"How long do you reckon this quarantine is gonna last?"

And on and on. Danica had done her best to be reassuring, pasting on a brave smile she was far from feeling, but for the most part, these were questions for which she had no answers, voicing the same fears she was barely able to contain in herself.

The floor nurse behind the counter turned and glanced at Danica from behind a face mask.

Danica noted she was also wearing protective gloves. It struck her as odd. The station was well away from the isolation unit and behind a series of air-locked security doors. Theoretically, there was only minimal risk of contamination at this distance. She studied the cold blue eyes in what appeared to be a sharp, middle-aged face.

Those eyes stared back at her, taking in her ruined face and swollen, puffy eyes.

"I don't think we've met," she said, trying to break the awkward silence. "I'm Dr. Diza. Danica Diza."

The nurse raised an eyebrow. "Liz Bishop. I pulled this rotation and I'm not happy about it. I was perfectly fine over in Cardiology. And the sooner they send me back there, the better. Meantime, I'm just doing my job."

"Thanks," Danica murmured. "It's been a challenge. For all of us."

"If you say so," the other woman replied curtly. "Just another day as far as I'm concerned. So don't get any big ideas about needing me for a shoulder to cry on, okay? I keep things on a strictly professional level. You remember that, we'll get along fine."

Danica stared at her, bewildered. "I beg your pardon?"

Nurse Bishop slid the charts across the countertop. "You think I can't see you've got some stuff going on? Been crying all night, from the look of you. Well, it's not my business and I don't want to hear about it, either. Take your drama to your mama, I always say. Meanwhile, you have work to do. Best get to it. Here are the current stats. Dr. Wong's upgraded to stable. The chaplain is deceased. Three-thirty a.m. this morning. Nguyen is still critical. And the rest? Well, Jesus, take the wheel, I guess. All I'll say. Get suited up and I'll buzz you in. I'll be on the monitor if you need anything. But just so you know, I'm not setting foot inside that unit. Not for anything."

Hot words bubbled to Danica's lips as she snatched her charts across the counter. Who the hell did this woman think she was, anyhow? She knew well enough that working relationships, especially between the younger doctors and older nurses, might get strained from time to time, even in the best of circumstances. And these didn't even come close. But still, a certain amount of respect was always called for. On both sides.

She managed to hold back her own remarks and settled for a brief, curt nod. "Anything else?"

Nurse Bishop shrugged. "Ribavirin's running low. Oh, and some nutcase wandered up here from 3R about 4 a.m. Claimed she'd caught the fever and was going to sue. Abdominal pain in the upper right quadrant. Turned out to be mild appendicitis. Dr. Stone took care of it."

Danica nodded and turned away.

"And don't forget to initial those charts when you're through. Can't afford to be forgetful, can we?"

Danica only paused her steps to indicate she'd heard but did not turn around. *Bitch*, she thought as she headed for the decontamination chamber. Once inside, she stripped down and donned new scrubs and the usual layers of HAZMAT gear, going through the motions on autopilot, as sure of each step by this time as she was of her own name. She could almost feel Nurse Bishop's cold, efficient eyes, watching her every move.

A sudden thought struck her with an almost brutal force, and she paused for a moment in front of the mirror, taking in the dark circles under her own eyes, and her hollow, distant expression under the still-puffy lids. *Was this what Shaka saw?* she wondered. *Just duty? Just cold professionalism, devoid of compassion or emotion? Am I really any better than somebody like Nurse Bishop?*

A chilling wave of regret washed over her as she completed the suit-up and signaled the doors to open, colder even than the temperature inside the isolation unit. How could she have been so wrong? About him? About herself? One thing was certain: she had to find him, talk to him, try to make amends. That is, if he'd talk to her at all.

CHAPTER THIRTY-TWO
Galveston University Hospital

Slivers of painful sunlight stabbed through the slits in the blinds and penetrated his eyelids, causing Shaka to groan and turn in his sleep, slowly becoming conscious of the fact that every move was agony. Every muscle screamed, every cell throbbed as though some monster had come in the night and stolen his very skin, exposing only raw, shredded flesh and quivering nerves.

Bits and pieces of the previous day floated back to him as he tried to make sense of his condition. His rounds in the morning, then laughing with the other men on the loading dock, the stink of rotting fish and the blessed sight of gulls and buzzards wheeling overhead, circling a cloudless sky. The storm had passed. The water surge was receding. The smoke from the blast was still dense, but they were still alive. Then, his argument with Danica came back to him full force, crushing his chest and replaying in his mind like some awful, ugly movie, her words stinging him worse than his tortured skin.

Dimly aware that he needed to pee, he swung one leg at a time over the bedside, gingerly testing his weight on the floor. He realized he was naked, having fallen asleep in a call room after his shower last night without even bothering to dry himself. Eyes still half-closed against the too-harsh sunlight, he staggered to the bathroom and relieved himself, then cautiously flipped on an overhead light.

Shaka was proud of his body and took good care of it. He'd always been strong and well-built and rarely ill. Even in med school, when so many of his fellow students had succumbed to the perils of self-diagnosis and hypochondria at the hands of Dr. Internet, he'd somehow managed to escape all that and had always stayed healthy and strong.

So when he managed to finally, fully open his eyes, he was utterly unprepared for the vision that stared back at him from the mirror. His normally-bronze skin was a dark, sickly yellow; the whites of his eyes were tinged with red. A two-day stubble of beard shadowed his jawline. Then his gaze traveled downward, over his broad chest and well-muscled arms, while the truth of what he was seeing struggled to become a conscious thought. His skin was mottled purple in places under his arms and along the hipline on the side where he'd slept; the lividity glared at him like an accusation, even as he broke out in a fresh sweat along his brow.

He knew it now. He had the virus. He'd seen the symptoms too often over the past days not to recognize them in this moment.

He took a deep, shaky breath and turned to the door. He knew what he had to do.

Fifteen minutes later, Nurse Liz Bishop glanced up from the romance novel she'd been reading to see a naked, purple-mottling body staggering down the hall in her direction, half holding himself onto the wall as he made his way along the corridor.

"What the—" she shrieked. "Get out of here! Has everybody in this damn hospital gone fucking crazy?"

He stretched out his arms and fell heavily against the counter. "Dr. Shaka Sen," he gasped. "Let me into the isolation unit. Stat. I've got it—the fever. CC—" he stopped, his bloodshot eyes rolling in his head.

"I can't take you in there," she said. "I told them—I won't."

"Goddamn it, woman!" He lurched across the hallway, grabbed a wheelchair parked against the far wall. "Buzz me through!"

With her fingers trembling, she buzzed open the airlocks, jabbing at the buttons until he was inside.

Danica glanced up from her rounds at the flurry of buzzing to shout at the monitor. "Bishop? What's going on?"

As quickly as it had begun, the racket ceased.

The door swung inward, and with a mighty effort, a man in a wheelchair pulled himself across the threshold and rose to his feet.

Danica stared at him, repelled by the tell-tale bruising that all but covered his skin. She threw herself, sobbing, into his arms, HAZMAT suit and all.

"Shaka!" he heard her scream. "Oh God, oh God! No. No!"

Chapter Thirty-Three

Exurban Houston, Texas

The trip from Houston to Galveston should have taken an hour, but when Billy started out on I-45, headed south, he had no way of knowing what awaited him.

Traffic was light coming out of Houston. Most evacuees from Galveston would still be safely ensconced in shelters until they got an official okay to return, and FEMA and the Red Cross had already set up aid stations and soup kitchens around the city. News of the quarantine had gotten around by then; what news stations were back up and running managed to broadcast the occasional drone shots of the hospital grounds and the devastation left by the storm. As grieved as they were at their losses, those residents who'd been lucky enough to evacuate were in no hurry to return.

What little traffic there was consisted mostly of late-afternoon commuters who turned off the exits to nearby Baytown or Pasadena or the various farm roads on either side. Absorbed in his thoughts, Billy navigated the first twenty miles of his journey easily in his ancient Toyota. He was captivated by hundreds of wind turbines, towering over the flat, ceaseless landscape, their mighty arms whirling in a strange, alien ballet. Given the landscape, spread out in a flat, soggy network of marshlands and bayous on either side, the windmills were pretty much all there was to look at. He fiddled with the knob on the radio, hoping to tune into something besides the local religious station where a high-pitched preacher exhorted the audience to atone for their sins, lest the Lord in his wrath again rain down the kind of awful destruction they had just seen.

"Hurricanes don't work like that, moron," Billy said irritably and snapped off the radio. "Read some science, will you?"

Around the turnoff to Missouri City, just north of Pearland, the landscape views changed. The road was utterly empty of traffic. Billy was forced to slow to a crawl as he navigated the nightmare of wreckage left behind by the storm and those desperate to flee. Hundreds of overturned cars, RVs, and tractor-trailers were scattered on either side of the sodden highway like abandoned toys in a child's playroom. As he made his way at a snail's pace, weaving in and out, had noted that there had been more than one pileup in the mass exodus of those heading north. Telltale burned-out vehicles, jackknifed eighteen-wheelers, and passenger buses were tossed together with crushed subcompacts, rolled-over SUVs, T-boned Cadillacs, and twisted pickup trucks, their hulking, deserted remains sending up shimmering waves of heat into the desolate landscape.

The whole scene was surreal. The forsaken atmosphere of the place reminded him of some of the scenes in those post-apocalyptic video games he liked to play. Only this was no game, and each looted suitcase or child's doll or overturned cooler reminded him it had been ditched out of necessity as the panic-stricken populace ran for their lives. His old Toyota tended to overheat in stop-and-go traffic, and he was moving at ten miles an hour. Watching the needle on his temperature gauge, he narrowly missed puncturing his tires as he edged around a torn-off bumper. He'd be damn lucky if he made it before dark.

He passed a sign for the old Calder Oil field, a place they called the Killing Fields back in the day when the bodies of dozens of young women gone missing from Houston and Galveston had been discovered, all buried in shallow graves. Authorities had investigated for years, trying to identify the serial killer, but the crimes were never solved. The thought of being killed, then tossed out on the side of the road, forgotten and left to rot out here at the edge of nowhere, depressed Billy more than he could say.

He eyed the landscape to either side of him. The ditches ran with seawater from the surge, the marsh gases steaming in the heat and rising up like spirits in the first glints of burnt orange over the western horizon as the sun began to set. To the east, the chemical fire in Texas City still belched black smoke that cast a pall over the blue sky, mixing with the colored sunlight in a way that was almost beautiful, yet it terrified him to his soul. Nowhere in any direction had he seen a single form of life. And he could only wonder, when he got to the hospital, if what he'd find there would be even worse.

Eventually, the road wreckage opened up a bit, and the Toyota chugged along valiantly for a few more miles before it gave off a telltale blast of steam and coasted to a stop. Billy got out of the driver's seat and waited for the steam to abate before popping the hood to survey the damage. It didn't take long for him to figure it was more than a radiator hose; the head gasket had blown. He would have to make the rest of his journey on foot. Cursing a blue streak, he snatched his backpack from the back seat, tied a bandana around his head, and set out, with a pair of mirrored sunglasses to keep out the glare. He reckoned he was no more than four miles from the beach, and with any luck at all, he could make the hospital before full dark.

He spent the time reviewing everything he could recall about CCHF and the strain he was working with. He'd been lucky, in some respects, successfully generating enough of the antigen to induce an immune response and isolating the pathogen. But those results had been unstable, unable to withstand the usual purification necessary to produce a viable vaccine. But then he'd only had lab samples at his disposal. Depending on the antibodies present in any survivors, assuming there would be survivors, they would be fresh enough not just to grow in the necessary proteins, but to stabilize and purify as well. He'd been lucky before—maybe he would be again.

A huge, displaced water moccasin reared up from the asphalt, ready to strike.

Billy jumped back and froze in his tracks.

The creature apparently decided he wasn't worth the trouble and slithered on its way.

Still trembling, Billy snatched off his sunglasses and mopped his brow. *Wow*, he breathed. His luck had almost given out.

He caught a new blast of the acrid smoke coming from the east and fixed his bandana over his mouth to filter the smell. His mind continued to work frantically. He faintly recalled that the venom of a water moccasin was rarely fatal, yet in severe cases could cause widespread hemorrhaging as CCHF also affected the circulatory system. And more recently, snake venom was being studied to develop treatments to kill cancer cells, inhibit their growth, and to be used as therapy against viral and bacterial pathogens. Could there be some relationship? Might a less virulent form be harvested from the snakes? Enough to trigger an autoimmune response that lessened the fatality rate of fever victims? If so, then south Texas had a readily available supply.

Still struggling to connect the dots, at last he saw the white dunes rising up along what used to be the north shoreline of Galveston Bay. With the last of his strength, he half-pawed his way up the incline and stood at the top, surveying the scene before him in the gathering twilight. Here, as elsewhere, the landscape was littered with filth and debris, upturned boats, wrecked docks, and dying fish. But there, across the now-calm waters of the bay, the hospital stood in the far distance, seemingly untouched by the storm. The sight of it lifted his heart with joy. He'd been right to come, after all. He knew it.

After a few more minutes, he noticed a single figure hunched over near the water's edge, a huge pile of shrimp nets piled on his left, and miracle of miracles, what appeared to be a small, but intact motorboat pulled well up onto the sand, its shiny black rudder catching the last of the sun.

Half running, half sliding, Billy made his way down, approaching what he could now see was an elderly Mexican fisherman, hunched over and patiently mending his shrimp nets by hand. Yanking his bandana down around his neck, Billy approached the old man, smiling and waving. "*Hola!*"

he shouted. "Glad to see somebody around. You make it through the storm okay?"

The fisherman glanced up at him with a bland, unreadable expression, then went back to his nets, his fingers moving as if by memory.

Billy squatted to his haunches, withdrawing his wallet from his back pocket. "I need to get over there," he said, pointing his thumb toward the hospital. When there was no response, he opened his Google Translate app and tried, *"Necesito ir por allá al hospital. ¿Puedes por favor llevarme allí?"* He peeled off a hundred-dollar bill and waved it under the old man's nose.

The fisherman stared at him with the same implacable expression, then slowly shook his head. *"No. No puedo señor … ."*

Frustrated, Billy rose to his feet. "It's just a quarantine, dammit!"

He glanced around frantically until his eyes settled on the boat. He peeled off four more hundreds and threw them in the old man's lap. "Look, I'm sorry, man. It's all I've got."

With that, Billy waded into the water and began tugging on the boat, until the fisherman got slowly to his feet and pushed from the other end. Once in the water, Billy lowered the rudder and pulled the starter until the engine finally coughed to life. With a whoop of triumph, he headed out into the bay, sending the old man a thumbs-up and a final wave. Billy had to cleverly get past the National Guard patrol. Although they didn't want people getting off the island, he doubted anyone was stopping people from getting to it. He decided he would wait until nightfall and slip past the patrol.

As Billy's boat roared away from the shore, he watched the fisherman finger the bills and tuck them safely in his pocket. The fisherman then withdrew the silver crucifix that hung from his neck, made the sign of the cross three times, and kissed it before tucking it safely back inside his shirt. When Billy was out barely out of hearing distance, he thought he heard the fisherman say, "Wasn't even my boat."

Chapter Thirty-Four
Galveston University Hospital

A thunderous knock woke Danica in the call room. She made her way to the door in protective gear, unsure if she had been infected.

"We've been trying to get a hold of you for hours! They need you in the unit," said Shannon in a panicked tone rarely heard from a veteran nurse. The nurse turned and left back to the unit.

Danica hated being put on the spot like that. She quickly got up and tied her hair into a ponytail in the dark. She noticed the bump on her head resolving. She fixed her protective gear and headed out.

From the other side of the door, she could hear muffled voices and rushed footsteps. She made her way to the door and stepped into the hall. In that moment, there was a palpable sense of fear. It was pitch black. Patients and staff were colliding into one another, falling onto the floor, some grasping in front of them to feel their way toward a sense of security.

Danica caught up to Shannon and asked, "What's going on?"

"We're truly up a creek without a paddle," Shannon replied.

Danica reached into her lab coat, fumbling for its contents. She discovered a dying penlight from her neurology rotation three weeks ago. She shone the flickering light in front of her as her eyes accommodated to the scene that was unfolding. She caught a glimpse of the nurses' station and the hallway leading to the elevators she would normally take when power was available. To her left, though, she saw the door to the emergency exit and the windowless staircase. She passed through the door and started her climb down the stairs. None of the signs were illuminated, including the ones indicating which floor she was on.

Fuck. The last thing I need is my penlight to die and be stuck in this stairwell. She remembered from the time when she got a step-tracker and entered a ten-thousand step challenge with her fellow co-residents that each floor was separated by two flights of stairs with twenty steps each.

I can do this. I'm on the sixth floor. Unit is on the third floor. That's one hundred twenty steps. She started to count.

Danica got to what she thought was the third floor and reached into her pocket for the penlight once again. Nothing. She tried in vain to muster some juice by switching the on/off button over and over again.

She started to panic.

Danica felt for the wall and leaned against it as she began to hyperventilate and a sense of doom closed in on her.

She bent down to calm her breathing.

Just then a door opened wide and a beam of light shined into the stairwell.

"Glad you could finally make it, sleeping beauty," said Dr. Stone.

Danica caught a glimpse of the familiar double door entrance that had been propped open, labeled "Intensive Care Unit."

A cacophony of voices all asked for the same thing at once.

"I need another set of hands!"

"I need an ambu bag!"

"Does anyone have a stethoscope?"

Dr. Stone explained, "We're down to our last barrel of diesel for the back-up generators. We need to keep it for the lab and isolation unit, so we've been on battery power for these vents the last four hours. Now they're starting to die. Find an ambu bag and start ventilating some patients manually."

"How do we monitor their vitals without a pulse ox?" Danica asked.

"You need to read an old book every once in a while, Danica. Look at their conjunctiva, monitor their heart rate with your stethoscope, and don't stop bagging," replied Dr. Stone.

Danica went over to the next patient bed to help with the efforts as others ran around looking for supplies.

Grunting noises filled the air, but no one questioned the order as everyone took their places in the room to begin the tasks at hand.

Chapter Thirty-Five

Galveston Island

The power outage had finally convinced Dr. Kirsten Stone to let Jason Carter investigate what remained of the city as close to the hospital as possible, if only to salvage what they could. Their other supplies were running dangerously low and even the most basic medications were in short supply.

True to his promise to Corporal Mendoza, Jason and his team had managed to fashion a rough barbecue out on the loading dock, but even with that, it would be a few more days before enough scrap lumber or charcoal could be dried out enough to use.

When Dr. Sen had come down with the fever, word had spread through the hospital like wildfire; every new case of CCHF meant at least three more weeks of quarantine. Thus far, there hadn't been a whole-scale panic, but that didn't mean it couldn't happen. Three times now, the drug storage rooms in the pharmacy had been broken into and an ugly rumor circulated that some among the staff were hoarding morphine and oxy, ready to take their own lives if rescue didn't come. Jason reflected, standing in the early morning light out on the dock as he waited for the others to assemble.

Scarcity either brought out the worst in people or it brought out the best. And when survival was at stake, anybody could turn on a dime.

Jason peered out on the nearly-unrecognizable landscape, trying to get his bearings. Mountains of refuse lay between the hospital and the A&M market to the east, if indeed it was still standing. Worst of all was the utter absence of life. Only the ceaseless cry of the gulls overhead, accompanied by the low whine of automated drones that circled like monstrous dragonflies over the island, punctuated the eerie stillness. Five days after the storm, there was no sign of rescue, no hint of human life anywhere outside the hospital. Which either meant that the Guard had managed the most successful evacuation in hurricane history or those they'd left behind hadn't lived to tell the tale. As yet another drone circled above, he lifted his eyes again, suddenly struck by an idea. He hastily scanned the dock, then bent and gripped a broken brick. Mentally measuring the distance, he glanced at the drone once more and began to scratch out a message on the concrete, in big block letters three feet high:

PLEASE HELP US

He was getting to his feet as the others emerged onto the loading dock, armed with pistols, ammunition, and whatever wheeled-transport carts might be practical without slowing them down.

Corporal Mendoza eyed the message scrawled on the concrete and wordlessly placed a hand on his arm.

"I just hope one of them drones catches a picture," he said. "Maybe somebody will see." He drew a deep breath. "Now, we better get moving. Let's roll."

CHAPTER THIRTY-SIX
Galveston University Hospital

One week after Hurricane Beatrix made landfall

Dr. Kirsten Stone sat alone at a nurses' station in the ICU, trying to take a power nap even as daylight started to creep into the unit. She was unable to stop the endless loop of possibilities that skirted through her thoughts—though even that distraction was preferable to the certainty of betrayal that had settled around her heart. Try as she would to deny it, it appeared as though the remaining staff and patients of University Hospital in Galveston had been utterly abandoned, ruthlessly left to die, casualties of not just a hurricane, but of a system that cared nothing for the helpless. She slid open a drawer to her desk and was shocked when her own image—from a makeup mirror she kept there—stared up at her, reflecting the deep shadows under her hollow eyes and the taut lines of despair that settled around her mouth. She struggled to keep up appearances for others, but she couldn't lie to herself. Almost overnight, her face had transformed from a confident, competent professional to that of someone who had lost all hope. And every passing hour offered nothing by way of reassurance.

She glanced reflexively at the wind-up watch on her wrist. Every day since the storm had passed, they'd been in touch with the CDC via an old analog ham radio set left behind by the National Guard. They'd asked for research, information, findings, anything that might be of aid in developing even a crude vaccine. The first few days, the CDC had answered with sketchy information and no concrete answers. But for four days now, there had been no response from their headquarters at all. Her mind fought the certainty that their silence was deliberate, yet the tentacles of despair tightened around her heart until she thought it might burst.

Dr. Stone stared up from her chair as Billy Andersen strode into the unit dangling his ID badge in her face. Stupid with exhaustion, she could only gawk at him. "So," she began after a moment. "How in the world did you even get here? This island has been under lockdown since—"

Billy grinned at her and swung up a chair. "Real nice Mexican fella sold me his boat to get across the bay," he replied. "And then I walked, crawled, and swam once I got to Galveston to get to the hospital. And as for the building, well, let's just say there isn't much to stop anyone from getting in. Took me a couple of days with protein bars and scarce water, but I'm here."

Dr. Stone pressed her lips together. No one was more aware than she as to just how isolated the hospital was. As for security, only the lab and isolation units had electrical power. They'd cut everything else from the ICU— general wards, elevators, door locks, and monitors—in order to conserve what energy they had left.

"Just think of me as what you'd call a first responder," Billy said, and for the next twenty minutes, he filled her in on his work with CCHF and wanted to know what progress her team had made thus far.

"Not much, I'm afraid," she admitted. "Aside from supportive care like fluids, and airway support, we've relied on steroids and Ribavirin for actively infected patients. We have had multiple fatalities: an intern, a chaplain, and, I am sorry to say, your lab partner Cory Finch. A few patients with a compatible crossmatch to a volunteer who survived the virus while on duty in Iraq are getting his convalescent plasma. This isn't enough, though. Two of our staff volunteers have still fallen ill."

Dr. Stone looked away in shame, thinking of Dylan Nguyen and, now, Shaka Sen.

Billy's heart dropped. Remorse and sorrow filled him as he thought about the last time he saw Cory. Cory was a good guy; he hadn't deserved to go out like this. Billy should have been here. Cory's death fueled Billy even more, determined to fix this mess.

Taking a moment to gather his thoughts, Billy pushed on. "The first step is testing convalescent plasma. What happened with the volunteers?"

"The first had a very rapid onset of the disease. The second had a prolonged prodrome and incubation took almost a full week. Both are still with us, but in Nguyen's case, I fear not for long."

Billy's face sank. "I had hoped there would have been a better response."

"So how can you help us? Dr. Wong tells us you're the man with the answers," Dr. Stone turned to him and asked.

"It's classified," Billy said, immediately feeling foolish. "That clearly doesn't matter at this point," he continued. "For the last three years, I've been working on a vaccine for all strains of CCHF as part of a Defense Department grant by determining virulence and altering the lambda factor, or the force of infection of the pathogen. That is, the rate at which individuals become infected. We took a vaccine developed by Bulgarians for one very specific local strain of the virus and created a much better vaccine based on our predictions. Problem is, we've never tested on humans before."

Dr. Stone nodded in understanding. "Well. No better time than the present. Let's go. Someone has been anxiously waiting for you."

Relief washed over Dr. Stone, and she felt as calm as she looked.

***

Somehow, finally being released from the isolation ward back into a private room was more disconcerting than Dr. Wong planned. He stared morosely out at the wreckage of the city from the wheelchair parked in his room. And the view outside told him just how much the world had altered during his days of delirium. A vision of his wife and children danced in his mind's eye, even as his heart prayed for their safety. He knew he was not a brave man, not really, but he had no other choice than to remain here in the hospital. He had to help develop some kind of weapon against this virus, which had ravaged so many, in the same way the storm outside had ravaged the countryside.

A light knock interrupted his reverie. "Enter," he said.

And in the next instant he was on his feet, throwing his arms around Billy Andersen like he was his long-lost son.

"You have no idea how much we need you, Billy," Dr. Wong said after a moment, falling back into his chair and dabbing his eyes with the edge of his robe. "I'm doing all the research I can to find a stable therapy, and damn, I'm so grateful to have survived this, but—"

"But," interjected Dr. Stone, walking into the room behind Billy, "I've had to severely limit Dr. Wong's time in the lab to run tests for a vaccine. After his bout with the fever, he's still very weak. And the last thing we need at this stage is to have him collapse on duty. Or worse, succumb to some infection acquired in the hospital."

Dr. Wong held up his hand. "Fair enough. One more casualty isn't going to do anybody any good."

Dr. Stone smiled. "I'll leave you two to catch up. When you're done, Dr. Wong or the floor nurse can direct you to decontamination. And, Mr. Andersen? Thank you for coming all this way."

Billy turned around to face her with a glimmer of hope. "I think I have an idea."

CHAPTER THIRTY-SEVEN
Galveston University Hospital

Beep-beep, beep-beep, beep-beep.

The timer finally rang and a new group of volunteers started to manually ventilate the patients.

A sense of dread filled the air.

I don't know how much longer we can do this, thought Danica, as exhaustion settled into her body.

Danica had been doing this work every two hours for the past four days. Every volunteer in that room had. The lives of each patient rested in the volunteer's tired hands.

"This is unsustainable," whispered the charge nurse to one of the respiratory technicians.

Dr. Stone then walked into the room, weariness evident across her face, mirroring the look of everyone in the room.

Dr. Stone took a long deep breath. She took command of the room and gathered everyone at the nurses' station. Danica made her way to the crowd assembled in a circle. Dim light coming from the flashlights illuminated the faces and the makeshift huddle.

Dr. Stone spoke loudly so everyone could hear. "I know everyone is tired. I am too. We're understaffed. We're running out of medication, fluids, catheters, and the like. We can't keep doing this. We simply don't have the manpower.

I don't know when help is coming—if at all. We have some hard decisions to make in the next hour."

The room went silent, followed by hushed whispers. Dr. Stone had explicitly said what everyone was thinking but couldn't express.

Dr. Stone took a deep breath and swallowed the bile coming up. "I want you to know that the University Hospital is not a charity hospital. I need a group of you to be my ad hoc ethics committee. Help me triage which patients will receive priority treatment—and our resources—and which patients will receive palliative care only. We have to make this decision collectively."

How do you prioritize? thought Danica as she looked at the ICU census.

"I'll be on your committee Dr. Stone," said Alondra the charge nurse.

"So will I," said Dr. Amy Dunn, the ICU fellow.

"And Dr. Diza," asked Dr. Stone, "you're being volun- told."

The group of four reconvened in the empty family waiting area room outside the unit, shutting the doors behind them.

CHAPTER THIRTY-EIGHT
Galveston Island

The team of six—Jason Carter, Katie Mendoza, Rick Johnson, and three others from the hospital—moved along what had once been one of the main traffic arteries east did so in the half light of dawn, slowly making their way through a landscape devoid of markers, as unrecognizable as the moon. Carrying a couple of hand trucks and some pickaxes, and armed only with Katie's service pistol, they moved in an eerie silence oddly in keeping with the changed world in which they found themselves. They remained alert for any cries of survivors trapped in the never-ending rubble, but there was only the whisper of the ocean, the whine of the occasional drones, and the mockery of the great, fat buzzards and greedy gulls that circled high in the sky in a sinister ballet, biding their time till the next victim fell.

According to Katie, the A&M market, if it were still there, was a little more than a mile from the hospital grounds, yet it took nearly two hours to travel the distance. Time itself had ground to a slow crawl in this abandoned place, and the whole island had been torn from the world of the living, even as the ruins of what it had been filled up with the ghosts of its dead. They had to keep moving; the days heated up fast and the nights fell quickly. And if they were fortunate enough to find any supplies, the way back, loaded down with food, water, and medicines, would be far more arduous than the way in.

Suddenly, Katie Mendoza halted and peered off to the right, shielding her eyes from the fully risen sun. "Is that it? I think I see it! Over there, in that parking lot!"

Squinting, Jason circled up to her left. Five hundred yards further east, a couple of lone structures rose up in the distance. "Hard to tell with that rolled-over semi in the way," he said.

He signaled the remaining team with a whistle and pointed in that direction. "This way," he shouted. "We veered off the original road someplace, but at least we're not as lost as we could be!"

Navigating over embankments of garbage and floodwaters that stood between them and the parking lot, they finally stood sweating and wet, the structure they were seeking barely visible in the hazy sun. A full view by a huge eighteen-wheeler jackknifed on its side in front of a lone, seemingly untouched cinder block structure in the foreground with a sign that read, "Sandy's Nail Salon—Manis, Pedis and Spa! *Se habla Español.*"

"Hang up a minute!" Jason yelled to those ahead.

At his elbow, Katie raised an eyebrow. "Dude, I mean, I could use a mani-pedi myself, but is now really the time?"

He stared at her, not understanding she was joking until she broke into a wide grin. He shook his head apologetically.

She laughed. "Just trying to lighten the mood."

"It's not that," he responded, circling the jackknifed semi. "This box here's refrigerated. Or at least it was before it crashed. And he was headed toward that market, most likely. So there may be supplies in there too. It's still locked, so it should be airtight. Might not be any good by now, but we should check."

"Good thinking!" Katie raised her hand in a high-five.

"Gimme that gun," Jason instructed. "Everybody else, stand back." Holding his breath and taking aim at the back doors, Jason Carter murmured a silent prayer. *Please Jesus, whatever's locked up in there, don't let it be full of people ...*

He fired. Once, twice. And the doors of the mighty truck swung halfway open, hanging crazily on what was left of their hinges.

A sudden scent filled the air, and Katie crept forward from the rest of the crew to the back doors, trying to peer inside. She beckoned wildly for someone to come forward and give her a boost up. Two of the men grasped hands to give her a foothold so she could scramble inside. A searing pain caught her attention. She glanced down. She had cut her leg on the door. She bent down to look at it and noticed a sliver of blood trickling down. One of the guys gave her a piece of cloth to wrap her leg. She thanked him, then turned around and continued into the truck.

The men waited breathlessly, until incredibly, the sound of her laughter, joyful and free, echoed from inside the box and out into the silent landscape, loud enough to frighten the gulls.

"Hallelujah!" she shouted, appearing once more to push the doors open wide. "What we got here, gentlemen, is a load of none other than Texas ruby grapefruit, oranges, and limes, and yeah, even mango. There must be fifteen hundred pounds of produce here. Some of it's gone off, some of it's bruised, but some, thanks to shipping underripe, is perfectly edible. Thank the gods!"

With that, she began pitching oversized grapefruit to each of them like baseballs, laughing as she did. Then she jumped down, three more grapefruits tucked under each arm. Jason Carter expertly sliced open one of them and handed her a segment, gratitude brimming in his eyes.

Watching her suck greedily, he chuckled around his own mouthful, "Lord, woman. You'd think you'd never seen a grapefruit before."

"I don't care!" Katie insisted. "I feel like I haven't seen a piece of fresh fruit in a hundred years!"

"Well, you're right about that much," he admitted. "But what are we gonna do with it all?"

Katie's face fell. "We'll take as much as we can on the return trip, then send another team in the morning. Now that we've opened the truck, it won't last long in this heat, but it'll keep us hydrated and stave off starving, anyhow. We could do a lot worse, Jason. Much. Much worse."

He lifted his head and gazed uncertainly in the direction of the market. "True that. Let's keep on."

As the team drew closer, their spirits rose when they saw the old-school neon sign rising above the steaming asphalt of the parking lot. The building, like the nail salon in front of it, was oddly untouched by the surrounding chaos. The windows had been boarded up all around, and when Katie got closer, her eyes filled with tears when she saw the handmade sign hanging in the front window.

PLEASE NO LOOTING
THE FRONT DOOR'S OPEN
TAKE WHAT YOU NEED TO SURVIVE.

Angela and Miguel

Jason came up behind her and gave her shoulder a reassuring squeeze as a choked sob escaped her throat. "They must have put that up just before they evacuated. Glad to know there's a few decent people left in the world. 'Course, that doesn't mean we'll find anything left inside, either."

He cautiously elbowed his way through the front door. Beaming a flashlight over the interior, his heart sank. As he feared, the shelves had been stripped bare, or nearly, the floors scattered with a haphazard array of crushed cans, scattered dry goods, and odd items likely dropped in the rush to grab as much as possible, as fast as possible. Aiming their lights toward the higher shelves, they could see some larger bags, stored out of the reach of floodwaters, too large to be hauled away in the general frenzy.

A slow grin spread over his face. "Damn," he said. "It just might be our lucky day, after all."

"What? What do you see?" Katie asked him. Since her head barely reached his shoulder, the bags pushed back against the wall on the highest shelves escaped her line of vision entirely.

He pulled over a plastic crate and helped her stand on it. "Rice, beans, and grits from what I see. Might be some kind of cereal up there, too. The bulk bags would have been too big for one or two people to make off with by themselves, most likely. Besides, most folks in a panic ain't thinking real far ahead; they always go for the perishables first."

He turned and shouted at the rest of the team. "Hey, guys! Who's gonna give me a boost up there so we can get these bulk bags down?"

Twenty minutes later, they had a fifty-pound bag of dried pinto beans, two twenty-five-pound bags of grits, a hundred pounds of rice, some industrial-sized tins of tomato sauce and pickles, and two gallons of corn syrup. It wasn't much for the three hundred-odd patients and staff who remained on the island, but it would stave off starvation for a while, at least. They'd loaded up most of it into the rolling carts they'd brought with them when Katie emerged from the back of the building. "I almost forgot," she cried. "The freezer and the pharmacy!"

Standing at the door to the deep freezer housed at the far end of the store, Carter examined the locking mechanism closely. "Doesn't look like anybody's messed with it," he said. "Give me your gun and stand back, everybody."

A blast of decidedly cooler air, though tinged with the smell of spoiled meat, greeted them as Jason pushed the door open wide. Cautiously, Katie moved forward. The frozen poultry and smaller cuts had spoiled in the prolonged power outage, but as she moved toward the two hanging sides of beef and touched them, she smiled. Her hunch was right. Not only were they not spoiled, they were still cool to the touch, dry aged in the airtight chamber. One of the men whistled through his teeth. "If we can find a way to get them back and cooked, we'll have meat for a week, at least. I can taste that steak right now."

"That ain't all," Jason said, as he and Johnson emerged from a small, dark room off to the left. "Had them a smokehouse, too. Look what we found."

He pitched a vacuum-packed ham the size of a small toddler to another of his team. "Genuine country ham. No refrigeration required. Must be fifteen pounds."

Rick Johnson dragged two dilapidated grocery carts from the depths of the smokehouse storeroom, along with a roll of aluminum insulation they used for the smokers. "Wrap that beef up in this and throw it in the carts. We'll make it back, okay."

A young, rangy-looking orderly, whose name Katie didn't recall, emerged from the pharmacy section, looking oddly out of sorts, despite the others' elation. "I don't know what you expect me to do back there," he said. "Fuck if I know what any of that stuff is or what it's for. Just a bunch of pills and shit."

Katie stood in the doorway of the pharmacy, looking perplexed. The kid had a point. They faced a bewildering array of pills and medicines, but the brand names and dosages were as much a mystery to her as they had been to him. "Take whatever you can carry," she instructed. "Just keep them separate and don't mix them up. We'll have to let the staffers sort it out."

Despite the sweltering heat, the team was elated as they dragged their burdens back toward the hospital, laughing and joking with one another, borne by thoughts of the meals to come.

Katie Mendoza hung back a little, staggering under the weight of her two backpacks and scowling at the buzzards that circled overhead.

Jason circled back around to where she lagged behind the rest, concerned that a heat stroke might be creeping up on her.

"Want me to take one of those?"

When she looked up, he saw that she was crying, tears streaking her dirty face, smudging as she furiously wiped them away.

"Corporal? Katie? What's wrong? By God, if I were you, I'd be dancing right about now. You sick?"

"No!" She made to hurry away but was hampered by the weight of the foodstuffs.

He had no trouble catching up. "Then what is it? You saved the day, you know that, right?"

"I haven't saved anything—" she insisted, guilt holding her heart in a vise grip. "It's all my fault …."

"I don't get it. You're wrong there. This food's going to go a long way to keeping us all alive, at least until—"

"Until what?" she demanded. "Somebody shows up to rescue us? Not happening, Jason. Or haven't you figured that out yet?"

He sighed heavily, the air escaping his lungs in a rush. "You can't torture yourself. And you can't give up hope. Hell, I learned that much back in Iraq."

But Katie wasn't backing down. Her heart hurt too much, and the tumult of emotions caused her to blurt out the first words that came to her lips. "And what happens to us if we do get rescued? Even if we manage to stay alive? A court martial? More prison time? They don't care about people like us, Jason. They never did."

Jason's face fell. "Look, lady, if you want to take that attitude, I ain't gonna argue with you. But I'm not going to agree with you, either. I got better things to think on than being prosecuted."

Already ashamed of her outburst, she straightened her shoulders, yet remained angry and defiant. "Yeah? Well, think on this. None of the stuff we got today is going to do us a damn bit of good without some water. And unless you know how to change seawater to fresh water or feel ready to drink your own piss, we're practically out and still have no diesel for the generators."

The weight of her statement hit him like a punch to the gut. He stopped in his tracks, staring mindlessly at the bay that sparkled in the sunlight, then at the ocean that stretched out to sea. He stared at the water's edge in the distance as he trudged along, as if the sun-drenched shores might hold an answer. *Water, water everywhere ...* played in his thoughts in an endless loop. She was right, of course. They'd die of dehydration sooner than starve.

Chapter Thirty-Nine
Hart Senate Office Building, Washington, DC

General Drucker sat fidgeting in front of a microphone across an empty bench reserved for the Committee on Homeland Security and the Secretary of Defense. He was visibly uncomfortable with all the scrutiny. To his left sat the head of the CDC. To his right, a representative from FEMA. There was also a uniformed officer from the Coast Guard. Military police stood at the threshold of the room. Drucker didn't like the look of it, not a bit. He knew nothing good ever came out of an investigative hearing.

The chairman, Senator Crowley, cleared his throat unnecessarily as he entered the room and stepped behind the podium. "I must remind everyone in this room before we begin that this is a closed investigative hearing. Nothing you say or hear leaves this room. Your attention, please. Lights?"

The ceiling lights dimmed as a wide-screen TV monitor slid silently from the ceiling. After a moment, black-and-white drone footage of the Cynthia Mitchell Causeway appeared on the screen, followed by an endless lazy loop of images that showed the extent of the hurricane damage:

the wrecked bridges, buildings, and shopping malls reduced to matchsticks; upended cars and trucks; ruined boats; the odd house still standing; and piles and piles of once-majestic palms and tropical vegetation rotting in the sun. Last but not least was a series of aerial shots of the University Hospital medical complex, showing first the gaping holes and shattered face of the huge glass wall, then as the drone circled around for a final view, it hovered for a final, long moment above the loading dock on the inland side where Jason Carter's hastily scrawled message could be read as clear as daylight:

PLEASE HELP US

The room was utterly silent as the screen went dark and the lights came back on. No one knew where to look.

Crowley stepped back to the podium and cleared his throat once more. "What we have here, ladies and gentlemen, is a real clusterfuck."

Senator Crowley went on: "General … " and paused for a brief second that felt like ages, "can you tell me about the current activities at the Dugway Proving Grounds?"

"We have been America's testing site for chemical and biological weapons since 1942. We also house the US Army Chemical, Biological, and Radiological Weapons School. We used to conduct open-air tests of various pathogens that cause disease in humans, animals, and plants. Most of the work we currently do is classified," Drucker replied, in a clearly-rehearsed manner.

Based on the evidence he had received, Crowley wanted to push General Drucker to admit what he was up to. Crowley tried a different approach. He turned his attention to the Coast Guard representative.

"Captain Lennox," said Crowley, "can you tell me about the Coast Guard's role in the response to Hurricane Beatrix?"

"Thank you, Mr. Chairman," replied Lennox. "The Houston-Galveston Command has several airborne and sea assets in the area but they have been unable to provide logistic support due to poor visibility and weather conditions. We are in the dark, to put it simply," stated the captain.

"So you mean to tell me that, effectively, the Army is running the show?" asked the senator.

"As much as I hate to admit it—yes," replied the captain.

"Thank you, Captain Lennox. You are excused from this hearing."

Senator Crowley looked down at his notes for a moment before addressing the representative from the CDC.

"Dr. Singh, can you tell me more about the Crimean Congo Hemorrhagic Fever and what you did after Hospital Galveston reached out to you?" asked Senator Crowley.

Oh, for Chrissake, thought General Drucker. *Get on with it, can't you?*

"Crimean Congo Hemorrhagic Fever, or CCHF, is a viral illness that causes a coagulopathy, which can kill its host. When University Hospital in Galveston reached out to us, we did not know how to proceed. There is no effective medical treatment or vaccine. There are only a couple of labs in the entire world that work on the CCHF virus. We made a call to our counterparts at the Army and mutually decided this pathogen needed to be contained before this incident became a public pandemic mistake. Dugway assured us they would work to get an appropriate quarantine in place," said Dr. Singh.

"Thank you, Dr. Singh. You are excused from this hearing," said Senator Crowley.

The general was alone. His heart sank deep in his gullet and he wished for nothing more than to disappear completely.

"General," Crowley continued, "so we have established the Army was in total control of the situation on the ground with a total monopoly of information. The CDC has told us that they completely deferred to the US Army regarding conduct of the quarantine in Galveston. Can you tell me more about Operation Sunset, or are you going to continue to feed me bullshit?"

The General was stunned. He wasn't prepared for this. *How does he know about Sunset?*

After taking a moment to regain composure, Drucker sputtered, "Operation Sunset is a project to study the Crimean Congo Hemorrhagic Fever."

"I know that, general!" replied Senator Crowley sternly. "I'll ask you again. Tell me about Sunset, and I'd like to remind you that you are under oath."

"Operation Sunset is a project to test a weaponized strain of the CCHF virus," Drucker stated.

"Why are we developing weaponized strains of *any* virus? No legitimate country in the world is doing this. Even North Korea is a signatory of the Biological Weapons Convention," said Senator Crowley.

"Emerging threats, Mr. Chairman. We live in an era of asymmetrical conflict where cyberattacks and disinformation campaigns on Twitter go hand-in-hand with military campaigns. We saw that in Ukraine. We saw it in Syria. We don't even know for certainty if the 'Chinese virus' was indeed something that jumped from animal to human in the meat market or if it was manufactured and released by accident because other governments aren't as forthcoming. We need weapons with plausible deniability," said Drucker.

"You are no better than the terrorists or the insurgents we are fighting every day. Shifting the blame doesn't make you a hero. It gives you a delusional sense of safety and patriotism. You are by all accounts a murderer. It didn't matter to you that you instructed the local Guard unit to destroy the causeway and let a lethal virus run its course on a civilian population—on US soil, much less." replied Crowley.

Drucker was at a loss for words. He knew he was done.

"Dugway has been operating with little oversight for decades under complete secrecy. First, Skull Valley sheep incident. And now this? Your actions rival those of the Soviet Union, who covered up the Chernobyl disaster," continued Senator Crowley.

Drucker knew there was little he could say to help his cause. He couldn't defend the Skull Valley sheep incident—when Dugway released VX nerve agent into the air, killing six thousand sheep in Utah—just because it was before his time. This had led to a reluctant admission by the military, causing international infamy, which led President Nixon to ban all open-air chemical weapons testing.

Drucker pleaded to the committee. "Even the Soviets used their own soldiers to help remove radioactive debris to contain radiation spread to the public. Regardless of our difference in opinion, we have a vaccine, Mr. Chairman. We've never had a chance to perform a test in real world conditions, and we might never have gotten to it without this incident," said Drucker. "This vaccine could save the lives of our boys overseas. You don't see the sacrifice we make for people like you who've never fought for the flag. To you we are expendable," the general continued passionately.

"That's not your call to make, general," Senator Crowley replied.

Senator Crowley turned to the Secretary of Defense who had been silent up until now.

"Based on the testimony that I have heard today and by the power vested in me by the Uniform Code of Military Justice, I am recommending we proceed with detention and a trial for general court-martial. Good day, General Drucker."

Drucker felt nothing at all as he marched between the guards the short distance back to his rooms. Forty years of service repeated in his thoughts like a broken record, keeping time to the sound of their boots on the tile. Desert Storm, Desert Shield, Enduring Freedom, and Iraqi Freedom. Each of his tours of duty flashed before him in an endless loop. And not once, *not once*, in all those forty years had he believed he was fighting for anything but the greatest country in the world. And all for nothing, an entire career blown away in a puff of smoke. There would be a court martial, prison, disgrace.

Once inside his chambers, General Drucker listened as the guards locked his door and took their positions in the hall. He removed his uniform and folded it, lovingly fingering his Medals of Honor and evidence of rank. He walked over to the radio and switched it on just as "Carry On My Wayward Son," came blaring on. Going to the closet, he pulled on his favorite robe and sat heavily at his desk, where he pulled out a small highball glass and a flask filled with twenty-year-old bourbon he'd been saving for a special occasion. Pouring himself three fingers' worth, he leaned back and sipped appreciatively, looking out the window, absorbed in the way the brilliant sunlight played with the clouds, trying to pick out the shapes they made—a lion, a child, an angel.

He smiled then and reached into his desk to remove his M9.

He loaded a clip, turned off the safety.

With one last look at the angel in the clouds, he put the barrel deep in his mouth.

And pulled the trigger.

Chapter Forty
Galveston University Hospital

He's so strong, Danica thought. *He can't die. Please, not him.* Still in her HAZMAT suit, she wet a washcloth in a bowl of lukewarm water and carefully bathed Shaka's face, neck, and arms, gingerly lifting his mottled limbs and allowing the breeze from the still-running fans to cool and dry him as best they could. With every day that passed, she felt more and more as though time itself were going backward as supplies and food ran dangerously low. And every day, all use of modern medicine was rendered nearly useless, forcing her to rely more on her physical examination skills rather than monitors. The grocery store pharmacy raid had even yielded two giant jars of old-fashioned Mexican quinine, still used for malaria south of the border, which the hospital staff had decided to administer in minute doses to the fever victims on the chance that using anything they had was preferable to using nothing at all. It was a different kind of medicine than she was used to practicing—ironic, in its way. Before the storm, they'd had a wealth of technology, miracle drugs, and systems to communicate with experts all over the world. Now, as physicians, they had only their instincts, their experience, and their dedication. Not to mention that mysterious chemistry that existed between doctor and patient, their faith in one another and themselves that a patient could, and would, survive.

Danica's own emotions in turmoil raged in her head. She spent years building up a persona of not wanting to end up like her mother, stuck in a loveless marriage and completely dependent on the other person. Danica had been driven down this path to be different. She aimed to be self-reliant with a career she could be proud of, but in reality, all it had done was lead her to years of loneliness. Her past relationships kept haunting her, enabling her to build up walls. After meeting Shaka and almost losing him, she realized she was making a mistake by shutting him out.

Life can be taken away at any moment. Life doesn't pause for you to get your shit together, she thought. *You can't pencil in life moments to make them happen on your own timeline; they have to be experienced in the present.* Danica wanted to open herself up to the possibility of love and happiness, to an equal partner who brought out the best in her.

She looked at Shaka for a long, silent moment as his chest rose and fell in a slow, shallow rhythm. "You were wrong about me," she said softly. "I never felt powerful, only humbled. Especially now, with you. All I can do is be here for you in the present. I am so sorry for everything. Please come back to me."

After checking on the others, she sank wearily into a nearby chair and reached for his hand, his crazy warmth penetrating even the three layers of protective gloves she wore. And only dimly aware that she was almost certainly dehydrated and possibly hungry, she fell into an exhausted sleep.

When she awoke, Dr. Kirsten Stone was standing by her side, holding an ice-cold bottle of water. "Your blood work showed you are negative for the virus," Dr. Stone said in the speaker with no particular inflection. "You can't sleep here. Get up, decontaminate, and meet me in the hall."

Reluctantly, Danica did as she was told. Somewhat refreshed by an all-too-brief shower and a fresh suit of scrubs, she found Dr. Stone just outside the chamber, still holding the bottle. Danica stared down at it stupidly as the other woman thrust it into her hand. Bottled water seemed to be as much a thing of the past as ice cream or fresh eggs.

"Drink it. You need to. You're undoubtedly as dehydrated as the rest of us. Did you get a meal last night?"

Leaning heavily against the wall, Danica took the bottle and drank it slowly, swallowing gratefully, a host of questions crowding her thoughts. "Where?" was all she could manage to voice aloud.

Dr. Stone attempted to explain. "Apparently, some pilots over at the aviation school at Ellington saw Jason's SOS on Twitter and wrapped a few hundred cases of water bottles in as much bubble wrap as they could get their hands on. They loaded their Piper Super Cubs and left the bottles on the hospital's helipad. It's not nearly enough, but it will see us through a few days, if we're careful. I also had the orderlies harvest anything they could from every water cooler in the complex. It's not exactly fresh, but it will do for cooking and sterilizing, if necessary. God knows we can't boil anything from outside. Even if it weren't mostly seawater, the storm's stirred up a real toxic stew. Chemicals, bacteria, sewage, you name it. And we cannot afford to make anybody sicker than they already are. With our supplies of antibiotics running low, one more infection like CCHF could wipe us all out. Meanwhile, drink up—this one's on the house."

Danica nodded, marveling at the way Dr. Stone kept her cool, no matter how dire the situation. She might look like hell, just as Danica supposed she did, but otherwise it could have been an ordinary conversation, about ordinary things.

Dr. Stone continued, "When you're finished, see if you can find the kitchens. Follow your nose. I think they're on the fourth floor, east wing now. I know they're cooking up everything they have to delay spoilage in the absence of refrigeration. And you look like you could use a cup of bone broth or two."

"Yes, ma'am. Now that you mention it."

For just a moment, Dr. Stone, her expression an odd mixture of disapproval and compassion, dropped her mask of cool efficiency and looked Danica straight in the eyes. "And I'm afraid I cannot allow you to spend your sleeping hours in the isolation unit, no matter what your situation with Dr. Sen."

Her cheeks on fire, Danica glanced away, startled, her mind fumbling for some explanation. "But I was just—"

Dr. Stone held up her hand calling for silence. Any hint of compassion Danica had seen in her eyes was gone. "Spare me the heroics, doctor. I don't have the time or energy. Your personal life is none of my business, but you have spent the last three nights in the isolation unit at Dr. Sen's bedside. That alone puts you at greater risk of infection. As you are essential personnel, I cannot risk you. Do you understand? I'm taking you off the isolation rotation entirely for now."

Stricken, Danica stared at her. "You can't—"

"I just did," Dr. Stone replied coldly. "Unfortunately, Dr. Sen's survival does not depend upon your presence in his room, Dr. Diza, no matter how pure your intentions. On the other hand, the survival of many of our other patients depends on your treatment. You can't focus on one at the expense of the others or of yourself, understand? None of us can."

Just then, Billy Andersen interrupted. He and Dr. Wong had readied the first batch of vaccines for willing volunteers in the quarantine unit.

"What's your background in immunology?" he stopped to ask Drs. Stone and Diza.

"I'm not a fellowship-trained immunologist or anything, but I did take three semesters in medical school and worked in a virology lab the summer before I joined medical school," replied Danica.

"Fine, I'll keep this as simple as I can," Billy continued

Danica hated the mansplaining, but she would set aside her lecturing for another time.

"Our initial experience with the Bulgarian vaccine was that it generated a response; however, the antibodies it generated could not neutralize the CCHF virus without—"

Danica nodded. "Periodic booster shots."

"Exactly," continued Billy, still unaware of his faux pax. "We've isolated the PLA-2 protein from the snake venom. Due to its virucidal properties, they've used it against hep C, dengue fever, and yellow fever with good results. This vaccine utilizes a complementary approach using short RNA to increase PLA-2 expression which gets upregulated like it does during envenomation from a snake bite. It is effective at reducing the hemorrhagic complications during an active CCHF infection. So after isolating and growing the living virus, we needed to find the right protein medium to render it inert enough not to spread or destabilize during the purification stage. Researchers have years to experiment; we don't. We did have a crude vaccine that looked promising in a murine model, but we haven't tested it on primates and usual lab animals. They were largely evacuated before the storm, so we had very limited choices. Funny world, isn't it? To think the authorities would see fit to rescue lab animals before people."

Danica was glad Billy and Dr. Wong were there. Even though animal equivalency was a long shot, it was better than nothing given the current context. She knew that at the end of the day, if they survived, it would be thanks to their efforts, not hers.

"Anyway, the kitchen's that way, two floors up. Get something to eat, Dr. Diza. Your regular rotation begins at the usual time. I'll alert you of any changes," said Dr. Stone.

Danica found she could indeed follow her nose as she made her way to the kitchen. As she turned a corner in the corridor, the rich scent of soup followed by a tantalizing mixture of citrus and spice filled the air, making her stomach growl. As she got to the door and peered around the bend, she saw the tall lithe form of a woman standing over a couple of pressure cookers that merrily belched steam into the stifling atmosphere. Huge piles of roasted meat lined the countertops, interspersed with vats of rice, beans, and, miraculously, whole crates of grapefruit.

The woman turned and, seeing Danica on the threshold, raised an eyebrow. "Yes?" she asked. "Can I help you?"

"Dr. Stone sent me up for something to eat. Just came off duty." It was only partially a lie. "I'm Dr. Diza. Danica. I don't think we've met."

Katie managed a thin smile and shook Danica's extended hand. "Pleased to meet you," she said. "Katie Mendoza. I used to be a corporal, with the Guard. But I don't suppose that matters now. Sorry about the chaos. We managed to forage some supplies out on the island, but we have to get them cooked as fast as we can. Nothing's going to last long without refrigeration."

Danica glanced around. "Can I help you at all?"

"Maybe. But first, when was the last time you ate anything?"

Danica hesitated, trying to remember. "I'm not sure," she admitted. "Maybe thirty-six hours?"

"Sit." Katie gestured to one of two stools shoved under a counter. She pushed a small, saran-wrapped container of what looked like Jell-O in Danica's direction. "Bone broth," she explained. "I've been using the beef bones and the cooking water in the pressure cookers. Pure nutrients. When we cool it off like this, it makes a kind of gelatin—easy to digest but hydrating too." She watched as Danica brought the cup to her lips and slurped appreciatively. "Don't go too fast," she cautioned. "It's richer than it looks. No use in having it all come back up again."

When she was finished, Danica sighed gratefully, amazed at how fortified she felt. "That was wonderful. Thanks."

"You're welcome," Katie smiled. "Did you get water?"

"I'm okay. Dr. Stone gave me some."

"Sorry I have to be so stingy," Katie replied. "But we have to ration. Especially with water. Just no other way to get us through. Take one of those grapefruits, though; they're going fast in the heat. Might as well use 'em rather than lose 'em."

Danica spied another stack of cases in the far corner of the room. "Baby formula?" she asked.

"Yeah," Katie answered. "Weird, isn't it? One of the guys found a whole room of the stuff up by what used to be maternity. Dent and scratch stock. I guess, before the storm, the hospital would send back whole cases if even one can was dented or had a torn label or something. Only this time, nobody came to pick them up. You'd think they'd have sent them off to one of those godforsaken internment camps, wouldn't you? Up at Crystal City or Tornillo even. But no, assholes. Pardon my language."

"No argument here," Danica replied.

"Don't get me wrong. America's a great country and I was proud to serve it. For a while. Anyways, when I found out there was only one infant here with us, I commandeered a few cases for down here, to cook grits and rice and things like that. We can even give it straight to those who are too sick to eat. Fat, protein, vitamins, and calories. That's all that matters."

"You all are amazing, Jason, you—the whole team. Thank you, truly."

"Not so much." Katie shook her head. "Hell, I never would have thought of it myself a week ago. But like they say, necessity is a mother, isn't it?"

Just then, one of the pressure cookers let out a high squeal, making them both jump. "Those will be the breakfast grits," Katie said, reaching for a potholder to release the valve. "Once that cools a bit, you can help me portion them out."

Katie turned then, bumping her shin on a stainless-steel cart and letting loose with a yelp of pain. "Shit!"

Danica rose. "What is it? What's wrong?"

"This damn leg." Katie flinched, settling herself on a nearby stool. "I scratched it the other day, jumping off that grapefruit truck. It bled some, but not much, so I wrapped it up. When we got back to the hospital, I cleaned it up and found some ointment. But it didn't seem to help at all. I don't know what's wrong with it."

Danica pulled over her stool and propped up the other woman's leg. "Let me have a look. Does it hurt?"

"Not much, aches a little. At least, until you smack it hard as I just did." A sheen of sweat broke out on Katie's forehead and she sucked in deeply. "I guess I've been too busy cooking to notice much."

Grabbing a set of latex gloves from a nearby dispenser, Danica put them on and gradually peeled back the large bandage that covered the wound. She had to fight back the bile that rose in her throat at what she saw. A huge, red and purple gash, roughly the size of a baseball, pulsed angrily against Katie's olive skin, its center oozing blood in a slow, inexorable stream.

Katie's hand flew to her mouth, her eyes wide and terrified. "Oh God! It's not that fever, is it? Have I got it?"

Danica tenderly drew the bandage back over the wound. "No, no. But you've got a wound with a possible infection, a bad one. Probably from the water outside. Did you get it wet at all?"

Katie nodded, fighting back tears. "We had to come back through some of the floodwater, but I was careful to clean it in seawater from the bay before I bandaged it up. My mom always did that; she said the saltwater helped things heal."

"Well, she may have been right, but not this time. That is how you contract necrotizing fasciitis, which happens when a wound is exposed to floodwater. I don't think this it is what we're looking at, but it is a deep wound, and we will need to take cultures and clean the wound properly. Good thing we caught it early. I'm going to need to get you upstairs. Do you think you can walk?"

At that moment, Danica's beeper went off and a text from the nurses' station near the isolation unit flashed before her eyes. *Mr. Nguyen has passed. 4:08 A.M. RIP*

She fought back a terrible desire to scream as rage, fear, and helplessness rose like fire from her insides. She tore off her latex gloves and began texting frantically.

Prepare a room away from CCHF patients. I'll need an antibiotic IV set up stat. Broad spectrum cephalosporin, fluoroquinolone or tetracycline, whatever we've got left, as strong as you can make it. Get whatever lighting you can find. We're on our way.

As if by magic, Jason Carter burst through the doorway, smiling and rubbing his hands together. "I swear to Jesus, once this thing is done with, I'll be up before dawn for the rest of my days. What's for breakfast, beautiful?"

Katie looked up at him, shaking her head, her lips trembling in the effort not to cry.

He glanced first from her face to Danica's, confused. "What's wrong? What is it?"

Danica stepped closer. "You think you can carry her down to the third floor?"

"If I carried you, I sure as hell can carry her."

"Lift her in your arms, not over your shoulder. We need to get her to a room upstairs, stat."

"But you still haven't told me what's wrong!"

Danica drew a deep breath. "She has a nasty gash on her leg. We need to clean it up and close it to make sure the infection doesn't spread. Thankfully we caught it early."

Scowling, Jason bent and lifted Katie into his arms as though she weighed nothing at all. Danica held the door as they passed her.

"Let's go quickly."

She led the way down what seemed like the endless corridor, into the stairwell and down what seemed like an eternity of steps. And with each step, each breath echoed the thought. *All of these immunocompromised patients and poor sanitary conditions mean an increased risk for bacterial infections. One good festering bacterial infection could kill us all.*

And with each step, Danica Diza fought the specter that dogged them—her words part mantra, part plea, part prayer.

Not today, please. Not today.

CHAPTER FORTY-ONE

Galveston University Hospital, ICU Conference Room

Members of Dr. Stone's ad-hoc ethics committee stood outside a small conference room on the fourth floor at 7:00 a.m. for their first meeting. It was one of the few non-clinical spaces with power, owing to its shared electrical supply with the isolation ICU. An uneasy feeling permeated the room as the participants trickled in and took seats in faux-leather office chairs around a circular particle board table.

Danica looked at the painting of a sandcastle hanging in the otherwise blank, unadorned room. It seemed out of place to have such a difficult meeting with heavy consequences against such a whimsical backdrop. But the image also strangely gave Danica hope. It reminded her of the annual sandcastle competition that the city of Galveston sponsored in the summer, which was her absolute favorite. She loved watching the artists' imaginations come to life in intricate castles and designs. Galveston was known for its many festivals, such as the crawfish boil festival, Lone Star Biker Rally, Oktoberfest, Dickens on The Strand, and, of course, the biggest festival of all, Mardi Gras. Galveston's Mardi Gras was the second biggest in the country after New Orleans'. Each festival was more splendid and over the top than the other. She didn't know when they would emerge from all the death and despair, but she knew it couldn't last forever. She hoped she might even make it to see another Sandcastle Day or maybe even dress up for the first time to attend Dickens on The Strand.

Dr. Stone entered the room, still in the same navy-blue scrubs from the day before. She hadn't slept yet so she had to be mentally and physically spent. She was still working around the clock to ensure operations remained ongoing. Dr. Stone distributed a neatly-printed census to each member in the room. Her obsessive tendencies were evident and helpful during times like this. She had grouped patients by the equipment and medication shortages by which the hospital was affected. Danica glanced at the first four names on the census arranged by diagnosis:

Sixty-five-year-old female Eva Jons with chronic myelogenous leukemia.

Eighty-nine-year-old female Leonarda Gamboa with liver cirrhosis.

Sixty-seven-year-old female Dorothy Wichmann with bilateral subdural hematomas on aspirin.

Thirty-two-year-old male Art Lindley with perforated bowel from ulcerative colitis and severe anemia.

"Thank you all for participating in this meeting. As a physician here in the US, I never expected to have to make these sorts of decisions. For those of you who don't know me, I am Dr. Kirsten Stone. I trained in Emergency Medicine but currently lead as chief medical officer. How about we quickly introduce ourselves before moving on?"

"Hi, everyone, I am Alondra Partida. I have been an ICU nurse for eight years. Previously, I was a social worker for the prison system, working with inmates who delivered in prison and placing the newborns either into the foster care system or with families. I did that for over ten years, but watching these babies going through withdrawal was life-changing. Addicted moms delivered babies that were then shoved into foster care where they were potentially abused and neglected. That took a toll on me. Those kids were set up for failure from the moment they were born. So I decided I needed a change and went back to nursing school."

Alondra grabbed her cup of coffee and gulped a big sip, waiting for the next introduction.

Dr. Dunn took off her long white coat and hung it on the chair, revealing clean purple scrubs. "Good morning. I am Dr. Amy Dunn. I completed law school at the University of Houston Law Center, then decided I would rather be a doctor and did medical school at Baylor College of Medicine. I went on to complete my internal medicine residency at UTMB and now am a pulmonary critical care fellow here."

Danica was next in the circle, "Hi everyone. I am Dr. Danica Diza. I did my medical school at UTMB as well, and now I am finishing up my last year of family medicine residency as the chief resident."

Last but not least, the pastor was ready. "Good morning. I am Father Patrick McDaniels. My daughter is a patient here who was too sick to be transferred. I want to thank everyone for the exceptional care you all have provided to patients. I know it is not easy being away from your own families and the comforts of home, then to have to put others first. Needless to say, it is much appreciated."

Dr. Stone led on. "Good to have you all on board. I appreciate it. The first order of business is how to ration our blood products amongst the first four non-CCHF patients on this list," she continued. "As you know, our CCHF ward has consumed quite a bit. Volunteers are still donating, but our blood bank is out of O negative completely."

"I think we should prioritize blood products by age," said Dr. Amy Dunn. Dr. Dunn had a certain stoic quality about her but was still an obvious choice for the ethics committee. She'd had a legal background prior to her change of heart and switching careers in medicine. She had never practiced law, owing to big picture challenges, but she knew more about it than anyone else left on campus. "Like how they used soft utilitarian guidelines with the ventilator shortage during the early stages of the COVID-19 outbreak in Italy."

"Hang on, now" Danica piped up. "Our situation is more complicated than age alone. The thirty-two-year-old with a perforated bowel needs a real surgeon. I can debride wounds and struggle my way through a section, but I don't fix bowel perfs. We also can't life-flight him off the island. What would be our rationale to give him PRBC units that could otherwise be used more successfully elsewhere?"

A pang of guilt suddenly overcame Danica as she spoke those words. Somehow, she thought avoiding Shaka's name would make her think less about him struggling with the infection.

Others nodded in agreement.

Danica continued after swallowing a lump in her throat. "Maybe we can reach out to the Houston hospital's transfer center or even send out a Hail Mary communication to the Guard to evacuate any remaining surgical patients. It's clear that someone with a surgical diagnosis needs a surgeon, or at least someone capable of operating."

Dr. Stone said, "That's a great point, Dr. Diza. We need to evacuate surgical patients. We didn't foresee that Dr. Sen would be out of commission."

Just then Alondra, the veteran ICU charge nurse, piped up. "You really mean to say that a sixty-five-year-old with chronic myelogenous leukemia—a terminal cancer— is going to get blood products over a thirty-two-year-old?"

The room went quiet as everyone pondered the question she posed.

"This is just nuts. I can't believe we are making calls like this. This whole committee is bullshit," Alondra elaborated.

"This is not about what we would do under normal circumstances with all the resources available to us. We have to make a decision. We can save one life—or let both perish. It comes down to our ability to take care of these patients first. Then the medical risk factors for each particular diagnosis," said Dr. Stone, trying to moderate the tension in the group.

Danica flipped through the census. She could see there were forty-four names in total. She thought to herself that this was going to be a long meeting.

Alondra continued, "You people are out of your fucking minds. We are going to have to answer to someone—the law, the media, family members—after all is said and done. I don't want to be in an orange jumpsuit after this hurricane."

Dr. Stone relented. "Okay, how about we table the discussion on blood products? Everyone has made some good points."

Next, she said, "We are short working dialysis machines. We can't do scheduled dialysis for the pre-existing renal patients who are still on the island."

Dr. Amy Dunn said, "This doesn't even need to be discussed in an ethics committee. There is a simple clinical answer to this. We only dialyze symptomatic patients. Check their labs for acidosis or hyperkalemia. Done."

Danica was exasperated with Dr. Dunn not seeming to understand they were in the middle of a hurricane. "Hang on, it's more complicated than that. We don't have the capacity to draw labs daily, so we can't see if patients are developing acidosis or electrolyte problems. What really matters is preventing these dialysis patients from getting pulmonary edema bad enough to need a ventilator."

Alondra nodded in apparent agreement. There was no one else Danica respected more in the ICU than Alondra. Danica remembered her first night as an intern covering the surgical ICU, getting called by Alondra about a myocardial infarction patient developing cardiogenic shock. Without hesitation, Alondra was ready to hang a bag of norepinephrine while Danica was still fumbling for the cardiology fellow's phone number. It had been a humbling experience she wouldn't forget. Alondra had never rubbed it in her face. The event taught Danica that it's not just the degree behind your name, but also the clinical experience.

"So, let's do daily EKG checks and auscultate for rales every four hours?" said Danica. "We have an almost unlimited ability to get ECG tracings, and everyone should have a stethoscope. If anyone develops a peaked T wave, rales, or other signs of fluid overload, we dialyze."

"Couldn't have said it better myself," said Dr. Stone.

"Finally, something that makes sense," said Alondra in an approving tone.

"Next item on our agenda are infusion pumps. The power is gone, so all are functioning using their internal batteries. Once those are depleted, any patients who are on intravenous medications given in a continuous manner are going to be in a whole lot of trouble. Any ideas?" said Dr. Stone

"Let's try to find out who really needs to be on continuous dose intravenous medications," said Danica. "Those who can be weaned to a scheduled dosing wouldn't need to be consuming any valuable pumps."

"It doesn't need to be that Draconian yet, Dr. Diza. How about we just place the IV bags underneath the patient themselves?" said Dr. Dunn. "The patient's own mass will help push fluid and any piggyback medications with it like a hydraulic pump. We could titrate the rate by putting a roller clamp on the line."

Alondra was visibly astonished by the practical, timely, and applicable comment Dr. Dunn had made. Perhaps she had gotten Dr. Dunn all wrong.

Danica took a surreptitious glance at her phone one more time. What had started out as a brief meeting had already taken more than an hour.

"We've done a good job so far, but still haven't addressed what we are going to do about the blood products," said Dr. Stone.

An uneasy realization finally dawned onto everyone in the room that a thousand little decisions about every aspect of patient care were going to be made each day the quarantine continued. Sometimes ingenuity would solve a problem before it became an ethical crisis, but that wouldn't always be the case.

"This discussion can go on for days without getting anywhere. We aren't going to have a perfect algorithm. We need to make some decisions," said Danica.

"I know," said Alondra. "But I'm worried what's going to happen to us after this quarantine is over. We are going to be scrutinized for our actions."

"That's the whole point of assembling this committee," said Dr. Dunn. "There is legal precedent for that if we look back at natural disasters like Hurricane Katrina. Do any of you remember Dr. Anna Pou?"

"Vaguely. I remember she was an ENT here before Ike and would come by occasionally to do a bedside trach in the unit," piped up Alondra.

"Well, after Katrina, she was charged with criminal felonies regarding the handling of several patients at the Charity Hospital in New Orleans. Many organizations expressed concern that the case would set a bad precedent, causing practitioners to reconsider whether to help during a disaster. Ultimately, the indictment was unsuccessful," Dr. Dunn continued.

"Well, that's just perfect," Danica muttered sarcastically.

"I'm not saying that you're wrong, Alondra. This can still come back to bite us, but this committee will be helpful in defending whatever decisions we have made," Dr. Dunn concluded.

Dr. Stone chimed in. "Okay, so let's move forward with the recommendations we have made in this committee, effective immediately."

Dr. Dunn, Alondra, Danica, and Father Patrick looked at one another and nodded in agreement.

"In the meantime, let's get in touch with the transfer center of different hospitals in Houston to medivac surgical patients from our hospital. I've also instructed Jason to prepare a team to retrieve the supplies the Guard had dropped off since the surge receded. Hopefully we can find some diesel for our generators. Is there anything anyone else would like to add?" Dr. Stone asked.

"I'd like to pray for our patients before we adjourn," said Father Patrick in his heavy Irish accent. "You have made some decisions today with a heavy heart, but I have seen your intentions are pure. I'd like to say some words from the Church of St. Francis."

He continued, "A Blessing for the Sick: Lord Jesus, when you were on earth, they brought the sick to you and you healed them all. Today I ask you to bless all those in sickness, in weakness, and in pain. For those who are blind and who cannot see the light of the sun, the beauty of the world, or the faces of their friends: Bless your people, O Lord."

Alondra bowed her head in silence.

Father Patrick continued, "For those who are helpless and who must lie in bed while others go out and in: Bless your people, O Lord. For those who must face life under some handicap, those whose weakness means that they must always be careful: Bless your people, O Lord."

Danica paused in reflection. Her thoughts turned to the patients intubated and sedated in the ICU. Each patient was probably separated from a loving family member out there, someone who was agonizing over what was happening to their loved one.

"For those suffering from a debilitating or terminal illness and for their caregivers: Bless your people, O lord. For those who are near the hour of death and in their final struggle: Bless your people, O Lord," continued Father Patrick.

Danica's mind drifted back to Shaka. He was alone, lying there in the CCHF wards, probably in a febrile delirium. She hoped with all her heart he wouldn't succumb to this virus. Danica wasn't a religious person, but the pastor's words were evocative and moved her.

He finally ended, "Almighty God, as we ask your help for our brothers and sisters who are ill, we ask you to help us to be healing people in our time and place. May your love touch others through us, and may we help all people to live in peace. We ask this through Christ our Lord. Amen."

CHAPTER FORTY-TWO
Harborside Drive, Galveston, Texas

A week-and-a-half after Hurricane Beatrix made landfall

The team of six, consisting of the old supply run crew of Jason Carter, Katie Mendoza, Rick Johnson, and three other volunteers from the hospital, looked out onto Harborside Drive. Equipped with pickaxes, ropes, and the pistol, they moved together in utter silence, surveying the landscape. Once a crowded area where numerous festivals had taken place and crowds from all over Texas gathered, Galveston now lay as a wasteland. Cars were toppled and pieces of junk faced opposite directions, piled against one another as toys in a junkyard. Evidence of the water damage on the buildings and landscape was apparent, marking how high the surge had been. Boats that were once parked in the harbor were in the middle of the streets.

They moved in formation, protecting each other, looking for any sounds that would alert them to survivors, but there were none. The only sounds were of waves crashing and the gulls squawking at anything salvageable. The scent of salt mixed in with the musk of death and decay rolled through with every breeze.

According to Katie, her kayak was close to the port near pier twenty-one, less than a mile away. They were going to retrieve the kayak to use as a vessel to put supplies in to drag back. Billy had traveled in the middle of the night and had had to abandon his boat due to the debris. Unfortunately, he didn't remember exactly where his boat was, but he felt hopeful that it was close to the kayak and retrievable to use.

Going through the ruins of the city, the team remarked at how time seemed frozen. They took longer than anticipated to travel. The sun blazing down was torture enough, indicating the scorching heat wasn't going to have mercy. They needed to work quickly and efficiently to make it back before nightfall.

Jason looked at Harborside and gazed at it as what could have been—the hustle and bustle of city life. Jason was from Galveston and had lived here for a while before deployment, so he was familiar with Galveston's history. The city was no stranger to outbreaks. In the 1800s, Galveston had suffered yellow fever and cholera epidemics. The city became Texas's largest city and the busiest port. For a time, the Strand was known as the "Wall Street of the South." The Strand had weathered through civil war, fires, and hurricanes, and now it would survive an outbreak as well. Since Jason was from around the area, it was hard for him to not get nostalgic for a place that had been through as much as this city had. He believed it would again come out of this disaster stronger than before.

Katie cried out, "The kayak is right there! Fifty feet to the left, tied up next to the dolphin watch boat."

Jason focused and said, "I see it. Help me get it out."

Working in tandem, Jason and Johnson grabbed the yellow kayak and pulled it out of the water, laying it out on the ground. The paddles were no longer there, probably at the bottom of the ocean. They tied the kayak to their waists with rope and dragged it along the street, making headway toward Harborside Drive again.

"Can't believe this, man. I grew up here, past Sixty-First street," Johnson said to Jason. "I had always evacuated, so I haven't ever been through a hurricane on the island itself. Experiencing a hurricane while it's happening in your hometown is a whole different experience."

"I know, man. It's tough. Nobody should have to experience this," Jason managed.

"You know, I had a job in the Port of Galveston over there on the right. The port handles all types of cargo. I worked in one of the cargo ships before it became a huge cruise ship terminal. Now all you see are these large Carnival Cruise Lines vessels, Royal Caribbean International, and Disney Cruise ships docked outside every week, ready to take another group of travelers out to sea. My family and I went on a Carnival Ecstasy to Cozumel and Progresso years ago. It was one of the best vacations of my life. If I survive this, I will definitely take my family on another cruise. This event has taught me that life is too short. Might as well start living now."

Jason nodded. "That sounds great, man. You should enjoy your time with family."

Walking along Harborside as fast as they could, towing their fashioned cargo, they continuously searched the landscape, but it remained devoid of any signs of life.

Suddenly, one of the other guys shouted, "Look over there on Twenty-Fifth street! It's all gone!"

His face turning from shock to sadness, Johnson asked, "Did you guys ever ride on the Ferris wheel on Pleasure Pier? That was a blast. Sucks that it's not there anymore."

Everyone stood a moment longer, looking at the ravaged area that was once Pleasure Pier, an amusement park that had opened in 2012. The pier had been destroyed before, by Hurricane Carla in the mid 1900s. It later housed the USS Flagship Hotel, which was demolished after Hurricane Ike.

"The ocean claimed it all back again, thanks to Mother Nature. Maybe they will build something else now. Let's keep moving," Jason urged them on.

Navigating over heaps of garbage, they got to the Pelican Island Causeway crossing. They made their way up the bridge, taking in the scent of the sulfur piles that once stood as mountains, now barely visible. At the top of the bridge, they stood sweating. They looked at the magnificent view of the bright blue ocean in the distance with the sun high above. On any other day, it would have been a beautiful day.

Jason saw the railroad tracks to the left and wondered where they went. "Johnson, is this the rail that connects to Houston?" he asked, circling up next to Johnson to get a better look.

"I think so. I think the railroad splits off once it gets to Texas City. Part of it goes to Houston and the other part to Fort Bend, I believe. Why?"

Jason continued, "I lived in Galveston for a while and I learned about the history of this area."

Johnson looked up at Jason with a raised eyebrow, "You a history buff? Wow, would not have pegged you to be into history."

"Not a lot to do when you are unemployed, looking for a job. Anyways, I remember learning about the Galveston-Houston Electric Railway, which ran from downtown Houston to downtown Galveston back in the 1900s. It started at the railroad museum in downtown Galveston and ran parallel to I-45. It's the old tracks you see next to the causeway when you're driving. It used to be the fastest inter-urban line."

"Yeah, I think I remember that, and there was talk about re-establishing some of the train service between Galveston and Houston. It would have made the commute a lot easier," Johnson chimed in.

Jason nodded. "I wonder if they ever got that railroad functioning?"

Johnson kept walking at a brisk pace. "Even if it was functioning, you said it yourself that it runs parallel to I-45, which they blew up to kingdom come, so the chances of the railway still standing are slim to none."

"You're right. Just wishful thinking, I guess," Jason retorted.

By the time they crossed the bridge, they had all taken off their shirts due to the heat and unbearable humidity. A few hundred yards directly in front of them was a rolled over sailboat with the sail ripped to shreds.

They approached slowly, taking in the vessel. Jason thought the boat had surely been a fabulous piece of work back in its pristine days, appropriately named Pandemonium. It was dirty white with brown wood and gold fixtures.

"Let's see if anything was left on the boat," said one of the other team members, Ross, as he strode off onto the board, taking off his gloves.

Johnson and Ross climbed onto the boat and went inside, lifting the door to where the living quarters were.

Johnson came back up with a grin on his face. "There are only a few beers and some water. Also found a first aid kit."

"Great. Let's start with the liquid hydration first and continue on," Jason said excitedly, also hoping no one would have a heat stroke.

They cracked open the beers on the railing and drank them in one long chug. It didn't even matter that they were warm. The taste was refreshing and crisp. The short drink break boosted their team morale.

They gathered their belongings and continued on.

Up ahead, they passed a ripped-up TxDOT I-45 exit sign, houses taken apart like delicate flowers, and storefronts left in shreds as though they'd been made of paper.

Solemnly, they continued their journey. Jason saw Katie limping on her injured leg as he caught up to her. "We are getting closer. How are you holding up?"

"Hanging in there. Feeling defeated in a sense. Wondering how some people just follow orders." Katie looked down.

"Everyone operates differently," Jason said, trying to catch her eye. "Some people just follow orders without feeling any remorse. I have done things as a soldier in Iraq just because I was told to do it and bullied by propaganda. The problems start when you develop a conscience and no longer want to be a part of the façade."

Katie's voice cracked. "If I hadn't … hadn't … blown up the bridge, we wouldn't be in this situation … ."

Jason stopped and grabbed Katie's arm, forcing her to look at him. He saw the tears streaming down her face. The rest of the team walked ahead, giving them privacy.

"Look, whatever you did doesn't matter. It is in the past. You can't change the past. If you hadn't done it, someone else would have and we would still be in this situation. The point is you came here to help in any way you could. Most people would not have done that."

Katie wiped the tears from her eyes. "You are right. When I joined, I just wanted to help people. Create a better, safer world. Wasn't that a grand delusion?"

Jason empathized with Katie, his own past constantly in the forefront of his thoughts. "Trust me. I get it. I wanted that too. But reality is far from the truth. Regardless, you came here by putting your own life at risk. That has to count for something."

Katie took a deep breath and gathered herself. She nodded her head, and, after a moment, she started to walk away with her head held slightly higher.

Jason slowly turned, unsure if he was able to convince her, but knew his words resonated with her. He caught up to her once again and pulled out the city map.

Katie pointed onto the map at the location where the military had dropped the supplies. The site was close to where Harborside Drive and the causeway meet, which was a six-mile trek in one direction.

"Why that location and not any closer?" Jason asked.

Katie shrugged. "I don't know. I imagine it had to do with logistics and the smoke haze that diminished visibility."

Jason knew this trip was going to be an excruciating all-day ordeal. Katie said there were generators and diesel tanks there, along with medicine and some food. Jason feared whether it was all still there, had been taken by other survivors, or lost to the ocean. He couldn't think about that right now.

"Holy shit. Over there," belted out Johnson.

In the distance, they could see the giant collapsed causeway that once carried people onto the island, now laying in pieces, with some parts submerged on the ocean floor. North of them lay six black rectangular plastic boxes of supplies, five diesel tanks, and three portable generators. There was also a torn-up life raft in the water near the supplies.

Johnson worried aloud, "How are we going to take all of this back? That's a lot of supplies, and we do need all of it—but we physically might not be able to take it all back with just us."

Jason told the guys, "Let's load up as much as we can into the raft and kayak."

They got to work, moving everything, unlatching the boxes to see which ones had priority, in case they had to leave anything behind. Taking inventory, Jason noticed different types of medical supplies, ranging from medicines to IV kits, along with non-perishable food. The most critical pieces of equipment were the generator and the refuel tanks. Even after they loaded, they had two of the black boxes, two diesel tanks, and a generator they couldn't fit and were going to have to carry back.

Crouching down to take a rest, Ross said, "Should we only take what we can drag back? Leave the other stuff? It took us a little over three hours to get here, and with this added weight, it's going to take much longer to get back."

Jason caught his breath. "No, we need all of these supplies. I don't even want to leave one piece behind if we don't have to. We don't know if we will be able to come back for it."

Johnson wiped his brow and looked around. "Let's see if we can concoct something from the debris around us," he said. "You know, build something we can use to pull back the equipment easier, rather than carrying it."

Ross rolled his eyes. "Yes, let me get some wood, a saw, and some nails, and I will get right on that."

"Don't be a dick," Johnson snapped. "I meant maybe we can use a piece of wood to build some kind of raft we can put some of the tanks on, instead of carrying them all the way back. We can pull it using the ropes."

"That might work. Getting everything over the bridge is going to be the hardest part," Jason chimed in.

Ross walked around near the edge of the harbor, closer to the water. The water was muddy brown and reeked of seaweed and fish. He saw some driftwood, but nothing big enough to use to haul supplies. He walked to the other side of an overturned Dodge Charger, to see around it. It was a shame to see a car that powerful laying waste. He turned his head and found exactly what he was looking for—a paddleboard. It was beaten up, its colorful neon colors chipped off. Part of the end was broken off, and shattered pieces of wood showed through. But it had survived the storm, so it would survive this, he thought. He pulled up the board where the group was.

"Put the rest of the supplies on here and tie them down with the ropes so they can be pulled, like the kayak and the raft," Ross ordered.

They worked in silence, quickly and efficiently.

Finishing the last knot, Jason asked, "Okay, everyone good?"

Mendoza and Johnson were wrapping the last of the supplies with rope. Once that was completed, they were ready to head back.

"All right, let's go home," Jason said.

Jason, Katie, and Johnson pulled the raft; Ross pulled the paddleboard; and the other two pulled the kayak.

The sun wasn't directly over them anymore, but they could still feel its sting. They walked in silence, only focusing on breathing and the task at hand, slowly making progress.

After what seemed like eternity, they finally made it to the top of the connecting causeway to Pelican Island.

"Hold on a minute! Let's take a break. I need some water," Jason yelled to those ahead.

Pausing, Jason looked out to the ocean to observe the sunset, feeling hopeful and appreciating nature's beauty even after its fury.

After the sun had set twenty minutes later, Ross said "Ready to go? I don't know about you guys, but I don't really want to be here after dark."

In agreement, they resumed their posts and carried on. The way down the bridge was much faster and less taxing.

Every inch of Jason's body ached with pain and soreness. The military had trained him relentlessly so he would be physically able to carry out any orders given in his missions. He hadn't been on a mission in years, yet here he was, challenging his body to its core, in a different type of agony. He wasn't used to this level of workout anymore, and his body was letting him know that.

Jason's arms and legs felt like jelly and were ready to give out. He called out for another break. More than four hours had passed since they had begun their return, and the team still had a mile and a half to go. Jason sat down on what used to be the sidewalk, leaning his back against an old factory building. He closed his eyes to rest for a few minutes.

"You okay?" Katie ask with concern, handing Jason a bottle of water.

With a small smile Jason replied, "Yeah, I will be fine. Just worn out. I guess I'm not as young and fit as I used to be."

"Hey man, we wouldn't have gotten this far without—"

Katie's words were cut off by a bark close by. Jason and Katie perked up and tried to listen for it again. They could hear the whimpering and barking of a dog trying to catch their attention.

Johnson said, "I think the dog is in this building."

Jason got to his feet and walked all the way around the building, looking for an entrance. He spotted a broken window. He wrapped his shirt around his arm and broke all of the remaining glass in the frame. Slowly he climbed inside. It was pitch black.

Johnson rushed to the window, clicked on a long flashlight, and handed it to Jason. "Use this!"

Jason took the flashlight and shone it around, trying to get a better look at his surroundings. Big pieces of factory equipment sat on an assembly line. A breeze blew in a scent of something rotten—or dead. The smell was so strong, he gagged multiple times, but he continued. The barking was getting closer. At the end of the assembly line, he found a big, brown, rusted door. He stood close to it, trying to listen to the other side.

He heard a whimper.

He turned the knob and tried to push the door open, to no avail. He tried to pull it, but that didn't work either. He shook the door to break the lock. He hit it with his shoulder multiple times to break it, but the door was sturdy. He took out his pistol and shot the hinges. Part of it loosened up, and he climbed through the door. The vile smell was even stronger here, and he couldn't hold it in. He retched out all the water he had just drank outside until there was nothing left except acid.

Jason heard the bark again, and now he knew he was in the right room. He lifted his flashlight to get a better look. A stairway led to the storage basement that was still partially flooded. He looked at the stairs to see how far down it was, but he couldn't tell. He didn't like what he was about to do or the idea of it, but he had no choice.

In one swift motion, he jumped down into the water. It was ten to twelve feet deep. He swam around the debris, using his flashlight and the noises as a guide. At the end of the room, he abruptly hit a wall. He searched every inch of that wall above water to see if he could see the animal.

The dog kept whimpering and barking. Jason realized the dog was on the other side of the wall. Searching for another way across, Jason swam to the bottom.

He found another door. He jiggled it, but it wouldn't budge.

He had to go back up for air.

He was a decent enough swimmer, but he didn't know what was on the other side of this door. He didn't have an oxygen tank and had no clue how long he would have to hold his breath.

He contemplated leaving the dog and heading back, when he heard another whimper, he knew he had to save the animal.

Jason took a deep breath, dove down as fast as he could, and kicked the door a couple of times.

He was running out of oxygen.

After coming back up for air, he dove down again, throwing his whole body against the door. On the eighth try, it finally gave way.

Jason swam to the top of that room and caught his breath, treading water as he took in a few deep breaths.

Something licked his face.

He took out the flashlight and saw a filthy dog in front of him, overjoyed to see him. He couldn't help but smile at the dog, and he began to pet him. Carrying him back was going to be a challenge, since he couldn't tell the dog to hold his breath.

Jason looked around the room to see if there were any exits. He couldn't find any. He had to go back the way he came in. He got close to the wall with the door. Looking into the dog's eyes he pleaded with the animal to hold his breath at the right time to get to the other side.

Jason took a deep breath and plunged in, holding onto his new furry friend. Swimming as quickly and efficiently as possible, he made his way to the top. Jason's head broke the water first, and he quickly brought the dog out of the water and looked him over.

The dog barked again.

Jason looked him over with a flashlight and saw a few injuries. The animal was ragged, flea-bitten, and caked with mud, with knotted, tangled strands of fur. Jason thought the dog looked like a poodle or terrier mix with brown and white fur, no more than twenty pounds. The dog retreated as Jason got closer to examine his front paw, which looked broken, and he had a few scratches.

After Jason petted the dog a few times, it tried to get up, peered at Jason, and got closer to nuzzle into him.

Knowing the dog was terrified, Jason held the shaking canine. He tried unsuccessfully to dry the dog with his shirt. Now his shirt smelled like a dirty dog, and the poor thing wasn't much drier. Jason carried him the rest of the way out of the factory. At the broken window through which he'd entered, Jason whistled as loudly as he could to get someone's attention.

"He's back! He's coming," Katie yelled, panicked.

Jason handed the dog through the window, then crawled out.

The crew, delighted to see a furry friend, took turns petting their new member.

"We thought something happened to you," Johnson said.

"It just took a while to get through the doors in the basement. He either got left behind or got stuck. I couldn't leave him."

Jason put the dog on the raft on top of the supplies, and they continued their journey.

Ross, his thoughts clearly pained, looked at the dog. "Yeah, I get it. I miss my dog. He went with me everywhere."

***

When they finally dragged their haul to the hospital entrance and successfully completed their mission, Katie, Jason, and the rest of the team were thrilled. Despite the exhausting day, they felt a new sense of joy and accomplishment.

"Get this stuff inside, pronto!" said Jason. "Call everyone available to help unload. Play this right and you just might see a hot meal tonight! Some sweet tea too! How'd that be for a change, huh?"

Jason flashed a wide grin as he grabbed a portable generator in each hand and swung them inside, handing them over to Ross. Exhausted or not, this crew couldn't help but return Jason's enthusiasm. And no matter what their personal feelings, they couldn't help but offer him their respect.

The man closest to Jason took up the cry. "Hey, that mean we get fried chicken and fresh biscuits too?"

Jason forced a laugh and clapped him on the shoulder. "You dreaming, now, dude. You know that, right? Hey y'all, Johnson over here thinks he's some kind of comedian!"

Jason then turned his attention to Katie. "Can you take my new buddy and get him cleaned and patched up? I will come and get him after we are done unloading."

Joy spread across Katie's face. "Sure thing."

She picked up the grimy ball of fur and took him inside.

The laughing and jokes continued as the team headed for the first stairwell. They lined up bucket-brigade style and hand-to-hand passed the supplies upward. Half an hour later, the task was nearly done, and Jason had completed the inventory. Feeling accomplished, Jason squared his aching shoulders. He climbed the last flight of stairs toward the isolation unit in search of Dr. Stone to give her a bit of good news.

CHAPTER FORTY-THREE
Ellington Airfield, Houston, Texas

Governor Mark Willis looked through the Manila folder marked "Top Secret." Never in his five years in office had he come across confidential material like this, nor had he been personally briefed by the Secretary of Defense. This was one of those times when the truth was stranger than any fiction. From his office in Austin, the state governor stared glumly out the window, down into the broad boulevards below that surrounded the building. Thousands and thousands of protestors spilled out and lined the streets, shouting and chanting and raising a series of crude, handmade signs:

"Let Us Bury Our Dead!"

"Survivor lives matter!"

"Do Something"

"The buck stops with FEMA?"

And worst of all, they held what seemed like endless photos of the missing—smiling kids and waving grandmothers, beloved cats and dogs, even whole families, lost in the storm or separated in the chaos of the aftermath.

"I can't let thousands of homeless citizens back onto the island. The whole damn place is a poison pit. A garbage dump. Got the environmental report this morning," he said to his attorney general, Adam Briar. "It's going to take years to clean up. And without federal funds to do it, the private sector will have no interest in returning to the island."

The governor put his face in his hands and rubbed his weary eyes. "I have a press conference out there in fifteen minutes. The public wants answers. And now I'm bound by secrecy."

Silence fell until the nervous AG cleared his throat and coughed softly. "Governor? If I may?"

The governor opened his eyes. "Yes? What is it?"

Briar continued, "I'll go downstairs and field some opening questions from the press. Give them updates from elsewhere around the state and the usual refugee contacts and aid stations. It'll buy you a few minutes."

Governor Willis waved in the general direction of the door. "Fine. Go."

Briar rose to his feet and came around the table to clap an encouraging hand on the other man's shoulder. "Now, don't be so hard on yourself. Who was it that said, 'You can please some of the people all of the time, you can please all of the people some of the time, but you can't please all the people all the time'? Lincoln, wasn't it?"

The governor sighed again. "I think the word was 'fool,' not 'please.' And it was P.T. Barnum."

Briar shrugged. "Whatever. Politics is just another kind of circus when you get right down it. But I think you're missing the point."

The governor glanced at his watch as it bleeped a reminder. "Which is?"

"Those people out there are scared, okay? And they're angry. They've lost goddamn near everything—homes, businesses, family members, their livelihoods. And they don't know why. They feel like they're being punished for something they didn't even do. Shit, that hurricane was no more their fault than it was yours, but that doesn't stop them for looking for somebody to blame. That's why they're so fired up about those folks in the hospital. They didn't do anything wrong, either. And yet there they are, little more than prisoners. You can preach all you want about God's will, Governor, but that's bullshit too. They take it personally because it *is* personal. It happened to them. But you have to rise above all that, show them you're in this together. Throw them a bone, for Chrissake. Give 'em some hope. And you sure as fuck can't do that while you're sitting here feeling sorry for yourself and trying to cover your own sorry ass. Much less kiss somebody else's."

The governor's watch beeped another warning. He rose to his feet and pulled on his jacket, running a hand through his hair. "Nice speech, Adam," he said sarcastically. "Can I count on your vote in November?"

Briar chuckled. "No harm in baiting a bear every now and then."

"Fine. While I'm down there, get on the phone with Patriot Electric and get an update. Galveston needs to get back on the grid in the next twenty-four hours. I don't care what it takes. And call the Federal Aviation Administration to lift the temporary flight restriction. We need to let Red Cross fly supplies into Scholes while the bridge and harbor are out. You!" he shouted at a nervous-looking National Guard officer standing at the door. "Come with me down to the podium. A crowd just loves a guy in uniform."

Once in the elevator, Governor Willis cast the young officer a sidelong glance. "Can you sing, kid?"

"Sing?" He was clearly confused.

"You heard me."

"Uhhh … a little."

"Good, that's all you'll need. I have an idea. Got a phone on you?"

"Yes, sir."

"Good, get on YouTube. I want you to look up a song called Galveston by Glen Campbell."

Moments later they emerged from the capitol amid a flurry of cameras and an ocean of cell phones raised high to record the proceedings. Reporters, ready with a barrage of questions, waved frantically as Governor Willis stepped to the podium. The governor held up his hands for silence, waiting until the furor died down.

"Morning, everybody. Just to let you know, I won't be taking any questions right now; our attorney general has doubtless filled you in on as much as we know about the disaster at this time."

A chorus of angry "boos" rose from the assembly.

"As you know, we in the State offices have declared a state of emergency in Texas, but the wheels of bureaucracy turn far too slowly, and for Texans at risk, that is simply not good enough."

This time, angry cries of "Do something, do something!" echoed from the sea of faces before him.

Like some preacher leading a prayer, the governor again paused, this time for dramatic effect. "I know you are tired. And homesick and grieving too. I know only too well what it is to wake up in unfamiliar surroundings, not sure of what the next day will bring. Therefore, I want you to know that as of this morning, I have issued an executive order. Within the next twenty-four to thirty-six hours, Galveston Island will be restored to the grid, including the University Hospital Complex. We may only manage to give them a few hours at a time, but it will be something at least, to help ease their suffering. And when power is restored, we will have the National Guard and other first responders manning the pumping system to clear the floodwaters from the streets. It will take time, but it's a start. And the good Lord knows we have to start somewhere!"

Cheering erupted in a wild cacophony.

The governor smiled. He'd given them something. It sounded like hope. When the commotion died down, he spoke once more into the microphones. "Ever since this disaster befell us, I've had a song stuck in my head. You ever have that happen? This one was written nearly fifty years ago, I reckon. About a homesick soldier, yearning for a city by the sea. Well, here's another soldier, and I wonder if you might sing that song with us today. Let it rise from your voices as a new anthem. Not one of loss and despair, but one of hope and faith and conviction. Galveston will rise again, bigger, stronger, and better than before. And together, we will snatch her from the jaws of destruction to rebuild and reclaim our treasure—our jewel of the sea."

When the applause died down, the young officer stepped forward. In a shaky baritone, he began to sing. Almost immediately, a thousand voices rose with his own, and the moved officer could feel the tears rolling down his cheeks. Together, the crowd sang the kind of hymn the world would not soon forget.

Chapter Forty-Four
Galveston University Hospital

Lights came on, and long-muted, darkened TV screens flickered to life, drawing people's attention like worshippers to the altar. Monitors hummed and computers bleeped and door locks clicked. Within minutes, every possible outlet in every possible room was once more in use. Voices rose as arguments ensued and a couple of scuffles broke out over what to charge first—the portable battery chargers or their beloved cell phones.

When the lights first came back on, the ones left at the hospital didn't know what to make of it. Some cried, some laughed, and others stared around them in awe. Danica decided to take advantage of the newly-restored power to check out Katie's wound as she had just come back from the supply run.

As Danica walked through the hospital, she saw patients sitting up in their beds or, if they were able, moving out into the labyrinth of corridors like sleepwalkers, blinking in disbelief. "What is it?" they asked each other. "What's happening? Have they come? Are we being rescued?"

And everywhere, people gathered around the air conditioning vents and fans, enjoying the cool air that now blew into an atmosphere that for so long had hung with heat and humidity so dense it had been almost palpable. No ocean breeze could have been more refreshing or welcome, no mountain gust more invigorating.

Outside of Katie Mendoza's room, Danica put on her gloves, surgical cap, and mask, then entered the space, away from the isolation unit, followed by a nurse. Danica smiled behind her mask as Katie sat up in bed, then motioned to the nurse to raise the bed electronically so Danica's patient could better face her.

"I don't know where or how they managed to restore the juice," Danica said surprised to see the dog in Katie's bed. "But let's use it while we can. How are you feeling today and who is this little fella?"

Katie's eyes were grave. "Better." Katie began gently stroking the dog's fur. "This is Casper. Jason rescued him from an abandoned building on our supply run and I cleaned him up. He has grown on me."

Danica smiled at the adorable dog as he got closer to Katie either terrified or as a gesture of protecting his new owner. Danica motioned to the nurse, who began to cut away the bandage and packing from Katie's right leg.

Katie averted her eyes as the dressing came off and was duly deposited into a waste container.

Danica bent low over her small, healing, open incision, using a small, portable flashlight with a magnifier to illuminate the open gash. When Katie spoke again, her voice was barely above a whisper. She licked her dry lips. The whole scene reminded her of something out of an old war movie. Only this was no movie. Not by a long shot. Try as she would, she could not keep the terror from her voice. "What's the verdict, doc? It's been almost five days. Am I gonna lose my leg?"

Squinting over the incision for what seemed like an eternity, Danica finally straightened up and switched off her flashlight. She walked around the side of the bed and faced her patient, meeting Katie's eyes full on. "As you know, the wound was a bit deep and infected. But it is responding to the antibiotics, and it looks like it is healing well. And that's very good news."

The air escaped Katie's lungs in a rush. "Whew! I was thinking I might need that leg." She managed a wan smile.

Danica shook her head. "But you have to be patient," she replied. "With your immune system already compromised by the lack of water, an inadequate diet, and sleep deprivation, it will take everything you've got to continue to fight off the infection. So, you're just going to have to let your body heal. Try to take it easy now. So far, you're doing fine, but you're going to have a hell of a scar. It is going to take time." She motioned to the nurse to begin repacking the wound.

Katie leaned back against the bedclothes, relief washing over her like a river. "And here I thought my scars would come from being on active duty with the National Guard. Thank you."

Danica leaned against the wall across the room. "Jason told me that you were the one who blew up the last access point at the bridge, but that you didn't agree with the orders that were given, so you swam to join us to aid in any way you could."

Ashamed, Katie looked down. "I enlisted because I wanted to make a difference and be just. But everything about this order of seclusion was unfair and unjust and I couldn't stand by it. I followed my orders because I vowed to, but it didn't mean I couldn't ease my conscience. At that moment, climbing the ranks seemed trivial compared to the sentence I passed down to the island and everyone on it."

Danica reached for Katie's hand, holding it in her own. "You have gone above and beyond to ensure our safety and to allow us to make it thus far. Just remember, healing is sometimes a whole process, but given how these things can go, I'd say you are a darned lucky woman, Katie Mendoza. Forgiveness will come with time, but the first step is to not be so hard on yourself."

Katie managed a real smile this time. "Lucky? Wow, I've been called all kinds of things, doctor, but I think this is the first time anybody called me lucky. Can I ask you a personal question? Why did you go into medicine?"

Danica sat down on the chair next to Katie. "Honestly, I didn't know what I wanted to do for a long time. My mother instilled the value of having an education early on, but it wasn't until I was in junior high that I decided on becoming a physician. I lived close to the border, so my mother and I would visit an orphanage in Mexico, to distribute school supplies and clothes. It changed me drastically. The kids there had all sorts of medical needs.

"I vividly remember one kid, Joseph, who was ten years old. His mother was a prostitute, on various recreational drugs. When Joseph was born, he stayed in the NICU for a while, because he was so small and he was withdrawing. He was taken from his mother and placed at this orphanage. As he grew, the orphanage struggled to take care of him as an autistic child. They tried to do as much as they could, but Joseph was non-verbal and depressed. He would engage in self-inflicting harmful behavior. When I met him, he showed me his pictures. He was an artist and had these amazing paintings. He used these paintings to express how he felt. He would draw or paint pictures of people he would meet, places around the orphanage, and things he liked. They were so beautiful. Joseph played the piano and the xylophone and he was remarkably talented. He was a sweet child who was unable to get the care he deserved."

Danica became quiet for a moment, then took a breath and continued. "I came to the conclusion that donating materials and spending time wasn't enough. These kids, this community, needed true health care. I decided I wanted to pursue medicine. I did multiple mission trips after that to Peru, Puerto Rico, and helped out at relief hospitals during major hurricanes in Texas. It just felt so good to help others. It was a passion. I chose family medicine because you get to take care of all ages and do a little bit of everything. You build these long-lasting relationships that are truly special, and it makes it all worth it."

Katie had tears streaming down her eyes. "I want that feeling. I want to find purpose like that and aid others in any way I can. Thank you for sharing that."

Danica smiled back. "Anytime. You have a good heart. You came back to be with us, and that in itself says a lot about you. Katie, you will find your passion too. Just give it time. Anyway, I'll be back around again tomorrow to check on you. Just call if you need anything."

As Danica made to leave, Katie called after her. "What's with the lights anyhow? Did they drop any more supplies? Is somebody finally coming to rescue us?"

From the threshold, Danica glanced longingly down the hallway toward the isolation unit, thoughts of Shaka never far from her mind. "I wish I knew. But your guess is as good as mine at this point. The supplies you, Jason, and the team brought back that the National Guard dropped off should help and last for a while. There haven't been any new fever victims, at least. So this quarantine has to end sooner or later."

Katie smiled to herself as she laid back down in her hospital bed, for being able to help clean up the mess she had caused.

Chapter Forty-Five
Galveston University Hospital

In her makeshift office just off the lab, Dr. Kirsten Stone frantically typed a communication to the CDC and Guard:

No new cases of CCHF. Need to evacuate non-infected surgical patients via airlift. Immediate aid essential; supplies at critical lows.

She thrummed her fingers nervously on the desktop, awaiting a response. When it finally came, the answer only added to her frustration.

Awaiting further instructions re: evacuation. Advise current status of the infected. Perhaps we can assist from here. Utilize stork packs as needed.

"And fuck you too," she said aloud. "Fucking bureaucrats."

Forgetting for a moment that recently she herself might have been rightfully called a bureaucrat, she scowled at the computer and signed off, snatching up her phone as she left. She hurtled through the door of the lab, almost knocking down Dr. David Wong, who was standing transfixed in front of a flickering TV screen with tears running down his face. She glanced up to the screen, which was replaying footage of the statewide protests, this time from Dallas.

Dr. Wong wiped his eyes and pointed. "You see that? The woman in front? My God, that's my wife. My Patty. She doesn't know—she doesn't even know I'm alive because I haven't been able to get in touch with her."

Frantically, he fumbled through his pockets, hunting for his phone again.

"It's still on the charger, more than likely." Dr. Stone answered coldly, her professional demeanor descending on her face like a mask. "Look, I don't mean to be insensitive, David, but calling your wife can wait. CDC tells me they want our updates on the infected, and they aren't giving me any info at all about when they're lifting the quarantine. Or when they might begin airlifting non-infected patients out of here. We have power for now, but from what I gather, it's only for a few hours a day, at best. But at least we got more supplies that Jason and his crew retrieved to keep power going to the essential equipment. I also couldn't get any info on further supply drops. So, it looks like we've got to give them everything we've got before we get anything at all. You follow me?"

Dr. Wong nodded mutely.

Then both doctors focused their attention on Billy, who sat at a table nearby, staring at both of them, wide-eyed. Dr. Wong moved closer to the table.

"What the hell are stork packs, anyway?" Dr. Stone asked. "CDC said we should use them."

Dr. Wong shrugged. "Don't know. Never heard of 'em."

"I have," Billy piped up. "But I didn't think they were real. More like a rumor—an urban legend."

Dr. Stone pinched the bridge of her nose, trying hard not to lose her patience. "That doesn't answer my question, Mr. Andersen. What are they?"

"I first heard about 'em when I was getting security clearance to work in the biocontainment lab. Supposedly, in high-risk situations and facilities like this, the government stashes emergency supplies somewhere, either on the premises or nearby, for use in the event of a calamity. Hot locations are cities that are routinely hit by hurricanes or other natural disasters. These stork packs contain food, medicine, water, stuff like that. The exact locations are kept top secret and only shared with maybe three of the top dogs. So—"

"With a skeleton crew, we're not likely to discover where they are until we get out and can contact somebody who actually knows." Dr. Stone sighed heavily. "Terrific. That's just great."

Just then, a voice came over the intercom. After being silent for so long, the once-ordinary sound made them all jump: "Code Blue. All available personnel to the isolation unit, stat. Code Blue. All available personnel to the isolation unit."

"Damn it!" Dr. Stone cried. She shoved the phone in Billy's direction. "Keep sending that message about the stats of the infected until it goes through, then follow it up with location of stork packs. I'll be back as soon as I can."

With that, she ran out the door of the lab, sprinting in the direction of the isolation unit, just as the lights flickered and dimmed, and then finally went out. A soft but discernible moan echoed from everywhere at once, as the disappointed patients and staff once again fell into the stifling dark.

Dr. Stone managed to spare a single glance at the wind-up watch she wore on her wrist, the retro-style dial glowing eerily: 6:00 p.m.

Bastards, she thought bitterly. *Three hours? They give us three lousy hours?*

But with what seemed like the last of her strength, she kept on running. Maybe she could still save a life.

CHAPTER FORTY-SIX
Galveston University Hospital

Lost in a fever dream, Shaka tossed and turned in his bed in the isolation unit.

He saw himself as a child, no more than six or seven, holding tightly to his mother's hand as the mourners filed past his father's casket, the stern outline of his father's profile just visible above the edge. The scent of the funeral arrangements made his head spin. As did the never-ending array of perfumes and aftershaves of his aunties and uncles and cousins as they slowly moved past in a seemingly-endless procession, coming to offer their tear-soaked hugs; solemn, sweaty handshakes; and sniffling kisses. His knees wobbled in his short pants and he tugged irritably at the unfamiliar necktie and jacket he wore, too warm for the day.

His grandmother hurried forward and slapped his hand away, scowling at him. "Behave yourself, boy," she hissed. "Make your poor father proud, son. You're the man of the house, now."

The boy pondered what that might possibly mean. How could he be the man of the house? His father had been an international businessman, forever traveling to some other place, some other country. Shaka remembered the few exotic-looking toys his father had brought him—marionettes from Thailand, a puzzle box from China, and once, a windup robot from Japan. Shaka recalled the brush of whiskers against his cheek on the rare occasions his father was home long enough to tuck Shaka in, but the man himself was an utter mystery, as remote as that cold, waxy profile in the coffin.

In his dream, a kind of chorus rose, covering the casket in a lilac mist, as though those angelic voices were made of the air itself. The scene faded and the people filed out, floating into the ether.

Shaka cried out. "Mommy? Mommy? Do people know when they're going to die?"

Her warm, amber eyes looked down at him, blinking back a fresh bout of tears. "I don't know, Shaka. Maybe they do. Maybe sometimes."

"Did my father know?"

Her sigh was like an evening breeze. "I don't think so, Shaka."

He'd reached for her then and she lifted him in her arms, though he was too big to be carried. And for the first time and a long time after, only her embrace and hers alone could make him feel safe again.

And yet his mother had known—known for years—that she was going to die too. But she kept her secrets of living with breast cancer well-hidden. In the way we sometimes never really see those closest to our hearts, Shaka had never noticed the way the whites of her eyes had yellowed with time, or how frail she had become, or how pain had etched its signature in the lines of her forehead and the deep creases from her nose to her mouth.

"Just a little arthritis," she told him.

Preoccupied with his pre-med classes in college, Shaka had believed her and remained oblivious to the way illness worked on her like an artist's eraser, smudging away her strong lines into shadows, her light into shade.

When she passed away, Shaka sobbed openly, inconsolable and lost, staring down at her gentle face as she lay in her casket.

One of his uncles took mercy on Shaka and finally led him away. "Don't take it so hard, Shaka, my boy. Let her go. She was so brave for so long."

Dazed and disbelieving, Shaka only stared at him. "So long? What do you mean? I spoke to her just two days ago. From school. She said she was fine."

His uncle looked away, a little sheepishly. "You mean you didn't know? She never told you?"

Rage had boiled up in Shaka, then, tightening his heart in a vise. "Told me what?"

"Her condition." His uncle hesitated. "They offered her the surgery and chemotherapy, of course. Gave her a grim chance of survival even with both therapies combined. She chose to do a round of chemo and hated how it made her feel unlike herself. In those days, she thought quality of life was better than quantity, so she refused further treatment. Said she would rather live her life fully, no matter how short it turned out to be. She never wanted you to see her dying or be her keeper. And then, when you graduated, and she felt like a weight had been lifted, she was happy, truly happy. In that moment she knew you would be okay and she could let go."

The dream faded, and the mists rose around him, even as the pain in his heart cut through him like an angry knife.

She never told him. She never let him in. She pushed him away because she wanted him to focus on himself rather than being her caretaker. Right there and then he had chosen his path; he would become a surgeon, a fine one. The best he could be, even if only to honor his mother and to alleviate the guilt of missing his mother's sickness and pain.

He was on the beach then, transfixed at the sight of what seemed like thousands of candles fluttering in the ocean breeze. Everywhere, small memorials had sprung up in the sand, with piles of flowers and crude homemade tin and wooden crosses; some with sugar skulls and Styrofoam gravestones; some draped with rosaries; some with Mardi Gras beads. Others with photographs and endless messages of mourning to the missing and the dead.

"Have you seen Jorge Ochoa? Beloved husband and father …"

"RIP Maria Aldiz"

"Where is Lacey Chan? Last seen …"

"Tomás Rodriguez, only son. Our hearts are broken."

"Justice for Galveston!"

The mists grew darker, boiling around him like smoke. He could barely see the outline of the hospital in the distance. He panicked and began to run. Sweat poured off his body and his breath came short. Never once did that fiery grip loosen from around his heart. Gasping, he doubled over just outside the loading dock where a single candle burned by a makeshift memorial and some faded silk lilies danced under a portrait. He bent closer, hands on his knees, trying desperately to catch his breath, his vision swimming. He shook his head and thrashed, trying to make out the picture.

And it was his own face, smiling back at him. Scrawled across the picture was a question:

"Did you know you were going to die, Shaka?"

And as comprehension dawned, Shaka rose up out of his dream, thrashing against his hospital bed and crying out in an agony only he could hear.

"No-o-o-o!"

He fell back again, suddenly too weak to resist anymore, feeling his spirit rise up, liberated from his tortured flesh. And from what seemed like a great distance came the shrill electric whine of a nearby monitor as it rose, fell, then finally went dead.

CHAPTER FORTY-SEVEN
Galveston University Hospital

Dr. Stone arrived first after the code was called.

"He's flatlined!" bellowed an orderly. "I'll see if I can get the crash cart on portable charge."

"Find one now!" Dr. Stone slammed down the bed rail and straddled the patient, tossing aside the wires and electrodes attached to his broad, muscular chest. She tilted his head back and ran her fingers toward his throat, making sure to clear the airway, positioned her hands for maximum leverage, and began her compressions. *One, two, three ... .*

The orderly handed Danica the crash cart as she skittered into the room, hot on Dr. Stone's heels. She stifled a shriek when she saw who it was in the bed.

Dr. Stone barely spared her a glance. "Danica," she warned, intent on her task. "Remember yourself." *Nine, ten, eleven ...* "Prepare one milligram of epinephrine."

Fumbling through the crash cart, Danica extracted a packaged syringe and stripped away the wrapping with shaking hands.

Arms already aching, Dr. Stone continued massaging with all the force she could muster, keeping time with the throb of her own frantic heart. *Twenty-eight, twenty-nine, thirty.* She paused, bent to his lips, and blew two big breaths. She watched his chest as it rose and fell.

Then: nothing.

"Get some oxygen over here! And an ambu bag. Prepare to intubate on my call!"

And Dr. Stone began again. *One, two, three, four …* The thrusts were unrelenting and hard. "C'mon, Sen. You got this—c'mon! You're young, you're strong. Come back, we need you. Come back, dammit … ."

Danica stood at the ready with her hand in its protective glove, wrapped tightly around the syringe, her thumb poised at the plunger for the next move.

Twenty-eight, twenty-nine, thirty.

Danica gave two pumps of oxygen through the bag valve mask pump placed over Shaka's mouth.

Breathe, breathe … .

Had she seen a movement, some flutter of response, or only willed it?

Dr. Stone turned, leaned back out of her way, and shouted, "Now!"

Danica stepped forward, pushing the epi though the IV access.

Dr. Stone was back on Shaka in an instant, resuming her relentless rhythm, sending the drug coursing through the reluctant muscle that was his heart. *One-two-three-four-five … .*

Danica glanced around the room. How many minutes had it been? Three? Five? Time itself seemed to have stopped, the whole world suspended as they waited for a sign.

The nurse standing by at the opposite side of the bed announced, "His core temperature is high at one hundred and six degrees Fahrenheit." She listened with her stethoscope, felt for a pulse in his neck, and looked for a rhythm on the monitor, then stepped back, shaking her head.

Dr. Stone was now bathed in sweat, panting from the exertion, her own perspiration mixing with that of her patient, but she would not give up. None of them would. Not yet. Danica knew that as surely as she knew her own name. Thirty more compressions, two more breaths continuing the dreaded two-minute cycles of CPR before another injection would be given.

All at once, she spied the chrome casing of one of Jason Carter's makeshift air conditioners in a corner of the ward. An ice maker, pilfered from the kitchens. She turned to the orderly. "Did anyone turn this back on when the power was restored?"

The orderly shrugged.

Danica dashed for the machine, offering up a silent, fervent prayer as she ran. She flung back the lid. A blast of cool vapor rose like steam in the stifling room, greeting her. She frantically fumbled for a plastic bucket stored underneath and filled it with the half-melted slush that swirled at the bottom of the freezer. She ran back and, without waiting, dumped it over Shaka's body.

Dr. Stone continued CPR.

Then, like a miracle, the monitor started beeping with a heartbeat, and Shaka's temperature dropped down half a degree.

One.

Two.

Three.

Four.

Danica thought she might have heard a small sob rise along with the numbers, but it might have been her own. She shoved the bucket back at the orderly. "Get whatever's left in there. We have to cool him down."

"I have respiration," recited the nurse. "Shallow, but it's there." Then, in the next instant, "We have a pulse. Thready and fast, but YES!" The nurse grinned up at Dr. Stone as she helped Dr. Stone down from the bed, sopping wet and shaking with cold and effort. "He's back."

Dr. Stone's glance turned to Danica. "He's back," she said again, her eyes shining behind her protective mask. "That was some move, doctor. With the slush. What made you think of it?"

Danica shook her head. "That's the weird part. I didn't think at all. I just did it. I don't even know if I looked at his temperature, which was sky-high."

"Very unorthodox," Dr. Stone put in, then softened her tone. "But thank you. Even the best procedure can only go by the book for so long before gut instinct takes over."

She sank gratefully into a nearby chair and passed a hand over her eyes.

"Do we intubate him now, Dr. Stone?"

"Just a mask and oxygen for the moment. I want to see if he'll hold his own." Her gaze returned to Danica. "Stay with him tonight, Danica. I'm putting you in charge here. I'll find somebody to cover the rest of your shift."

Danica nodded and returned her gaze, her eyes full of gratitude and something else too. "Thank you, Dr. Stone. And now, the nurse here is going to escort you immediately to the decontamination chambers, followed by the showers. After that, you'll be confined to an isolation room. We're going to need to monitor you very closely for the next forty eight."

A look of surprise flashed across Dr. Stone's face. "What? But why? You can't do that! I'm needed back in the lab!"

Danica knelt in front of Dr. Stone and very gently took her hand. Danica had to break bad news before, but this time, the words stuck in her throat. "Dr. Wong can take care of the lab. I'll let him know as soon as you're settled." She paused for another long moment before she spoke again, doing her level best to mimic the other woman's chilly professionalism. "Dr. Stone—Kirsten. You don't have a HAZMAT suit on. No protective gear at all."

Dr. Stone glanced down at her sopping wet clothes incredulously, even as the enormity of her error took shape in her mind. "My God—I just didn't—how could I have been so stupid?"

Danica squeezed the woman's hand and helped her to her feet, trying not to meet the other woman's now-desperate eyes. "It doesn't matter; none of that matters now. It could have been any one of us, reacting in the moment. The important thing is, you've been exposed to the virus and we need to get you to decon and then to a private room right away. Okay?"

The attending nurse came around Dr. Stone's other side and took her firmly by the elbow, then led her to the threshold.

"You know the drill," Danica instructed. "Start her IV and keep her hydrated with normal saline and give her Ribavirin."

"I don't think we have any left," the nurse interrupted.

Danica stifled an exasperated sigh. "Then give her acetaminophen, for heaven's sake. Use what you've got! Anything to stave off this blasted fever. I'll be in for a blood sample in a couple of hours."

And as the door shut behind them, she sank into the chair nearest Shaka's bed.

The orderlies expertly stripped the sodden bedclothes and put Shaka in a fresh hospital gown. She never took her eyes off his oxygen bag and its reassuring rise and fall, rise and fall.

Only when they'd removed the soiled linens and closed the door softly behind them did she allow herself the luxury of doing what she most wanted to do most, to reach out and take his hand, softly uttering the words that bubbled to her lips. "It's all right now, Shaka. I'm here, I'm right here. You're safe with me."

She might have felt a faint answering squeeze from his strong fingers. But it was enough. At least for now, it was enough.

She bent her head and, for the first time that day, allowed her tears to flow. Though whether it was out of gratitude to a god who had spared him, or a prayer offered up for the life of one who'd risked her own, it was impossible to tell.

CHAPTER FORTY-EIGHT
Galveston University Hospital
Three weeks after Hurricane Beatrix made landfall

J ason Carter watched his team toss the contents of the three meager pallets of supplies the Red Cross had dropped on the beach before their helicopters turned and swung back north to Houston. *Combat fatigue,* thought Jason, and he had seen it often enough, felt it even in himself. The hollow eyes, the hair-trigger tempers, an inability to make even small decisions. Men so tired, stretched so thin, they could no longer reason; they had been reduced to mere reactions: *fight, flight, fuck, flee.* You could give them orders that might be followed, but if one went rogue, things could turn ugly fast.

He wasn't in any better shape himself, and he knew it. His mind refused to focus and he felt as if he were somehow existing outside of his body, three spaces to the left. But he was nonetheless resolved not to lose control of the situation. Like a hawk, he watched his team as they moved, robot-like, through their tasks. Tag-team style, they passed boxes of shrink-wrapped supplies hand-to-hand, to where he stood at the head of the line, ready to lift the parcels onto the loading dock. He passed a hand over his eyes. The heat shimmered in mirage-like waves and bathed him in his own sweat.

He caught a movement out of the corner of his eye as one of the men collapsed onto the sand.

Jason was on it instantly, jogging up in time to see Rick Johnson send a flying kick at Trace Jenkins's head. Jason managed to intervene, shoving Johnson far enough to the side that the kick missed its target.

"All right!" Jason bellowed. "That's enough, got it? Johnson, get a bottle of water. Whatever this is, it's done, understand?"

Johnson passed a hand over his mouth, but his pale blue eyes held a murderous glare. Finally, he turned and grabbed a bottle of water, taking Jason's place at the head of the line.

Jason stared down at Jenkins incredulously. To his astonishment, the kid was all but doubled over, cackling with laughter. "You too!" Jason barked. "Get up!"

Jenkins managed a sloppy mock salute, moving his limbs as though he were made without bones.

The rest of the team paused in their labors and gathered around.

Jason turned to one of them. "What the fuck was that about?"

A man stepped forward. "Didn't hear it all, but Jenkins was razzing Johnson about these here shit supplies."

"Shit? What do you mean?"

The man shrugged. "Nothing. Just that it's basic stuff and not near enough. You know, water, saline, some plasma. Syringes, a box of diapers. Protein bars. And some of them milkshakes, y'know, the kind they give old folks."

"That's it? No meds?"

"Not that I could see. Anyway, Johnson starts complaining about needing some real food, and Jenkins just laughs at him. Told him not to worry, if all we got was water and them canned shakes, pretty soon we'll all need them diapers, anyhow. That's when Johnson knocked him down."

Still snickering, Jenkins teetered to his feet.

Quick as lightning, Jason reached over and grabbed his jaw, forcing Jenkins to meet his eyes. "What the fuck, dude? Are you high?"

Jenkins drooled slightly now, and his eyes were red, watery, and unfocused. "Ohh," he managed after a moment. "You could say Imma little messed up. Can't hardly hold it against me, having a little fun. It's good shit too. Mighty good."

Rage boiled up in Jason from somewhere deep within himself and he reached up and cracked the other man on the side of his head, knocking him to his knees. "Where'd you get it, asshole? People are dying in there, and you're stealing from the pharmacy? You little punk!"

He picked up Jenkins by the scruff of his neck and hauled him to his feet, half dragging him across the sand. Jason's heart pounded mercilessly in his chest and he had to fight his own impulse to beat the kid to a pulp right then and there. Jason glanced wildly at the shocked expressions on the faces that surrounded him and fought to control himself.

"Get that stuff inside!" Jason bellowed. "Me and Jenkins here need to have us a little talk."

Together, they stumbled toward the loading dock, Jason shoving Jenkins roughly from behind with Jenkins staggering unsteadily forward. Inside and out of earshot of the rest of the crew, Jason grabbed Jenkins by the throat and shoved him hard, smacking his head against the concrete wall. "You ever been in the joint, boy? You know what happens to filth like you in a place like that? I do. And if you don't take me to your stash, I will shank you where you stand. You got that?" He slammed Jenkins' head against the wall again, for emphasis.

Jenkins was blubbering openly now, facing his captor with jittery, terrified eyes.

"I said, *understand*?"

"Shh, shh … Not so loud, man," Jenkins whimpered. "I can make this right, okay? Tell you what, I'll take you to the stash and cut you in on the deal. I just found the shit, man. Whole bunch of boxes marked Stork Packs in the bunkers near the big hotel, emergency use only. Meds. Food. Supplies too. I've been bringing a box at a time, but I could only get to some of it because of the water levels. They don't belong to nobody, right? Finders keepers. They lift the quarantine and we can sell it all, man. Out there, on the street."

Jason tried frantically to wrap his way around this information. "What are stork packs?"

Jenkins struggled against Jason's grip. "I overheard some of the hospital suits talking about stork packs, man. They've got emergency supplies, and I guess they're usually hidden in some underground spot in case of a natural disaster. I thought I hit the jackpot when I found them! I was gonna sell some of it, maybe, and you know, make some cash to bribe my way off the island. Survival of the fittest, dude."

Jason furiously wrapped his left hand around Jenkins's scrawny neck and squeezed slightly. "You piece of shit. Where have you been storing the boxes?"

Jenkins's eyes rolled upward as he struggled for breath. "Up above the regular floors, west wing. Big as a warehouse.

They store all kinds of shit up there. But these pack things were off in Fort Crockett at the coastal artillery battery. It was locked, but I was resourceful and busted the lock." Jenkins wiped his mouth with the back of his hand and tried to smile. "Don't you worry, though. I locked it all back up again. It'll just be our little secret."

Jason bent to one side, his left hand still clenched around the other man's throat. With his right hand, he reached inside his boot and withdrew an old kitchen knife, sharpened razor thin. Jenkin's breathing came out in a rasp as Jason contemplated killing him.

The silence between them stretched into minutes.

Jenkins's eyes bulged with fear.

Unable to look at him anymore, Jason dropped his weapon. As he lowered his gaze, he noted the purplish yellow tracks that snaked their way down Jenkins's arms. With all the precision of a pitcher on the mound, he reached back and clocked him squarely on the jaw.

Trace Jenkins crumpled like an old paper bag.

"Johnson!" Jason bellowed, as he tucked his knife back into his boot. "Get your butt in here."

Footsteps jogged down the corridor in their direction. When Jason glanced up, his eyes were composed, his face devoid of expression. "I need you and the team to come with me to Fort Crocket on the seawall. Get your supplies and meet me there in fifteen. I'm going to go round up some more help. If the lights come on again, we can load up the freight elevator. But if they don't, we're going to have to carry it down."

"Carry what?" Johnson only looked confused.

"That's what we're gonna find out. Some kind of supplies, I guess. This little piece of shit here thought he'd hit the motherlode. But he said there was food. Drugs too apparently."

Jason reached down and snatched a key from the cheap chain that hung around Jenkins's neck. "If we got any luck at all, this will get us inside that storage room. If not, we'll find some other way. So round up the guys. But first, find a room and lock him up. Watch yourselves. Judging by them tracks he's wearing, he's going to be hurting pretty bad when he comes around."

"You want me to tell one of the docs?"

Jason managed a smile. "Hell no. We're going to let this little punk do it the old-fashioned way like they do in the joint. Cold turkey."

CHAPTER FORTY-NINE
Galveston University Hospital

witch … .

Kirsten Stone felt it before she saw it. Lying alone in her bed in the ICU, she was counting the minutes, the hours, the days before she could return to the lab.

Twitch … twitch … .

She stared at her hand curiously, seeing the swollen vein and ugly bruise where the nurse had hooked up her saline drip, watching for the next, seemingly random spasm of the ring finger of her left hand. On another day, she would have written that nurse up for her clumsiness. But then again, maybe Kirsten herself had been the problem, struggling and fighting her confinement like the poor patient she was. She really didn't remember. Once she'd been forced to rest, so much of the last four weeks had simply fallen away as she sank into hour after hour of uninterrupted sleep, washing her terrors and duties and shattered nerves away, like the sea washing storm ruins from the beach.

Five minutes passed by her reckoning and she checked her phone to be sure. The power had been coming on more frequently now, twice today already, and remained on for longer periods of time. Those left at the hospital were delirious with anticipation, buoyed by the luxuries they'd once taken for granted. The nurses seemed almost cheerful as they dispensed meds and delivered meals. The doctors on routine rounds made jokes and small talk as though nothing was amiss. They were sustained by the influx of food, water, and medicine provided by the Red Cross drop off as well as the stork packs that had been retrieved by Jason and his crew from the bunker. They dared to hope once more for rescue—real rescue. Even if life on the outside would never be the same, life was worth living, after all.

Yet the guilt of Kirsten's carelessness haunted her. If she hadn't exposed herself to the virus, then she might have shared their enthusiasm. If she did somehow contract the fever, none of the progress they'd made would be enough to stay the awful reality awaiting them. With each new case of CCHF, they were sentenced to yet another extension of quarantine. And even with the influx of emergency supplies, it wouldn't be enough to keep sane. And it would be all her fault.

Twitch … .

She closed her eyes again, mentally mapping the electromagnetic signals from her brain through her heart and down her left arm, counting her breaths, shoving aside a single, terrifying possibility. *It couldn't be back, could it? After so many years?*

No one knew about her epilepsy, not even the staff. Feeling it was unnecessary, she'd chosen not to wear her medical ID. Eighteen years had passed since her last grand mal and, with only a couple of minor episodes since, she was so well-regulated through Keppra she simply didn't consider her seizures anyone's business but her own. Guarding her privacy about her past, she had kept her secret and maintained her distance from all but a chosen few. No one, it seemed, knew Dr. Kirsten Stone all that well, and that was just fine with her. She was all too conscious of the fact that many thought her cold and unfeeling. Maybe she was, as she'd thrown herself into her career and her love of art with the same fervor that other women put into their families and friends. That, too, had been her choice. She knew all too well how cruel people could be, especially when faced with a disease that, in her case at least, had no cause. Her seizures, however, could negatively impact her career and quality of life.

She thought about the cruel kids in junior high who'd laughed when she soiled herself after an episode. She'd sunk into a deep depression for many years afterward due to uncontrolled seizures and endless bullying. No one knew how dark her life had gotten or that she had become suicidal.

One day, after seeing how her failed suicide attempt had affected her parents and siblings—the only people who had always been there for her— she knew she needed help. She entered an inpatient psychiatric facility where they controlled the seizures better and bolstered her mood. Kirsten met many individuals with stories similar to hers. Those experiences led her to a passion to help others like her, and she drowned herself in medicine.

Twitch … twitch … .

Stop it, Kirsten. It's not a sign. That stupid nurse just hit a nerve or something. She glanced at her phone; half an hour until her latest test results came back. So far, she hadn't shown any signs of anything worse than exhaustion, but she wasn't foolish enough to think she was out of the woods, either.

Frantically, she texted Billy Andersen: *What's going on down there?*

Lunch. Billy replied. *Beef jerky never tasted so good doc. They give you any?*

Never mind that. What about the vaccine? she responded.

Waiting on the CDC. They were going to send their best guess on how much anti-venom to use once they ran it through their computers.

When was that? Kristen asked.

Yesterday, before the power went down. They sent one estimate yesterday morning. I made up a sample, but it didn't feel right. Asked 'em to repeat their analysis to see if they got the same result. Still waiting.

Shit, Kirsten thought. I need to get down there. The only thing guaranteed to make the CDC move slower than usual was for some yee-haw hotshot lab assistant to challenge their findings.

Where's Dr. Wong? she texted.

Talking to his kids. He finally got some FaceTime a few minutes ago. It's real sweet too. Only the kids think he looks funny with that half-ass beard.

Beard? Kirsten struggled to recall, suddenly realizing it had been so long since she'd actually looked at anyone, it was little wonder she hadn't noticed.

Twitch … .

They were all working as hard as she was—or as hard as she had been—moving from task to task like robots remotely controlled by some invisible hand. Pressing her lips together in a straight line, she kicked back her covers and struggled out of bed. When she stood, she was astonished by her own wobbly legs and how the overhead light swayed and spun with an onslaught of dizziness. Using her IV caddy to steady herself, she counted breaths till her head cleared, then willed her bare feet forward, pausing at the threshold to check the deserted hall. One wobbly wheel squealed on her caddy and she kicked at it with one foot to silence it. The lab was to her right, two floors down. She recited the directions in her mind as she teetered toward the tired red flicker of a red Exit sign that marked the stairwell. *I will be all right,* she assured herself. *I can do this.*

Near the end of the hall, another doorway, marked *Authorized Personnel Only,* stood slightly ajar. The skeleton crew had stopped locking the doors to the drug storage closets weeks ago, on her own order. It was simply too complicated to locate keys and security codes among limited personnel, especially on emergency power, and with supplies running, as there hadn't seemed much point in securing what was left.

She entered the small room on impulse more than anything, nagged by a little voice in her head that she may go into sudden withdrawal since the ICU staff didn't know about her condition and she had run out of her usual meds, which posed its own set of risks. That wasn't a gamble she was willing to take. Using her phone flashlight to better illuminate the shelves, she finally located a lone bottle of lorazepam and some sodium valproate. They weren't her usual scripts, but they were better than nothing. Hastily, she shook out two of each and swallowed them without water. Doubling her dosage but having gone without anything for a few days, she preferred to err on the side of caution. Then, feeling oddly reassured and somehow stronger, placebo effect or no, she made her painstaking way to the lab.

CHAPTER FIFTY
Galveston University Hospital

Shaka awakened to the sound of Velcro peeling as the blood pressure cuff released from his arm. Above him, Danica's kind hazel eyes shone from behind the hazy eyewear of her HAZMAT gear. She glanced at the monitors above his head and recorded his stats on her chart.

"Good news, doctor," she said, her voice only slightly muffled inside the suit. "You're five days out and fever free. We're about to declare the all-clear on you and put you back to work. How do you feel?"

He propped himself up on an elbow and glanced around the room. "What the—when did the power come back on?" He fumbled for the pitcher of water and the glass on his bedside table.

"Take it easy." She reached over and poured some for him.

As he swallowed, she said, "Four days ago, I think, might be five. Every day, they keep it on for a few hours longer. They need it to keep the flood pumps going. From what they tell me, the east end of the island is almost clear enough for the dozers and rescue teams. Rumor's got it they start the helicopter evac of critical patients day after tomorrow."

Danica waited while he absorbed the new information.

After a moment, she reached out for him and asked again. "Really, be honest now. How do you feel?"

He glanced down at himself, flexing fingers and toes, stretching his calves first, then his arms, high over his head. He fingered the remains of the yellowing, purplish welts that covered his biceps. "Kind of like an old bruise, I guess. But hey, happy to be here. What's that they say? Any day above ground is a good day?"

He managed a ghost of his usual smile.

Unable to restrain herself any longer, she threw her arms around his neck. "Shaka, I want to apologize for earlier. I thought that it was easier to not get entangled and to do our jobs. Relationships are messy and emotional. But then you coded, and we almost lost you. It was so horrible. I realized I didn't want to be without you, and how much I care about you! I didn't want to get attached, but you already had me. You had me the moment you kissed me."

He returned her embrace, and even with her protective gear crinkling between them, she could feel the blessed warmth of him once more.

"We need to talk," she murmured. "I have to explain."

As gently as he could, he removed her arms from around his neck. "Oh, we'll talk, all right. But not right now. I have another, more urgent appointment."

"I see." She backed away, crestfallen, and tried to regain her composure.

"Not yet, you don't." He threw back his blanket to display his full manhood, tenting up his hospital gown. "You have got me so pumped with fluids I need to get to that urinal in there, pronto."

"Oh!" she said, startled. Then, with as professional a face as she could muster, she said, "Let me get a bedpan."

He shook his head.

"I can help you get to the bathroom, Shaka."

He held up a hand. "Please, allow me some dignity in the presence of the woman I love. I got this; I promise."

A single, joyful giggle rose from her throat. *The woman I love* … . And she lowered the bedrail.

"Clearly, your circulation has returned to normal," she said dryly. "Help yourself."

"I thank you. See if you can find me a clean set of scrubs, will you? I need a shower and to get down to the lab. I bet they're just itching for some fresh antibodies." He discreetly disappeared behind the bathroom door, locking it behind him.

"The lab? What for? Don't you think you've done enough? That volunteer stunt for the vaccine damn near killed you, remember?"

Danica struggled to keep her voice from rising in hysteria. "Just … wait. I'm coming with you, but I have to go through decontamination first. Stay where you are!" she shouted. "Promise!"

After a moment, the reluctant reply rose over the sound of running water. "Okay. For you. I promise."

CHAPTER FIFTY-ONE
Galveston University Hospital

Kirsten met no one on her way to the lab, for which she was grateful. Maybe it was just the medication kicking in, but she took it slowly through the deserted corridors, feeling oddly more alive with each passing step, as though some sort of veil had been lifted from the world. After weeks of rationed electrical power, every light was brighter, and the faraway sounds of muted television monitors and beeping medical equipment and human activity all came to her with preternatural clarity, like some sort of symphony only she could hear. It was all perfectly ordinary—and yet, it wasn't.

She took a breath, feeling fatigued and energized at the same time. Relishing her feelings of unreasonable happiness, even euphoria, she felt like she'd been suddenly endowed with superpowers. Even the troublesome twitching in her finger had ceased. She paused and closed her eyes, mentally mapping the neurons firing in her brain, lighting up like shooting stars across a clear night sky. In another part of her mind, she wondered if this is what it felt like to be high, something she'd never indulged in for fear of an epileptic episode. The loss of control was what she feared most—

only this didn't feel like that at all. This seemed powerful, sending a surge of energy through her exhausted body and wounded spirit; the hope, now almost a certainty, that for all our frailties, a human life was a kind of miracle in the end.

An elevator door slid open as she passed and the lone passenger, a haggard-looking young nurse, got out. Kirsten couldn't recall her name and searched for an ID.

The woman recognized Kirsten readily enough, and she blushed sheepishly as her fingers fumbled for her badge. "Dr. Stone! Glad to see you up and around. Did your blood work come back with the all clear? Wow, what a relief. For everybody and the quarantine and everything. But especially for you. I mean—" The girl paused, stumbling for words.

Kirsten studied her with an odd, detached expression. "I'm fine," she lied. "I showed no signs of infection, if that's what you mean. The saline IV and the mask"—she paused and gestured to the caddy—"are for hydration and are only precautionary at this point."

Her thoughts raced to the bluish-purple splotches she had seen this morning on her body. In fact, her latest blood work wouldn't be back for hours, but she saw no reason to wait for it because she already knew what it would show. And, in any event, this scared-looking young woman was unlikely to report Kirsten as MIA from the isolation unit in any event. Kirsten was fine.

"Have a good one," the girl murmured.

At the last moment as the doors closed, Kirsten turned around with an unexpected smile. "You too. And don't worry. It's almost over. Remember that. We're very proud of each and every member of the staff. Thank you."

Kirsten leaned against the back of the elevator and pressed 3R as she had far more pressing matters to attend to in the lab. Walking away, the nurse looked relieved.

Kirsten got off of the elevator and headed toward the lab. At its door, Kirsten steeled herself once more, the neurons in her brain still firing at breakneck speed. It wouldn't be so easy to get past Billy and Dr. Wong. Resolutely, she waved her ID at the security lock and the door swung inward.

Dr. Wong had his back to her, bent over a microscope when she came in. Billy was nowhere to be seen, but with the same supernatural clarity, she saw a newly-filled syringe on the tray beside his desk and headed toward it like a moth to a flame.

Dr. Wong looked up and did a double take as she moved into his peripheral vision. "Dr. Stone! Kirsten? What are you doing here?" He came closer, his welcoming smile fading quickly as he glanced her over. "Are you all right? You don't look well. Your pupils are dilated and you seem tense. Why are you out of bed? We don't even have your latest results yet."

Edging toward Billy's desk, she all but ignored Dr. Wong. "Never mind that," she snapped. She reached the desk, her breath coming rapidly, and she forced herself to slow down. She had this. Without quite managing a smile, she met his eyes. "What's the latest progress on the therapeutic vaccine?" Slowly, almost casually, she picked up the filled syringe, squinting at the label in the now-haloed light. "Is this it?"

Something was terribly wrong. Dr. Wong knew it in every fiber of his body, yet couldn't put his finger on it. He approached her slowly, hastily scanning her face and body; except for the eyes, she didn't appear to be ill. She showed no signs of hemorrhage or even pain. In fact, she looked at least marginally better than she had before she'd been exposed to the virus.

"That's one version," he finally answered. "But Billy kept saying it didn't feel right, like it was too heavy on the anti-venom stabilizer. Too much could damage the nervous system, maybe even paralyze. So he asked the CDC to run the numbers again, just to make sure. He's checking on that now. Kirsten, why don't you sit down? He'll be back in a minute."

He took another step closer, but not close enough.

She plucked up the syringe, tore away the cap, and plunged it into her left bicep.

Well, that's one way to test out the vaccine, Dr. Wong thought.

A split second later, she fell to her knees, her bright eyes blank and unseeing, rolling back in her head as she toppled to her side.

"Oh my God!" Wong shouted. "Help! Somebody! Get over here, she's convulsing! Use isolation precautions."

Billy and two other lab assistants burst through the doors of the adjoining chamber with gowns, masks, and protective gear.

They froze at the sight of her thrashing wildly on the floor. "What the—quick! Roll her over on her side!"

"Somebody call a code! We need a crash cart down here!"

One assistant called the code, and the other began to count time. "Forty-five seconds ... one minute."

Dr. Wong knelt down next to her. "An airway! We need to keep her airways open." Reluctantly he reached for her mouth to hold it open.

Billy pulled his hand away. "Don't! You can't get her jaw open like that. She could choke."

"A minute thirty."

The crash cart burst through the door along with two nurses, followed in the next instant by Shaka and Danica, both in protective gear, close at his heels. They stared in disbelief at the agonized figure on the floor as her back arched violently, curved and arched again, exposing the colored splotches in between her gown and a telltale wetness spreading on the floor between her legs.

Shaka clenched his teeth and bent to examine her jaw. He tilted Dr. Stone's head back, while pushing upward, and then he grasped the jaw on both sides, lifting it to better visualize the airway. As he opened her mouth, he noticed a slight bluish tinge slowly making its way slowly over her skin.

"Respiration dropping," intoned the nurse stationed at the monitor. "Intubate?"

"Two minutes, fifteen seconds."

Dr. Sen shook his head. "I can't get a clear view of her airway. It would be very difficult and time-consuming to get an endotracheal tube down there, and it might end up causing more damage than good. Find me a scalpel. I'll do a trach if necessary."

He snatched on another pair of gloves as Danica and another nurse laid out the tray. "Time!" he barked.

"Three minutes."

"Damn it! Dr. Stone stay with us, okay? It will pass, it will pass—"

Dr. Stone continued thrashing helplessly, oblivious to his pleas.

In the next instant, she went utterly still, the seizure over as quickly as it had begun, though her limbs remained contorted.

Shaka rolled her over and, feeling frantically at her neck cricoid cartilage, made a quick incision.

Danica passed him the endotracheal tube.

He glanced up, his desperate eyes meeting Danica's. "There's a lot of scar tissue and the trachea is narrower than I expected!"

Danica bent over the wound, a sponge in her hand, and passed him a smaller probe.

"There is just too much fibrosis from previous tracheostomies," Shaka frantically stated as he tried to push the tube through the scaring on Dr. Stone's neck.

Shaka futilely tried to give her the last lifeline.

Eight minutes without oxygen.

Irreversible brain damage had already set in.

"No respiration," the nurse intoned softly, just after the monitors for heart rate slid into a silent flat line.

Nobody moved.

Numb with shock, Shaka stared helplessly at the senseless tableau before them, unable to react.

"Call it, God help me," said Dr. Wong after a few more minutes. "Somebody call it."

"Time of death: Fifteen hundred hours," Shaka said, feeling completely defeated.

Dr. Stone had saved his life by risking hers and he hadn't been able to return the gesture. She had been selfless and he was alive because of her. He would be forever indebted and grateful to her. Sometimes being a physician and putting others' lives before you takes a toll no one can imagine.

"Rest in peace," Danica whispered finally, watching as the orderlies gathered her up to place her body on a gurney that was waiting outside. Two prescription bottles rolled across the floor.

Billy Andersen scooped them up in his hand. "Lorazepam, 2 mg, and Depakote, 500 mg," he read from the labels. He glanced at Danica. "Was she on these meds when you had her in isolation?"

Danica shook her head. "Nope. Nothing—well, except for the Ribavirin we found in the stork packs. And we had to ration that."

"But dosages like this"—he gestured with the pill bottles—"they're strong, right?"

She nodded.

Billy looked at him. "But they should have prevented the seizure, right?"

"Yes, most likely they kept her epilepsy under control, but since being isolated to the hospital, she might not have been taking the medications every day or been low in supply," Danica said.

Billy scratched his head. "Nobody even knew Dr. Stone had it. She was asymptomatic and hid it well. Fully functional, able to run a big hospital."

The others could only nod their agreement.

Billy paced the floor. "So, could drugs to prevent a seizure actually cause one?"

"Not likely," Dr. Wong put in. "Especially if these were her usual meds, and in these dosages, but we don't know if she was taking those doses. We also don't know what happened when she injected herself with the vaccine; her medications could have reacted with the vaccine." He shrugged.

"Wait a minute," Danica put in. "You're not saying she deliberately OD'd on her meds, are you? With the quarantine about to be lifted? Why would she?" She and Shaka exchanged a shocked glance.

Billy put up his hands in protest. "No, of course not. But look at her bruising. She knew as well as any of us that she was going to test positive for the CCHF and that the quarantine would be extended. Her diagnosis of epilepsy and CCHF puts her at a higher mortality rate."

"Shit." Dr. Wong stepped forward. "That's why she injected herself with the raw vaccine! It was her Hail Mary. I tried to stop her, but she was too fast for me. Oh my God, she wasn't trying to kill herself, she was trying to save the rest of us and see if she could get rid of the quarantine and test the vaccine—"

"Not sure," replied Billy. "Maybe she had no way of knowing what would happen. But there was clearly some sort of interaction between the raw vaccine and the meds already in her system." He paused and turned to one of the lab assistants who hovered on the periphery. "Take Dr. Stone's blood samples and get them down to toxicology. I need their full report as soon as they can get me one. And Dr. Sen? If you don't mind, I'll need some blood from you as well."

"Fresh antibodies? You got them."

Billy nodded and stared once more at the pill bottles in his hand. "I'm not sure what happened, but she didn't die for nothing. None of them did. Not if I have anything to say about it."

Danica stepped forward and placed a hand on his arm. "Are you saying you might have the answer? About the vaccine?"

His bright blue eyes, shining with enthusiasm, met hers. "No," he said. "But I do have one hell of an idea."

CHAPTER FIFTY-TWO
Galveston University Hospital

Hours later, Shaka and Danica were still holding an informal wake in the residents' lounge over weak coffee and a plate of protein cookies someone had pilfered from the stork packs. Stunned by the news of Dr. Stone's unexpected passing, staff members wandered in and out, some alone, some in groups of two or three—stricken, shocked, or merely curious, each expressing in almost-reverence their inexpressible sense of loss. They realized how much she had kept them together through the past weeks, in the face of the biggest crisis any of them had ever known.

For his part, Shaka remained inconsolable.

Danica tried to be more encouraging and urged him to rest. Like all physicians, she'd had enough experience with death to know that each person grieved in their own way and it was best not to insist. The truth was, even she had no clear idea of what to do next or where to turn for direction, Dr. Kirsten Stone had led the various teams of the hospital staff with all the cool efficiency of a general leading her troops, as willing to take her place beside them in the trenches as she had been to lead from behind her desk—and the impact of her absence was devastating.

At one point, weary of the small talk, Danica wandered to the window. A fingernail's worth of moon scattered light across the bay, illuminating the silhouettes of a few brave souls, human and gull, who picked their way along the shoreline, seeking some treasure amid the ruins, while the near-constant thrum of hundreds of flood pumps sounded a dirge into the night. She knew they had finally turned some corner. Things couldn't help but irrevocably change, yet the road ahead remained obscure. And though they had survived so much—the hurricane, the loss of life, and the terrors of the quarantine too—she couldn't yet see how the future held anything less by way of struggle. It was more like she was learning for the first time just what people meant when they said: "It's always darkest before the dawn."

Suddenly, from another corner of the lounge, came a voice. "Everybody! Listen up! Check this out!"

A tall, rangy young male nurse held the television remote aloft and turned up the volume. On the screen scrolled edited footage of helicopters and drones circling the skies above the hospital. It was nothing they hadn't seen before, but as the closed captions scrolled across the bottom of the screen under a Breaking News banner, a female reporter's voice began the announcement:

"We have just received confirmation that the emergency helicopter evacuation of the more than three hundred left stranded in the subsequent quarantine of Galveston University Hospital prior to Hurricane Beatrix will commence at eight a.m. tomorrow morning. Responding to continued pressure from relatives, citizens, and human rights protestors, the governor has ordered a joint airlift effort, coordinating the Red Cross and National Guard with area hospitals in Houston.

"The effort marks a breakthrough in the stalemate that developed between federal and state authorities following an outbreak of Crimean Congo Hemorrhagic Fever, for which there is no known cure. Though a significant number of patients had been evacuated prior to the hurricane, many were left behind, under the care of a skeleton crew of hospital staff, in quarantine once the disease was identified.

"While we do not yet have exact statistics, we have been assured that only non-infected patients will be allowed to participate, while fever victims and essential remaining staff will remain behind. The CDC states the public is not at risk for further infection under this protocol. The news was greeted with tears and shouts of approval by protestors as they look forward to being reunited with loved ones in the aftermath of the biggest disaster Texas has ever seen … ."

In the residents' lounge, the assembled company erupted into whoops and shouts and hugs. A flurry of activity ensued as the veil of grief was abruptly snatched away, replaced by a ripple of excitement. Staff members rushed for the door, anxious to share their news and vie for some position in the long, slow parade that would begin the next morning.

"Strange," Danica murmured in a kind of wonder. "It's ending the same way it began. Remember, Shaka? The bagging and tagging?"

Lost in his own reverie, he didn't appear to have heard her.

Suddenly, Dr. Danica Diza's path became clear to her. She gathered up her notes and charts and headed for the door, pausing only to drape an arm around Shaka's shoulders; he alone seemed unaffected by the news.

"Try and get some rest. I'll be back as soon as I can," she said, bending to brush his cheeks with her lips. "I have rounds and—something else I have to do."

He glanced at her, a trace of his old sardonic smile playing around the corners of his mouth. "Ahh yes," he said. "Ever the dedicated physician. Duty calls?"

If he was trying to bait her, she refused to take it, all too aware that he was speaking out of his own, still-fresh pain.

Resolutely, she headed for the door. "No, Shaka," she answered softly. "More like respect."

He sighed heavily and passed a weary hand over his eyes. "Yeah, well, you do you, I guess."

***

After Danica left, Shaka got up and switched off the light as he left the lounge and headed into the corridor. Shadows gathered, and his own footsteps sounded unnaturally loud as he made his way to the stairwell, not even sure of where he intended to go. He figured it was well past midnight but couldn't be sure.

He sank down onto a step at one point, felled by a sudden vision of his mother in her casket, the certainty that he could have done something more, if only he had known.

Did you know you were going to die, Dr. Stone? Like my mother did?

He cursed himself all over again, endlessly replaying in his mind what he could have done better, faster, differently to save the life of the woman who had saved his own. Dr. Stone's death opened up an old wound for him, one he feared he might never be able to heal. The familiar old guilt closed around his heart like a vise.

He had exposed Dr. Stone to the virus; there was no escaping it. Dr. Stone had only done what she did to try and save everyone else. His training told him he shouldn't take the actions of a virus personally, but at the moment, at least, he was taking it very personally indeed. Even with his years of training, he couldn't shake the sense that he might have saved her, if only in return for her efforts to save him. *It wasn't supposed to happen this way—people don't die from seizures.*

Shaka had been resentful after his mother died. He had pushed everyone away, had spent years building up walls, not allowing anyone to get close. He couldn't bear that pain again. What right did he have to try to live and be happy with a woman like Danica Diza, anyway? Everyone he loved or cared about ended up leaving him one way or another.

Twenty minutes later, a familiar voice echoed over the public address system. He perked up. Danica, tone as cool and efficient as she could manage. What was she up to?

"Good evening, everyone," Danica began. "As you've probably heard by now, we regret to report the passing of Dr. Kirsten Stone, our acting chief of staff, this afternoon, due to complications from a seizure. I hope you will remember her in your prayers and honor her service to this hospital with your own."

There was a faint sniffle, then a long pause before she went on. "For those of us not yet acquainted, I am Dr. Danica Diza. I will be temporarily taking over her position for the duration, so if you have any questions, please feel free to ask. I only hope I am adequate to the task. As you also may be aware, confirmation has just come in that the Red Cross, in combination with the National Guard, will begin helicopter evacuation of non-isolation patients beginning at eight o'clock tomorrow morning. All available personnel are required to report to the fourth floor, west wing, to begin the necessary bagging and tagging procedures at six a.m. All staff attending the CCHF isolation unit will remain at their stations until the quarantine is officially lifted. You know the drill, people. The more efficient we are, the faster this will go. The faster it goes, the more people will eventually be allowed to leave. We are all anxious to return to our lives and loved ones, but this is a hospital and patients still come first. Thank you. Now get some rest. We've got a long day ahead of us tomorrow."

After another pause, she spoke again, her tone only slightly changed. "Paging Dr. Sen. Dr. Shaka Sen, report to room 4312, east wing. Your immediate assistance is required."

CHAPTER FIFTY-THREE
Galveston University Hospital

Shaka caught his breath at the sight of Danica, her slim silhouette standing in the window, clad only in a bra and panties. The moonlight that danced over the waters of the bay outlined her perfect slim profile, and it shone on her brunette hair, which was falling in waves around her shoulders.

She turned and smiled, extending her hand. "Come look," she said. "It's so beautiful."

Shaka took her hand. The energy of her touch coursed through him, drove back his demons, and flooded him with an all-too-familiar desire. His breath came faster as she pulled him close. He traced a line down her neck and between the rise of her breasts as he bent and murmured in her ear. "I remember this room," he said. "This is where we first … ."

She turned and smiled shyly, circling her arms around his neck. "I was hoping you might."

They paused, drinking in the other's scent, relishing the heat of living, breathing flesh, savoring the slow beginnings of an eternal dance—one bigger than sorrow and stronger than death.

Danica looked up at him, her dark eyes shining in the moonlight, her face flushed with anticipation. She smiled. "One of the nurses told me, weeks ago, that sex was the opposite of death. But it isn't, Shaka, love is. And I know you're hurting, believe me, I do. I just wanted you to know— whatever else happens—you *are* loved. So very much."

Unbidden tears sprang to his eyes as he crushed her close to his chest, and his heart seemed to beat in time to her own throbbing pulse. "Oh Danica ... I don't deserve you. Honestly, I don't."

She backed up and placed a finger over his lips. "I'll be the judge of that."

His grin was suddenly interrupted by a soft knock on the door. He rolled his eyes to the ceiling in disbelief.

Danica stifled a squeak as she threw on a nearby lab coat and buttoned it, tugging her hair back into its usual ponytail. The knock came once more and she positioned herself behind a nearby chair, hoping whoever it was wouldn't notice her bare legs and feet.

Shaka crossed the room, and she switched on the lamp and nodded. When he finally opened the door, both were surprised to see a somber-looking Jason Carter, along with Katie Mendoza, leaning on a hand crutch close behind him.

Shaka waved them forward.

"Evening, doctors," Jason said. If they noticed Shaka's rumpled hair and Danica's embarrassed blush, they were discreet enough not to mention it. "We've been looking all over the hospital for you. Then, when I heard Dr. Diza here over the PA, we figured we could find you both here."

"Good thinking." Shaka nodded, a little impatiently. "What's on your mind? Great news about the evac, right? Is there some problem?"

Jason shook his head. "I've already got my team assembled. They'll be ready to go when you are, helping to get folks to the helipad."

"Great, Jason, just great. Thanks!"

Jason hung his head. "Thing is, me and Katie here, we've been talking. And well—both of us hate to do it, but we're not going to be there in the morning. We're pulling out tonight. We've come to say goodbye."

"What? What do you mean, goodbye?" Shaka and Danica exchanged a bewildered glance. "Why leave now? My God, it's almost over."

Jason nodded. "Maybe for some. But not for us. Here in the hospital, we were safe enough, but out there? We're still fugitives. Soon as I set foot in Houston, somebody's going to try and slap my ass back in prison, and I ain't going. And Katie here? Well, she's AWOL. She's looking at a court martial at best. And when the military needs a scapegoat, they won't hesitate to throw her under the bus. Besides, even though she's been in service and is a US citizen, born right here in Texas, that doesn't mean so much to ICE these days. With a last name like Mendoza, she could wind up in one of them detainment centers. And I won't see that. Not ever. They'll have to kill me first."

Katie took his hand and kissed it. Chuckling wryly, she tried to lighten the mood. "Some hero, huh? A girl doesn't come across a Jason Carter every day."

Danica put her hand over her mouth, her eyes wide, recognizing the truth in what they'd said. "But, after everything you've done for us, surely your service here could count for something? A pardon?"

Jason smiled a little. "Pardons take a long, long time, ma'am. And mostly they never come at all. Especially here in Texas. Better we're gone. Both of us and our dog Casper. I don't reckon they'll be looking too hard for either one of us initially. Plenty of chaos out there to remedy first. But they will come looking. Eventually. Hopefully they will think we're dead."

He paused and drew a deep breath. "Anyways, both of us, we just wanted to say goodbye. And to thank you. I'm leaving here a better man than when I came, that's for sure. And if it wasn't for you taking a gamble on me, I'd never have met Katie. And she's the finest woman I ever met. We both need to go is all. Make a fresh start somewhere."

Shaka sank down on one side of the bed, struggling to process this newest change, his mind working fervently. "But where? How?"

Jason cleared his throat uncomfortably. "That's the other thing I wanted you to know about. We thought about heading out the bay into Mexico on a trawler, but it's just too dangerous. Then I got to talking with one of the first responders down on the beach yesterday. Fella from up in Utah, owns a trucking company. He was trying to find his sister and her kids. They didn't make the evacuation with the rest. So he loaded up a truck with water and drove straight through. He had no idea how bad it was till he got here. Day I saw him, he was circling the place where their house used to be. I guess it finally hit him. He wasn't ever going to find them because there was nobody left. No house, nothing at all."

Jason glanced up, his eyes gone sad. "I mentioned me and Katie. How we could help with the driving back to Utah and then go our own way. Anyways, I wanted you to know."

"Of course, it's all right! My God, man," Shaka put in. "Without you two, we all would have never made it this far!"

"Well, this fella says if we make our way from Utah to San Francisco, we can hitch a ride on a fishing boat heading north and into Vancouver. He says there's quite a little pipeline in place doing just that. Guess there's some folks left willing to show illegals some mercy, anyhow. At least for a price. I never worked a fishing boat before, but I reckon I could learn."

Meanwhile, Danica was rummaging through a nearby supply cabinet, bagging up bandages, gauze, and other essentials. She located a prescription tablet and wrote out three or four slips of paper, then handed them to Katie. "Keep that bandage clean and change it every two days. You'll need to stay on a course of antibiotics for at least another two weeks, so take those from the supplies that were retrieved and get these filled wherever you can. But if there's a change in your leg wound, any change at all, get to a hospital right away, hear me? Promise?"

Katie nodded solemnly. "Yes, ma'am. I will. And thank you again. For everything."

Shaka's voice suddenly rose. "Danica, what happened to my personal stuff? Where did they put it after I checked into the isolation unit?" Shaka stared at her.

"I don't know, probably at the nurses' station outside the ICU. Who checked you in? Do you remember?"

"I checked myself in," he said. "I know I did."

"Then your stuff must still be here. This wing's been mostly empty since. Did you look in the locker?"

Shaka rose and went to the locker, reaching deep into the far corner of the top shelf. "Yes!" he cried as his fingers closed around his wallet, cell phone, and keys. "Thank God!" He hurriedly opened the wallet and pulled out a wad of bills, thrusting them in Jason's direction.

Jason gaped, his eyes wide. "Doc, wait! I can't take this! There must be five thousand dollars here!"

Shaka reached out and closed Jason's hand around the money. "You can, and you will. You're going to need it. Call it traveling money. Hell, call it combat pay. You've earned it, both of you. Divvy it up and don't keep it all in one place, some in your pocket, some in your duffels, okay?"

Reluctantly, Jason nodded as Shaka handed over his phone. "Take this too. Dr. Diza's number is already programmed on speed dial. Check in with us as soon as you can, then trash it and get another one somewhere. Something that can't be traced, okay? They'll have a harder time tracking you that way."

Danica could only stare at him, wide-eyed. "Are you sure you're not the fugitive, Dr. Sen? What did you do? Rob a bank or something?"

He grinned. "Nothing so glamorous, believe me. I was an intern when I joined up to volunteer with the Red Cross in the aftermath of Katrina. Before we left, they warned us. When the grid goes down, everything goes with it. Debit and credit cards, cell phones, apps, wire transfers, the works. They said to travel with as much cash as we could, because down in New Orleans, cash would be king. Everything else was pretty much useless. They were right. So when Beatrix started rolling in, I went to the bank is all, just in case. Turned out it's come in real handy."

Jason shook his head, still marveling. "I'll pay you back. I don't know just how, but I will."

"Don't. If I've figured out anything, it's that you can't always pay people back. All you can do is do the right thing because it *is* the right thing. Get on your feet up there in Canada. Someday you'll run into somebody else who needs help. Pay it forward, not back, okay? Besides,"—he turned to Danica and draped an arm around her shoulders—"we don't need it. When we get out of here, University Hospital is going to get billed big-time, believe me. By the time they get done with our overtime and back pay, we'll be just fine. Trust me."

Jason inhaled deeply, looking as though the weight of the world had just been lifted from his shoulders. "Best be going, then. That ride of ours ain't going to wait."

"You sure he's all right?" Danica wanted to know.

Jason shrugged. "Sure as I can be, ma'am. We still got Katie's Beretta, in case there's any real trouble."

Shaka shook his hand and clapped him on the back, as Danica rushed forward to embrace them both. "Godspeed, you two. Stay safe."

After they had gone, Shaka and Danica stood together silently for a moment, each lost in their own thoughts— feeling at once bereft at the departure of two of the most remarkable people they had ever known and oddly proud to have known them at all. A strange sort of peace descended on them, mixed with a tumult of emotions. Whatever the future held, one thing was sure. As miraculous as it seemed, life sometimes gave people second chances, if they were willing to take them.

Danica draped her arms around Shaka's neck to pull him closer. "You are a good man, Shaka Sen. A very good and caring man. Never forget that. Now, where were we?"

He deftly reached over and turned out the light, caught her in his arms and carried over to the bed. He unbuttoned her lab coat, slowly, one button at a time. Once he exposed her lacy bra, he cupped each breast in his hands, running his thumbs lightly over her nipples. "No more duty calls?"

She smiled, shivering with anticipation. "Duty always calls. But then again, duty isn't everything."

CHAPTER FIFTY-FOUR
Galveston University Hospital

anica awoke in a flood of sunlight, snuggled up next to Shaka's side, a beautiful dream interrupted by the persistent bleep of her cell phone alarm. Never in her life had she been so tempted to pick the damn thing up and throw it out the window, as she clung stubbornly to the last vestiges of sleep.

In the next instant a voice announced over the PA paging system. "Dr. Diza, Dr. Danica Diza, please report to the isolation unit."

She squinted up at the speaker, but the voice persisted. "Dr. Diza, your presence is required in the isolation unit ... Paging Dr. Danica Diza ... ."

"All right! All right! I'm coming!" She kicked the sheet aside and struggled into her bra, then searched frantically through the bedding for her panties. Trying hard not to wake Shaka, she switched off the bothersome alarm and headed to the bathroom for a quick sponge off, snatching up her discarded scrubs as she went. Why hadn't she at least thought to bring some clean ones to the room last night? The thought almost made her snicker. *Because keeping your clothes on was the last thing you were thinking about last night.*

After a quick rinse, she dressed in record time. She pulled her hair into its customary ponytail and shrugged into her lab coat, grabbing her phone and ID as she went. Shaka was already sitting up in bed, a bemused smile playing across his lips. He reached out his hands and pulled her close, and she lingered a moment longer, drinking in his warmth and scent.

"Stay," he murmured into her hair. "They can do rounds without you."

"Can't," she replied, brushing her lips against his neck. "They want me in the isolation unit. Now."

His eyes widened with concern and he stared at the ceiling. "Oh, goddamn it! It's not a new case, is it? Please, tell me no."

Up till then, the thought hadn't even occurred to her. There were only eight fever patients remaining in the unit as it was, all critical. A new case could only mean an extension of the quarantine.

"Dr. Diza," the hollow intercom voice insisted again. "Dr. Danica Diza. Please report to the isolation unit ... ."

"I'm coming!" she shouted at the stupid speaker, trying to keep the panic from her voice. Turning back to Shaka, who was already out of bed and pulling on his pants, she nodded wordlessly before she turned and ran.

Ten minutes later, she was suited in full HAZMAT gear, punching in her code. Inside, she was shocked to find Billy Andersen, wearing with his scrubs only a mask and the usual gown and gloves for protection, along with two bewildered-looking nurses, who only shrugged as Danica walked in.

Billy drifted from monitor to monitor and bed to bed, oblivious to the rest of them as he frantically scribbled new data onto his tablet computer.

Danica walked up and tapped him on the shoulder. "I got a page. What's going on? Any new cases? Any casualties?" She glanced at the nurses, who shook their heads no.

Turning away from the last remaining bedside, Billy whirled around and fist-pumped the air above his head. "Yes. Hell, yes!"

Hesitating for only a moment, Danica came forward. For all she knew, the man was delirious. "Mr. Andersen? Billy? What's going on? Why aren't you in your HAZMAT gear?"

He met her eyes, his own shining with a crazy excitement. "You're the acting chief of staff now, right? The one in charge? Since, uh—Dr. Stone? That's what they told me." He jerked a thumb in the nurses' direction.

"For the moment," Danica answered. She was going to say that she'd volunteered more than anything, but it seemed rather beside the point.

"Then come right over here with me and sit down." He steered her to a nearby chair and flashed his tablet computer screen before her. "Look at this! I finally figured it out. I cracked the formula!"

She glanced from the rows of numbers and data streaming across the screen, then up again at Billy's ecstatic expression. His excitement was truly contagious, but she couldn't afford to make any mistakes, either. Gathering all her professionalism, she pulled up a nearby chair and indicated he should sit. "Okay, walk me through it, Billy, every detail. And don't leave anything out. I've been on the floor, not in the lab, so you're going to have to fill me in."

Billy passed a hand over his eyes, unable to keep himself from smiling. "Dr. Stone volunteered for the last round of experimental vaccine before I could stop her. That version had been approved by the first data that came in from the CDC, but I knew their numbers were off. I just knew it—in my gut. So, I was waiting on verification of their data, but she—well, you know what happened. You were there."

Danica nodded silently.

A shadow of grief and guilt passed over Billy's face before he went on.

Just then, Shaka burst through the door, like Billy, wearing only the rudiments of protective gear, but then, he'd already survived the virus. His voice held an unsteady edge. "What's going on?"

"Billy—Mr. Andersen here. He thinks he has the vaccine," Danica answered.

"I know I do!" Billy blurted out. "Look at their charts! Every one of them. They're going to live. Don't you get it? Viral titers in the blood are undetectable, temperatures are down, vitals are stabilizing … ."

Danica sat back, astonished. "You gave these patients your vaccine? Without an order?" Her voice rose without her intending it, but the risk he'd taken sent her mind reeling.

Billy got to his feet, clearly annoyed. "You know what they say about it being easier to ask for forgiveness than permission, don't you? Who was there to ask? Besides, with all due respect, ma'am, they were all on the verge of death, anyway."

"But how could you know it was safe? Especially after Dr. Stone?"

Billy was rapidly losing his patience. "Because I took it myself, all right? Eighteen hours ago, I noticed bruises on my arms and chest and I developed a fever. I knew it was only a matter of time. I had hoped the one Dr. Stone took would be the answer, but it was missing something. When Dr. Stone's epilepsy drugs interacted with the raw vaccine, I suddenly knew what was wrong! I'd used the purified protein from anti-snake venom in combination with an adjuvant, to retard the growth of the virus by neutralizing it and encouraging antibodies, but the proportions were wrong; it was too volatile."

"Slow down, Billy. What do you mean, volatile? How did they interact?"

Billy inhaled deeply and went on. "Dr. Stone knew she was already infected. What she didn't know was that the combination of the medications already in her system would lead to a catastrophic cascade of events. The combination caused an interaction between the venom and the seizure medications, rendering the vaccine volatile and allowing the venom to take over, inducing the seizure. Somehow that interaction made the vaccine unstable and unpredictable. So, I used a smaller amount of the isolated purified phospholipase type A2 protein from the anti-snake venom, added a second adjuvant containing vitamin E to the aluminum sulfate to help boost the body's response to the vaccine, and added more gelatin to stabilize the vaccine. You can test me right now. My viral titers are undetectable at this point."

Danica frowned at the screen, trying to make sense of it all.

"Look, you want to fire me or something? Go ahead! But these patients are going to get better. And nobody else has to get sick. See for yourself! We did it, damn it! We did it!"

Danica pressed her lips together behind her protective headgear. As a profound sense of relief flooded her limbs, she wasn't even sure she could stand, even as her more cautious side struggled to absorb this new information.

Hearing Billy's rising voice, Shaka walked into the room from the bedside of a nearby patient, the apprehension in his face mixed with something like awe.

"Okay, now everybody take a minute, all right?" His eyes fell on Danica. "He's right, Dr. Diza. I haven't seen all the blood work, but based on their clinical improvement, all I can say is—wow. We can worry about the procedures later. Billy, I think it's time you informed the CDC of these new developments in order for them to start mass producing the vaccine, for those left in Galveston. Dr. Diza, do you agree?"

All at once, her path was clear. She walked over to Billy Andersen and embraced him for a long moment. "Of course," she answered. Then she reached up and removed her protective headgear, grateful to be free of its prison. She took a deep breath and said, "Thank you, Billy. Congratulations. We owe you a lot. Everything. I'll come with you to the lab."

Then she gave him the benefit of a broad, genuine smile. "But first," she said. "You think I could get a dose of that vaccine?"

CHAPTER FIFTY-FIVE
CDC Headquarters, Atlanta, Georgia

Paula clumsily dropped the stapler to the floor, cursing as it fell right on her foot. She hated packing, but this was something she was not ready for. She was cleaning out her office. There was a feeling of dread and nostalgia.

Over the last week, numerous people had investigated and incessantly questioned her over her role in the cover-up and aftermath of the viral outbreak.

Someone needed to be the scapegoat and take the fall. The government pegged that person to be General Drucker, but he decided he would rather face death on his own terms than let someone else decide for him. General Drucker had been the one making the calls, but there was someone else pulling the strings in the background.

As for Hale, stepping down as director of the CDC was an easy decision soon after realizing that Drucker pulled the trigger and the government needed another person to take the fall publicly. Hale became uncooperative with the investigation, but he ended up making a deal. In exchange for not doing prison time, Hale stepped down and partially admitted to knowing about the virus and Drucker's involvement.

Paula packed up the last of her desk. She looked at her diplomas on the wall as a smile crept up her face. After all those years of hard work and endless nights—

Knock. Knock.

"Come in," Paula said, as she turned toward the door.

"Hey Paula, do you need a hand?" said Mark, the intern.

"Yeah, this is the last of it. Do you mind helping me move this stuff out?"

Mark walked over to the boxes. "Sure. Any last word on everything in Galveston?"

"Yeah. Everyone was evacuated and tested. It seems like the vaccine Billy Andersen developed worked. The sick patients in the ICU? Most of them recovered and were the last ones to be evacuated. The ones who recovered ended up having a robust antibody response." Paula responded.

Mark bent down to lift the box. "So it was contained?

Paula grabbed the last of her stuff. "Yeah, it would seem so."

Mark took a deep breath and paused. "So the government and Drucker wanted to create a more virulent strain of the virus, but also work on a vaccine at the same time to be used as biological warfare in the Middle East?"

Paula leaned onto her wooden oak desk. "Yes. How someone could commit a heinous crime like that is beyond me. What would motivate someone to willingly want to harm innocent people? Yes, the experimental strain was unleashed by accident on Galveston Island, but cutting them off and essentially using them as an experimental group to test the viral strain they created goes against everything the military stands for. They are supposed to protect the American people. What happened to duty, honor, and integrity? They used the American people as guinea pigs for experimentation as a delusion for the greater good for the future."

Mark looked her in the eyes. "This is why American people don't trust the government. I know from this experience that I will have a hard time trusting the government after this. It's a good thing you sent Senator Crowley the results of the tests and filled him in on the details."

"We may never know everyone who was involved," said Paula, "and I am sure there was a lot more than we know about. That bothers me, but I wanted to be on the right side of history. I did not want to be responsible for the deaths of hundreds of Americans, even if it meant I would lose my position here. I will sleep peacefully at night knowing what I did was the right call."

Mark laughed. "You and me both. Glad Hale didn't find out; otherwise we would have been the fallout people and all of this would have been pinned on us."

"Well, you are stealthier than you give yourself credit for. Come on. Let's move my stuff into the new office."

Paula walked toward the door.

"Yes, ma'am. Guess I am going to have to get used to you bossing me around as the new CDC director," Mark said.

"You do if you want to be my new lead lab researcher," Paula said as she held the door open for Mark.

Mark's face lit up in surprise. "Really?"

"Absolutely. Thank you for all your help."

Paula looked at him sincerely as he walked out the door. She smiled and walked through the door of her office after him one last time, closing the door behind her.

CHAPTER FIFTY-SIX

Galveston University Hospital

Eight weeks after Hurricane Beatrix made landfall

There are some moments in life when time itself seems to split in two, forever dividing the memory into "before" and "after." As she stood on the roof of University Hospital in Galveston on a beautiful September morning, Dr. Danica Diza watched the airlift of the recovering victims of CCHF as the helicopters sped north to Houston, savoring every detail, wanting to somehow imprint her mind with the images of this moment. One of the pilots gave her a last salute and she waved back, tears of gratitude and joy flowing freely down her face. She lingered there, watching the gentle rocking of the ocean against the brilliant, white sand of the beach beyond the seawall and the dunes in back, now almost cleared of the wreckage and havoc the hurricane had left behind.

A playful little wind whipped her lab coat around her and freed her hair from its usual ponytail. She caught the sharp, sweet scent of the sea on the breeze and heard the call of the gulls as they wheeled in joyous homecoming. Everywhere she looked, there were signs of life—shrimp boats out on the bay, spiky green seagrass that seemed to have sprouted overnight from the brackish waters of the marshlands, and most especially, the small, determined bands of residents and volunteers and day workers, clearing the city streets of all that had been ruined, and shoring up the remains of the structures that had survived. They might be living in tent cities and trailers, or even in their cars, but little by little, the people of Galveston were coming home.

She might have been gazing at the Galveston of the past, a sort of old-timey postcard with its layers of modernity and development all but stripped away. But at the same time, she was struck by how much a landscape could evoke a sense of healing, the same way a human body heals, cell by cell. Not all at once, not overnight, but evident just the same. The new city that rose in its place might be irrevocably changed; the process would take months or even years, but it would rise, beautiful and strong. And for now, at least, that was enough.

Her reverie was interrupted by a pair of strong arms encircling her from behind, and she leaned easily into Shaka's embrace, thinking his presence was the single thing she needed to complete the perfection of the moment. Whatever came before was past; whatever was coming would come. But this? This was perfect, indeed.

"Where have you been?" she asked. "I missed you."

"Sorry, had an early appointment in town. I, uhh—had some business. I needed to close a deal."

Danica turned around to face him, studying his expression carefully. Not for the first time, it occurred to her that there was much she had yet to learn about Dr. Shaka Sen. "What in the world are you talking about? What kind of a deal?"

He smiled with excitement, but just as suddenly, his eyes turned serious. "Danica." He inhaled sharply. "This may be way too soon, and way out of line, but have you thought—at all—about your plans? I mean, now that this ordeal is over, do you know what you want to do next?"

She suddenly realized that she hadn't really thought about any of it. "I don't know. I suppose I'll have to check if I still have an apartment. And then?" She shrugged. "Maybe go see my family for a few days, at least. After that? Who knows? Will the hospital reopen? Will we even have jobs if it does?"

To her surprise, he laughed out loud. "Hell, I hope so. I just bought a house this morning! A big one!"

Her mouth fell open. "You what? Where?"

"Here, in Galveston." He guided her to the other side of the roof and pointed west, toward downtown. "You see down there, the historic district? It's still in pretty good shape, considering. A lot of the newer condos and beach fronts have been lost, but those old buildings? They've been through more hurricanes than we know about. And that's the place to begin rebuilding the city, because with climate change, we haven't seen the last cat-five hurricane. We're going to have to stand a whole lot more."

She didn't want to dampen his enthusiasm, but she couldn't resist a little tease. "Agreed, but as real estate goes, it's not exactly a selling point, is it?" she said dryly.

He turned away, leaning heavily against the guardrail. "Maybe not. But being in a life-threatening crisis definitely puts things into perspective of what's important. It has also accelerated my timeline, and I know what I want. It's time I put down some roots, and I don't think I've ever loved a place as much as I love this island. This whole thing, the storm— getting sick, the quarantine—it's changed me. I almost feel like a different person. Maybe even a better one."

She nodded. "I didn't mean to make fun. And I know what you mean. I haven't processed it all myself yet."

He flashed a rueful smile. "You were right about me, you know. I was arrogant. At least at first. All set to be a hotshot surgeon. Go in with my scalpel and fix the problem. But real medicine doesn't work that way. I know that now."

He paused for a long moment. "My dad was a hotshot too. International businessman, traveling all the time—very successful. Truth is, I barely knew him. When he died, he left me and my mom very well off. Wealthy, even. But it was just me and her, you know? Everything I knew about roots, about family, I learned from her folks—and it wasn't much. She sacrificed her whole life for me, for what she thought was her duty. Just so I would be successful, have a career, like my father. But you know something?"

"What?"

"They were both wrong. I can see that now. If this experience has taught me anything, it's that people can only work miracles when they work together. No one person is more important than any other. That's why I want to stay here. Because Galveston needs help, and it needs the kind of people who are really invested to live here and continue to fight for it. Not just the thieves, developers, and oil companies who want to make a profit. It's not just about money, though having some of that myself can sure help. This city needs people who will fight to protect the wetlands and the wildlife, because our lives are all connected. The coral reefs are already dying, and if they go—then the oysters and the shrimp go, along with the livelihoods of thousands of people who have lived here for generations. I can't stand by and ignore that. Not anymore."

Danica reached over and took his hand. "It's funny," she said softly. "I was thinking pretty much the same thing a little while ago. How the island would heal and rebuild, but it would be more like the way a body heals, slowly, cell by cell. Not just by curing one thing and calling it done. There's always a bigger picture."

Shaka smiled gratefully. "I knew you'd get it. So, I took a walk the other day down in the district, and there was this house on the corner. It's been flooded, of course, but it doesn't look too bad. And that stuff can be fixed. But I don't know, it was the strangest thing. The place just drew me, like it was calling my name. Somebody had a put a *For Sale* sign in the yard, so I took down the number. This is where I belong. This is where I'll stay."

"Wow—looks like you got it all figured out!"

He turned to her again and draped an arm around her shoulders, flashing his old, mischievous, and completely seductive smile. "There is one piece of it missing."

"What is that, Dr. Sen?" she teased.

He leaned in and let out barely a whisper. "You."

Epilogue

*Ten years later, just outside Yellowknife,
Northwest Territories, Canada*

"Yo! Foreman? Hey, you the foreman of this crew?"

From his place in the cherry picker, twenty-five feet up where he'd been trimming the lower branches of a huge black spruce, Jake glanced down at the figure waving frantically at him from the ground. Jake turned off his chainsaw and gave the signal to be lowered.

Hell, what's the problem this time? he thought.

This was the hottest July on record, and the whole territory was going, one tree at a time. If it wasn't flooding along the coastline, it was drought further inland. He and his crew were shorthanded and even shorter-tempered. Today, they were culling a stand of virgin spruce infested by some beetles the First Nations boys couldn't identify.

That was why Jake had been up in the cherry picker. He didn't do it much anymore since his accident. His crew was comprised mostly of Native Americans, but something about the bug infestation had spooked them. The logging season was short enough up here, but every week brought some new struggle. Every day, try as he might to keep up morale, the sense of foreboding they passed to one another was almost palpable, as hard to interpret as the inscrutable expressions in their black, unreadable eyes.

His second-in-command, Ben Bellgarde, came forward and swung open the gate to the cab, silently offering him an arm to dismount. "Fella over there wants to see you," he said. "Says the Culpepper crew sent him over from the other side of the canyon."

Jake slapped his neck as a black deer fly landed on it, ready to feast. He glanced at the man leaning against a mud-splattered ATV, his work clothes topped with a neon orange vest and hard hat. Something about him was familiar, but he couldn't quite place him.

Jake limped in the man's direction, slowly and deliberately, ignoring the sweat that poured down his brow.

The other man waited, indifferent to his approach, then just as suddenly, rushed forward, recognition in his eyes. "Jason? Jason Carter? Is that you? Well, I'll be damned!"

The man he called Jason Carter halted in his tracks, feeling as though he'd just fallen through a trapdoor. Even with a bad hip, he had a good four inches on the guy and figured he could take him if he had to. He clenched his fists involuntarily and lowered his voice. "The name's Jake Carson," he said carefully. "Who wants to know?"

A broad smile broke over the other's man's features. "Don't you recognize me? It's Manny. Manny Ortega. We were cellmates for a while back at Huntsville. I was just a kid, remember? God, small world, ain't it? When you didn't come back to the joint after they took you to the hospital, I just figured you was dead. How'd you get all the way up here, man?"

Jake studied him for a long moment before recognition kicked in, noting a long, ugly scar that ran the length of the other man's face from his eye socket to his jugular that hadn't been there before. Manny saw the look and fingered his own cheek. "Them deportation centers weren't exactly a picnic. I wasn't out of jail a week before they rounded me up."

Jake took him firmly by the elbow. "None of that matters now. Name's Jake Carson, got it? I came up here with a woman who needed to get to where she was going. And that's all you need to know."

"I hear you, man. No worries. These days, Canada's full of ex-pats. I worked up the west coast through Vancouver, myself. 'Bout five years ago. My wife and kids were here already. That made it easier. Can't complain, either. Canada's been good to us."

"Us too." Jake nodded. "My wife's got herself a nursing degree. Works the hospital in Yellowknife. Guess she figured she'd take it up full-time after my accident." He slapped his leg. "Big alder fell one way when it should have gone the other. Hazard of the trade."

Manny nodded. "Least you're still movin'."

"So why'd they send you? The Culpepper crew. I got a whole parcel to get cleared here."

Manny's face went somber. "They want you to see something. It's back up the logging road about five miles. Climb in; I can have you there and back in a half hour."

Jake weighed his options, then finally decided to get in. "You all take a break," he hollered toward his crew. "I'll be back shortly."

As they headed deeper into the forest, they spoke very little. Jake was struck as always by the beauty of this place, a never-ending landscape of towering trees, rising thick and high enough to blot out the sun, bathing the world in its own enchanted light. It would be easy for a man to feel like an intruder here, among these silent sentinels, lost among the mosses and deepening rock canyons, the waterfalls and spring-fed ponds where the birds and bears and elk came to linger. But he never had, and instead he remained reverent in the face of such majesty. Jake Carson, in his time on earth, had never been quite sure there was a God, but if there were, he'd felt closer to him here than in any worldly church.

Then Jake caught it, a stench that wafted on the breeze, mixed with the smell of the engine's gasoline. It dissipated, then came back again, closer this time, stronger too. The smell of death and rot and blood and shit as only Nature could make it, and once imprinted on the memory, never quite forgotten, whether man or beast.

Jake sniffed the wind, trying to get a sense of direction, even as the black flies swarmed them by some silent signal, anxious for fresher blood.

Jake fought back the urge to gag as their ATV pressed further into that suffocating mist.

Manny pulled up abruptly, as close as he could manage. He tied a bandana over his own mouth and beckoned Jake to follow.

Wan sunlight filtered in from above, illuminating a small clearing where the bodies of what seemed like two dozen white-tailed deer lay haphazardly.

"What in the fresh hell is this?" Jake's left hand moved to cover his nose and mouth to block out the horrid smell. Jake peered in closer at the grotesque scene in front of him. "What happened to them?"

"We don't know what killed 'em," Manny said. "But we figured the foreman ought to know. Looks like they've been here a week or more, but in this heat, it's hard to tell."

The mysterious rotting carcasses, seething with maggots and black flies, lay dead and bloating in a small meadow. A flock of carrion birds had picked open the festering corpses, their filmy eyes, lolling tongues, and velvet antlers testament to some last, secret agony endured.

Jake swallowed the bile rising in his throat. His mind darted back to the cold, orange indoor corridor of the University hospital, lined with the stench of death and rotting flesh covered with purple splotches, and the steady hum of the oxygen masks being manually pumped. His palms became sweaty as he clenched his fists, and his heart started racing as he had to turn away to hide the sheer terror in his eyes. Jake had escaped to start a new life in Canada with Katie, living happily together. His first real chance at a new life. But as his luck would have it, trouble seemed to follow him everywhere. There was no escape. Jake ran back toward the vehicle, ready to go home and grasp onto everything he could, ensuring he wouldn't lose everything. He wanted to hold onto Katie and the life they had built for as long as he could.

Anxious of the unknown, Jake couldn't fathom reliving another possible outbreak.

This isn't real, he thought. *This can't be real.*